ST. MARTIN'S

MINOTAUR
MYSTERIES

ST. MARTIN'S PAPERBACKS TITLES
BY SUSAN HOLTZER

Something to Kill For
Curly Smoke
Bleeding Maize and Blue
Black Diamond
The Silly Season
The Wedding Game

The WEDDING GAME

SUSAN HOLTZER

St. Martin's Paperbacks

THE WEDDING GAME

Copyright © 2000 by Susan Holtzer.

Library of Congress Catalog Card Number: 99-089931

ISBN: 0-312-97866-9

Printed in the United States of America

St. Martin's Press hardcover edition / April 2000
St. Martin's Paperbacks edition / March 2001

St. Martin's Paperbacks are published by St. Martin's Press, 175 Fifth Avenue, New York, NY 10010.

10 9 8 7 6 5 4 3 2 1

This book is dedicated to my friends on the Little List, and to those on Alisdair's list. I miss you all; I hope that by the time this book appears in print, I'll be back.

And to Mr. D, with gratitude and affection. We miss you a lot.

Glossary of Internet Usage

Avatar: An online figure that represents the user, in games or chat rooms.

BTW: By the way.

f2f: Face-to-face; a style of interaction other than virtual (online) communication.

FAQ: Frequently Asked Questions; information provided for newbies to a newsgroup or mailing list, to avoid having to cover the same ground over and over again; what every newbie should read before posting.

Flame: An angry or hostile (often profane) posting on a newsgroup, usually in response to a previous post. A thread consisting of back-and-forth flames is referred to as a "flame war."

Header: The "Subject" line in a posting.

IDK: I don't know.

IIRC: If I recall correctly.

IMHO: In my humble opinion.

IMNSHO: In my not-so-humble opinion.

ISP: Internet Service Provider, the company through which a user logs on to the Internet.

LAN: Local Area Network. A means of linking several computers in a single office or business.

LOL: Laughing out loud.

Lurker: Someone who reads a newsgroup or mailing list without posting or making herself known.

Newbie: A newcomer to the Internet, or to computers and computing in general; usually a term of derision.

Newsgroup: One of Usenet's discussion groups.

Nospam sig: A signature line with a fake element inserted to prevent automatic e-mail harvesters from getting one's correct e-mail address; i.e, susan@aol.nospam.com. Used primarily in newsgroup postings.

OTOH: On the other hand.

ROTFL: Rolling on the floor laughing.

ROTFLMAO: Rolling on the floor laughing my ass off.

RPG: Role-playing game; a kind of game in which the player or players "becomes" a character in the game by selecting various qualities or attributes.

Shareware: Software that is marketed on a kind of honor system—the user tries it out at home and pays if he or she keeps it.

Sig: The signature line in a posting. Any sig of more than three or four lines is likely to be flamed.

Smiley: Text symbols meant to express emotions; sometimes called Emoticons. Basic smileys are:

>:-) Basic smiley. User is only kidding.
>
>;-) Winky smiley. User is winking about the joke.
>
>:-(Frowning smiley. User is unhappy.
>
>:-/User isn't exactly unhappy, but is worried.

Snail mail: The U.S. Postal Service.

Spam, spammer: Disgusting slimebags who advertise through newsgroups or unsolicited e-mail.

Thread: A series of postings under a single header, supposedly (but not always) on a single topic.

Topic drift: Moving away from the original subject of a thread without beginning a new thread.

Troll: A post (or one who posts) on a newsgroup intended to elicit flames.

UID: User Identification, sometimes called a "handle."

URL: Uniform Resource Locator; the address of a World Wide Web page.

Usenet: Derived from "Users' Network;" a collection of discussion groups, open to all Internet users.

*You are standing at the end of a road before a small brick building.
Around you is a forest. A small stream flows out of the building and
down a gully.*

> —OPENING SCREEN OF ADVENTURE: THE COLOSSAL CAVE

It hadn't occurred to her until too late that getting married
entailed having a wedding.

"One hundred and fourteen people." Anneke Haagen
tapped the stylus against the screen of her palmtop computer and stared at the number in dismay. "One hundred
and fourteen people." She glared across the tiny table in the
State Street coffeehouse. "Damn you, Michael, you swore
that at least a third of the people we invited wouldn't
show."

"So I lied." Michael Rappoport's classically handsome
face wore an unregenerate grin. Two tables away, Anneke
saw a pair of undergraduate girls staring at him and whis-
pering to each other. Female attention was always one of
the hazards of being out in public with Michael. "It's going
to be a great event," he said. "Just relax and enjoy it—it'll all
be over in another five days."

"Relax and enjoy it—like a Victorian wife, you mean?
Close your eyes and think of England?" Anneke snorted.

1

"Besides, we didn't want a 'great event.' We wanted a small private wedding with just family and close friends."

"We?" Michael winked broadly across the table, where Karl Genesko sat sipping coffee and trying not to smile.

"Don't drag me into this." He bit into a cheese Danish. "The groom never has any say about wedding plans. Thank God," he added fervently. "Oh, and it's only one hundred thirteen. Jay Banning can't make it."

"Jay? But he's your best man. Is he sick?"

"No. The Ravens are sending him to Seattle for the Washington–UCLA game. They want him to take a look at a defensive tackle they're considering for next year's draft."

"But that's silly," she protested. "Why can't he scout the kid at next week's game?"

"Because they want him to go *this* week." Karl shrugged easily, but Anneke could read his disappointment. "Jay either makes this trip or loses his job."

Which he needed, Anneke knew. Karl had been a star linebacker in the Pittsburgh Steelers' glory days; Jay Banning had never been more than a third-string defensive end. Karl, even then, had been intelligent, thoughtful, and forward-looking; Jay had been cheerful, extravagant, feckless. The two men had been teammates, and roommates, and friends, friends in some visceral fashion few people are lucky enough to achieve.

"Dammit, that really is obnoxious." She was furious for Karl's sake, but raging about the injustice of it would only feed his disappointment. "Who are you going to replace him with?"

"I've asked Wes Kramer."

"Oh, good." Of all Karl's colleagues in the Ann Arbor Police Department, Anneke was perhaps fondest of the grumpy, rumpled ex-Marine. "Does he even *own* a suit, do you think?"

"We'll rent him a tuxedo." Karl grinned. "And that is my *only* input to these festivities, I promise you."

"Liar." Anneke glared at him. "You're the one who's been encouraging Michael. If it were up to you, I'd be wearing a Princess Di wedding dress and getting married on the Diag while they played the wedding march from Burton Tower."

"I never thought of that." Michael's face lit up. "We *could* have the carillon, couldn't we? After all, the museum's right on the Diag." He turned to Karl. "Would they do it, do you think?"

"I imagine," Karl said solemnly. "Why don't you check with the carillonneur? He'd probably get a kick out of it."

"I have an even better idea." Anneke closed her palmtop with an audible snap. "Why stop at the carillon? Why not bring in the whole goddamn Michigan Marching Band?"

"Oh, I thought about it," Michael said. "But the uniforms would clash with the color scheme." He and Karl were both grinning openly now. "Besides, the museum director said no—he was afraid they'd scar the marble floors."

"How surprising," Anneke said drily, unwilling to admit she'd been had. "I didn't think there were *any* limits to your powers of persuasion. And speaking of the museum, will the east gallery hold this many people?"

"Not possibly." Michael shook his head. "I've already talked to them—we've moved it to the main rotunda."

"My God." The University Art Museum, a gracious, vaguely Romanesque building on the southwest corner of the Diag, had seemed an inspired choice for a small, elegant wedding. And Michael had seemed an equally inspired choice, indeed her only and immediate choice, for . . . what, exactly?

"Some maid of honor you turned out to be," she said bitterly. "I just want to warn you—when this is over, I intend to hunt you down like a dog and kill you with my bare hands."

"Ingrate." Michael contrived an infinitely sad expression. "And after all I've done for you, working my fingers to the bone, and all of it just to see you happy. I only want what's best for you, you know that. And this is the thanks I get."

"Oh, shut up." She threw the remains of a sweet roll at him. "You're worse than my daughters. One of them wants the wedding in Maui because it's such a romantic place and it would give her an excuse to go there, and the other one thinks I should be married barefoot in Gallup Park with sitar music and vows cribbed from either the *Kama Sutra* or the Sierra Club."

"You're not, are you?" For the first time, Michael sounded seriously anxious.

"Not what?" she asked crossly.

"Going to do something tacky with your wedding vows?"

"I haven't decided." She cocked her head thoughtfully, looking at him from under her eyelashes. "I *was* thinking about that verse from the Rubaiyat. How does it go? 'A flask of wine, a book of verse, and Thou beside me singing in the wilderness.' " She recited the words solemnly, but the look of horror on his face was too much. She broke out laughing as she got to the line about "Wilderness is Paradise enow."

"Relax, Michael. We're going to have a perfectly traditional ceremony."

"Including 'obey,' I assume," he said snidely. This time it was Karl who snorted with laughter, nearly upsetting his coffee cup. Michael joined him, and after a moment so did Anneke.

"The trouble is," she said, "weddings aren't *logical*."

"Sure they are," Michael contradicted her. "They have their own internal logic, that's all. Just think of your wedding in the same terms you'd think of your funeral."

"Why not? At the moment, believe me, it's no stretch."

"Your problem," Michael said, "is that you keep thinking this is *your* wedding."

"You mean it isn't? Hooray." Anneke clapped her hands. "Then for heaven's sake, let's find whoever it belongs to and let *her* deal with it."

"The thing is," Michael ignored her sarcasm, "both weddings and funerals may be *about* you, but they are not *for* you. They're not personal events, they're community events—otherwise why have public ceremonies at all? Life-passage events are intended to celebrate the link to your friends, your family, your tribe, if you will."

"And what if I won't?"

"All right, then, think of it as a game, with its own set of rules. Sure, you can ignore the rules, but then why bother to play at all? It's like cheating at solitaire—there's no point in playing if you don't accept the rules as the guiding parameters."

"But—" He had a point, she conceded. She thought about the cheat sheets available for all popular computer games, the ones that gave you step-by-step instructions for solving each puzzle. She understood their attraction—many people enjoyed games for the exploration rather than the puzzle-solving. Except, then it wasn't really a game, was it?

"What if you don't like the rules?" she challenged him.

"Then play some other game. Or write your own. But once you agreed to play the wedding game, you also agreed to play by its rules."

5

There was something wrong with his logic, Anneke was sure, but for the life of her she couldn't put her finger on it.

"Anyway," he sipped his latte—low-fat, no foam, sprinkle of nutmeg—"your real problem is stage fright, pure and simple. And that's something you're just going to have to get past, period. Thus saith the maid of honor."

Stage fright? She opened her mouth to protest, then shut it again. She loathed being the center of attention, hated the idea of being on display, being stared at and whispered about, but that was different. Wasn't it?

"Besides, you're going to look gorgeous enough to stop traffic," Michael went on. "You *are* going to look gorgeous, aren't you? Are you sure you don't want me to help you with your outfit? There are a lot of details, you know—selecting jewelry, hairstyle, et cetera."

"Michael, believe it or not, I'm perfectly capable of dressing myself. I've even been known to feed myself on occasion." She ran her hand through her hair, its short, shaggy cut like a brown-and-gray chrysanthemum. There really wasn't much she could do with it, surely. Should she have grown it out for the wedding? And her usual makeup would do, wouldn't it? With perhaps a glitter of eye shadow . . . She was saved from a serious attack of nerves by a low beeping sound.

Karl flipped open his open his cell phone and spoke into it. "Genesko." He listened in silence for a few moments, then said: "Right. On my way."

"Something major?" Anneke asked.

"An explosion." He slipped the phone back into his pocket. "An apartment building over on Oakland."

"Bad? Anyone hurt?"

"One person dead. I'll call you later." He dropped a quick kiss on her forehead and strode out of the coffeehouse.

6

Anneke was gratified to see that female heads watched him, too, and then was amused at her own reaction. At six-five, 250 pounds, he, like Michael, always attracted attention. Well, if those two could handle it all their lives, surely she could handle it for one evening.

"I wonder—"

"You don't have time to wonder," Michael declared. He slid a sheet of paper across the table. "Here's the final menu. And I warn you, the caterer is even more stubborn than I am."

"Impossible." Anneke sighed and returned her attention to the minutiae of shrimp-and-cucumber hors d'oeuvres.

Somewhere nearby is Colossal Cave, where others have found for-
tunes in treasure and gold, though it is rumored that some who enter
are never seen again. Magic is said to work in the cave.

—ADVENTURE: THE COLOSSAL CAVE

The worn corridors of the Nickels Arcade felt like a refuge, and Anneke climbed the stairs to her office with a sense of relief. Michael could say what he wanted, but computers were a lot more logical than weddings. She stopped in front of the door, with its frosted glass panel lettered in gold: HAAGEN/SCHEEDE COMPUTER SOLUTIONS, and smiled to herself. Work, she understood.

As she reached for the doorknob, she was suddenly aware of a throbbing beneath her feet. And when she pushed open the door, the sound of thick, bass-heavy music hit her in the face.

Computer screens blinked emptily—the two Pentiums, the Sun workstation, the single Mac, all sat abandoned. Instead, her entire staff of student programmers, the only kind she hired, were clustered around the Compaq against the far wall.

In a sliver of space between Marcia Rosenthal and Calvin Streeter, Anneke could see on the screen an underwater scene, dark and brooding, beautiful but filled with menace. As she watched, a huge sea creature swam into view, turned to face the screen, and lifted its lip in an ominous snarl. Along the right side of the screen, where a series of icons provided game controls and information, one gauge glowed an ominous red.

"Hurry up," Max Loeffler called out over the pounding of the music. "Your air supply is down to three millibars."

"I know, I know." The voice from the center of the cluster belonged not to one of Haagen/Scheede's young employees but to a student friend of Anneke's, Zoe Kaplan. "I can't get the damn airlock open. I must've been supposed to find a wrench or something before I went outside."

"No, you weren't," Marcia said. "You have to—"

"Don't tell her!" Calvin interrupted.

"Yeah, sure," Zoe said. "Just let me die out here."

"You don't die," he said. "FOX wants to keep you around for company."

"Wonderful. I've always wanted to be a girl toy for an insane computer. What if I— The electric eel!" Zoe's voice rose in excitement. "Where is the little bastard?"

"Oh, please." Max made a face. "Would we write a cliché like that?"

"Then what—oh shit, the *terminal*."

"Got it." Calvin nodded. "Remember, your antagonist is a computer—you communicate with FOX the same way you communicate with Windows."

"That bad," Zoe said ironically. The underwater scene looped and spun and finally zoomed in until a bank of dials and meters filled the screen. She dropped the mouse and pounded frantically on the keyboard. "What the hell is that password?"

She continued hitting keys. The music rose to a

crescendo, then stopped abruptly, replaced by the unmistakable beeping of a computer having an electronic tantrum. A ragged cheer arose from the group.

"Yes!" Zoe popped to her feet, pumping her arm in triumph. She caught sight of Anneke and grinned.

Anneke raised an eyebrow. "Enjoying yourselves?"

"It's great!" Zoe's face was flushed, and her mass of curly black hair was even wilder than usual. "I just escaped from the giant squid and got control of Airlock B. Boy, is FOX pissed." She pointed to the computer, where a baleful eyeball filled the screen. FOX—Focused Organic eXperiment—continued to beep angrily.

"He's still beeping," Anneke pointed out.

"That's because he's pissed. He's just—oh, shit!" Zoe hurled herself at the computer and grabbed for the mouse. The eyeball blinked rapidly, dissolved, and a small red apparatus slid across the screen. "Oh, shit, not *another* seabot." The seabot glided toward the door of the airlock; as they watched, the edges of the door glowed red-hot, melted into the frame, and the whole assembly seemed to dissolve. Within seconds, the steel-gray wall was a single featureless expanse. The door to the interior of the station was gone.

"Shit shit shit shit shit." Zoe threw down the mouse in disgust. The others laughed.

"Gotcha." Marcia clapped her hands.

Zoe clicked the mouse to end the session. "Does that mean I have to start all over?"

"No." Calvin shook his head, his dark face animated. "We don't want people to have to keep going over the same ground. That gets boring. FOX'll burn you another door. But it'll lead to where *he* wants you to go."

"But I can go back to my last save, can't I?" Zoe asked.

"Sure, but you don't have to. This way, you can keep

exploring even if you're not exactly on the right track. And remember," he added, "there are lots of different ways to win."

"The Group function worked properly, I take it?" Anneke asked him.

"Yeah." Calvin nodded. "It's a nested hierarchy of messaging groups, ending with a leafnode group."

"I thought the CreateGroupInGroup would work."

"Yo," Zoe interrupted. "If you people are going to break into a foreign language, I'm outta here." She picked up her blue bookbag with the University of Michigan logo.

"Sorry." Anneke laughed. "You've been around here so much lately, sometimes I forget that you're not a programmer."

"Puh-leeze." Zoe pantomimed mock horror. "Do I *look* like a geek?" She grinned widely at Calvin, who snorted back at her.

"That's why we keep her around here," he said. "If an absolute techno-illiterate can play 'Whitehart,' we figure everyone else can, too."

"Better a guinea pig than a computer wonk," Zoe retorted.

"Just remember that I'm the alpha wonk around here." Their eyes met and held, challenge flashing between them. Anneke blinked. Zoe and Calvin? She grinned inwardly.

"All right, children," she said. "Back to work."

"Right." Zoe hoisted the bookbag onto her shoulder. "I've gotta get over to the *Daily*, and then I need to go cover football practice. A whole morning watching great-looking bods in tight spandex." She sighed dramatically, carefully not looking at Calvin. "It's a dirty job, but somebody's gotta do it."

———

"It really is good, isn't it?" Anneke said to Calvin, when Zoe had left.

"You sound surprised." He laughed, teeth flashing white in his dark face.

"I think maybe I am. I've had that damn game in my head for so many years, it's kind of strange to see it actually come alive." She glanced once more at the monitor, where the words "Whitehart Station," in flowing white letters, floated against a dark seascape background. "You know, I started it so long ago it was originally a text-only game for the Apple Two. It seemed so easy to program."

"Primitive, you mean."

"I know. I couldn't even imagine . . ." She looked at the monitor again, even now amazed at the sophistication of it.

The broad outlines of the "Whitehart Station" scenario were simple—in a self-contained underwater station, the experimental control computer, named FOX, had run amok, killing the research team and taking over the station. Soldier of fortune Bailey Westron had been sent in by the government to regain control. Simple, yes—and, by the time Anneke finally got it into development, perilously close to a cliché. What made it different, she thought, was the way it played—not a shoot-'em-up, but a series of sophisticated challenges in which computer skills rather than fighting skills were paramount.

"You've done a brilliant job with the graphics," she said to Calvin. Which was true. He wisely hadn't attempted a photorealistic approach; the graphics had the stylized look of Japanese *anime*, all planes and angles, deceptively simple. Bailey Westron was an androgynous figure in his/her fatigues, gender identity only in the mind of the player.

"Thanks, boss-lady." Calvin's glance flicked to the screen

with proprietary pride. "How'd you like the music for that last bit?"

"Don't even ask. My musical knowledge ended with the Rolling Stones, and it wasn't much to begin with. The only thing I'm sure of is that it's loud."

"It's good stuff, trust me."

"I do." It was true, Anneke realized, and not just about the music. Calvin had walked into her office two years ago, a tall, skinny street kid out of the Detroit projects, with a chip on his shoulder the size of a two-by-four. How he'd taught himself the basics of programming was a mystery that Anneke avoided delving into too closely, feeling relatively sure that it involved unauthorized hacking at the very least.

Since then he'd grown into a tall, wiry, confident student, sailing through the University's computer science program without, apparently, ever bothering to crack a book. He was already, in fact, a better programmer than she was.

He was also her full partner in "Whitehart Station," a move that she thought had had a lot to do with whittling the chip on his shoulder down to popsicle-stick size. Well, he'd earned it. His eye for graphics, not to mention his ear for music, was clearly superior to her own. And nowadays, the multimedia aspects of a game were probably more important than any other feature, including even how well it played.

She glanced at the monitor once more. "You know, I think we're just about ready to go to beta."

"You think so?" Calvin sounded uncharacteristically hesitant. "I'm not sure about that jellyfish sequence. It's kind of out of perspective."

"Well, you can work on that during the beta phase." She

13

smiled at him. "We've got to send our baby out into the world eventually. Let's shoot for next month, okay?"

"Okay." Calvin straightened his shoulders. "When you get back from your honeymoon, I'll have it ready to go."

"Good." She picked up her briefcase and went down the hall to her private office, trying without much success to look forward to her honeymoon. She'd tried to suggest, delicately, that perhaps just a long weekend would be best—after all, they'd been living together for more than a year—but Karl would have none of it. The honeymoon, he declared, was the groom's prerogative. He would plan it, and she would damn well go along. All he would tell her was to "dress for fall."

Well, at least that eliminated the "long-walks-on-the-beach" cliché, an activity she knew would bore both of them speechless within twenty-four hours. Other than that, and knowing Karl, it could be anywhere from Sydney to Paris to Vancouver.

It didn't matter. The truth was, she didn't want to go anywhere.

Was she crazy? she wondered, as she sat down at her desk and powered on her computer. No. What she was, she realized with some surprise, was happy. She loved her home, she loved her work, she loved the man with whom she was sharing her life. Vacations, she thought, were for people who wanted to get away from their daily lives; she wanted to embrace hers.

She found herself humming the "Whitehart Station" theme as she logged on and downloaded her e-mail, and as she watched it sort itself into multiple mailboxes, she discovered she had a smile on her face.

She read and answered her personal mail first. No, she wrote her daughter Emma, I will not wear a green Save-the-

Planet ribbon on my wedding dress, but you are more than welcome to wear one on yours. Yes, she wrote her daughter Rachel, there's a market in town that sells organic food, and yes, I have a blender and food processor for preparing homemade food for Samantha. In truth, both blender and food processor were Karl's; she herself could have lived happily forever from local delis and Chinese takeout.

She worried for the tenth time about arrangements as she rapidly read and answered the rest of her mail. Maybe she should have put them all up in a hotel? Two daughters, a son-in-law, and a grandchild were possibly not the ideal house guests for the three days leading up to one's wedding. She read through her business mail with half her mind elsewhere, dumping most of it into a shared file for later consultation with her partner, Ken Scheede.

She sighed finally and put the problem out of her mind. The arrangements were made. One way or another, she only had to get through one more week. She turned to her third mailbox with anticipation.

You are standing at the southern end of a long valley illuminated by flickering red light from the volcanic gorge behind you. Carved into the walls of the valley is an incredible series of stone faces. Some of them look down into the valley with expressions of benevolence that would credit a saint; others glare with a malice that makes the heart grow faint. All of them are imbued with a fantastic seeming of life by the shifting and flickering light of the volcano.

—ADVENTURE: THE COLOSSAL CAVE

This was where she downloaded mail from GameSpinners, a private mailing list for computer game designers. Today there were twenty-seven messages from the list, and a quick glance told her that at least half of them were from the same half dozen or so people.

Which meant that the dreaded games-for-girls flame war had broken out again. And unfortunately, she herself was the reluctant center of the storm.

It had begun a couple of months ago, when she'd made a passing reference to her wedding preparations, and Kell Albright's antic imagination had caught fire.

Kell was their resident party girl, the one who insisted that "games should be fun, or why bother?" They'd never met face-to-face, but Anneke's imagination clothed Kell in short, tight skirts, multicolored hair, and several tattoos, dancing the night away at underground clubs before hitting the keyboard in the morning. It was hard not to envy her cheerful energy or enjoy her persistent humor.

Kell was also a true idea-hamster, notions spinning from her mind like sparks from a flywheel. She always seemed to be working on half a dozen game ideas at once, and never seemed to be seriously engaged in any of them.

Until now. Kell, it seemed, had decided to write a "Wedding Game."

<Kell>Wow, what a great idea for a game! It'd be for, say, young teenagers--maybe twelve to sixteen? You could have lots and lots of possible wedding scenarios, lots of different choices--players could even design their own wedding gowns. And then you could give them all sorts of problems to solve--nasty in-laws, fights about bridesmaids, drunken bachelor parties, stuff like that. It'd be great! Anneke, can I ask you questions about it while you're planning it?

Well, what could she say?

<Anneke>Sure, Kell, if you want to. But I think I'm probably not what you want. I mean, no traditional wedding gown, no mother of the bride, no in-laws at all, for that matter. And it's going to be just a small, private wedding. Wouldn't you be better off talking to a friend your own age who's having a traditional wedding?

<Kell>Au contraire. It's easy to get stuff about regular weddings from magazines and Web sites and stuff. It's the less traditional weddings that'll make the game really interesting, you know? Besides, you'll be making a lot of the same decisions every bride does--things like location, guest list, maid of honor, all that sort of stuff.

And anyway, none of my friends are even close to getting married. We're all still in girls-just-wanna-have-fun mode. ;-)

The smiley was typical of Kell. Most women computer professionals scrupulously avoided using them, but Kell happily, or perhaps purposely, sprinkled her postings with graphical smiles, winks, and nudges. Kell had a way of provoking flame wars even as she seemed merrily oblivious to them.

Today the battle had erupted under the topic heading "Finding decent beta testers." Not unusual for GameSpinners, where no one worried overmuch about staying on-topic. Generally, people just kept hitting Reply and posting away, even when the subject had drifted, as one had recently, from "Game Reviewers" to whether an AK-47 was better than an Uzi for taking out a Ninja attack squad.

<Kell>Why should girls get stuck with all those boring, repetitive shoot-'em-ups just because that's what boys like? Does every game in the world have to be written for 15-year-old boys?

A good question, Anneke thought, but in the context of the computer gaming world, not an easy one to answer. It was Seth Conroy (of course) who made the obvious comment. Seth spent his days slumming (his word) in the Information Systems department of a Los Angeles bank, instead of rapping with a hot game company. He wore suits instead of jeans and T-shirts; he punched a time clock instead of happily programming when and where he wanted to; he earned just enough money to be furiously envious of the Armani-clad hotshots above him in the rigid hierarchy. He felt overworked and underappreciated; he probably was; and it showed.

<Seth>::Does every game in the world have to be written for 15-year-old boys?::

Nope; only the ones that make money. If you want to be some kind of pro bono programmer, that's fine with me. But I want to do this for a living. And face it, it's boys who drop the big bucks in this marketplace.

Well, yes, but . . . Anneke selected the last sentence to copy it into her posting, and hit Reply.

<Anneke> Well, yes, but which is cause and which is effect? Maybe girls don't spend money on games because the only games out there to spend money ON are designed for boys.

She hit Send and clicked on the next posting. She was pretty sure Dani Noguchi would be in full attack mode.

Dani was young and bright and angry. She'd been on the fast track with a hot new startup, in Houston, a company that was going to "revolutionize the Internet." Well, weren't they all? Except, Dani had bought into the promise of a big payoff and had taken the fat stock options instead of a decent salary. When the company went belly-up, the "bold entrepreneurs" who'd run the scam walked away with a couple of million in their pockets and venture capital for the Next Great Thing. Dani had walked away with a pocket full of worthless paper.

<Dani>And what SHOULD girls like--some Martha Stewart game where the winner is the one who makes the best Christmas wreath out of used toilet paper? Come on, girls have as much anger and hostility to get out of their system as boys do. Maybe more--God knows we have more to be angry ABOUT. The

problem isn't the game TYPE, it's the game PLOTS. Give girls a strong female protagonist who isn't just boobs and ass, give them a real grrrl game, and they'll put their money down.

Not entirely true, though, Anneke thought. There were a few action games on the market that did just that, and while they did attract a certain number of girls, they still appealed more to teenage boys. Girls just didn't get into gaming young enough; by the time they're old enough for action and adventure games, we've lost them.

<Dani>Besides, girls NEED action and adventure games, for the same reason boys do--it's empowering, and it helps them learn about conflict. Shit, there's a lot more of the real world in Forsaken than there is in Barney's Great Adventure. The last thing we need is another generation of sweet little girls who never grow up and smell the shit.
<Kell>Sorry, but the last thing the world needs is another generation of women trying to act like men. The world already has a lot more testosterone than it can handle.

Anneke hit Reply, stared at the screen for a minute, then aborted. In essence, the argument was the central conundrum of the contemporary women's movement, and she wasn't sure herself which side she came down on. She moved on to the next message with the mixture of trepidation and anticipation that Vince Mattus's postings always engendered. Vince was *always* in attack mode.

<Vince>Why doesn't it surprise me that you're both wrong? Actually, there IS a market out there for girl games. And the great thing is they don't even have to be any good. All you have to do is package it in pink, and some dumb mother's gonna buy it for her

little Susie. I mean, it's not like she's gonna be able to tell if it's any good or not.

In fact, the chick market is a great opportunity for a third-rate programmer, because they wouldn't know a good game from a tic-tac-toe clone anyway. Girls don't really play games. All they want to do is jerk around and look at the pretty pictures.

As usual, Dani rose to the bait.

<Dani>Vince, you are such an indispensable icon of the women's movement. Every time we begin to get complacent, you remind us what men are really like. How far did *you* get on Tomb Warrior without a cheat sheet?

And as usual, Kell didn't.

<Kell>Poor Vince, you're so good at yanking people's chains, and so bad at everything else. When was the last time you actually had FUN? (I mean, without a centerfold and a towel. :-)

Anneke snorted with laughter as she read the rest of Kell's posting.

<Kell>Besides, the real problem is that teenage boys are so PATHETIC. I mean, the poor things are so hormone-sodden that they can barely speak in coherent sentences. Where's the fun in writing Yet Another game for an audience that feeble? >:->

<Seth>In a way, much as I hate to say it, Vince is right. But before you flame me, here's the thing--that's true of boy's games too. Most of the stuff we argue about here, like playability, is just a series of bullshit factors, at least for the action-adventure genre. If you give it enough flashpower, the kids'll buy it for the graphics and the scenario. Even if it's not the greatest game in

21

the world to play, so what? By then, they've already paid out their forty bucks.

Oh Lord, not the old playability-vs.-plot argument. She was about to pass on the rest of the thread when she saw Jesse Franklin's name at the top of the next response.

<Jesse>But where's the creative challenge? What's the point of being a gamer if you're going to think like that? You might as well be an investment banker.

Jesse was an icon in the computer gaming world, one of the great hackers back in the days when the word was an accolade, not an accusation. "Mordona," his brilliant adventure game written for the old Apple][, had been a triumph of programming, almost a tour de force. For a machine with only 32K of RAM, no hard drive, and a floppy disk that held a bare 128K, Jesse had created a game that grabbed you by the throat and dragged you into its world, all of it written in the tightest, most elegant code Anneke had ever seen. She felt privileged to have him on the list, but in this group, of course, not everyone felt the same. Maybe it was an age thing.

<Vince>Seth may be a money-grubbing whore, but in this case he's got a point. Jesse the Purist used up his One Great Idea twenty years ago, and he hasn't done anything since but sit around and pontificate, like he's the Second Coming of Steve Wozniak. If you want people to actually buy your games, you've got to give them something that grabs them by the balls in that first look. If they don't buy it, it doesn't matter how great it plays. And once they do buy it, who cares what they think of it?

<Dani>It figures that Vince would blow off playability, considering what he churns out. Anyone ever actually try to PLAY Tombs and Tokens?

<Vince>Anyone ever try to play any of YOUR games, Dani? No? Oh yeah, that's right--you've never actually written and marketed anything, have you? Now why doesn't that surprise me? Oh, right--you're a grrrrrl.

<Elliott>Yeah, but if the playability sucks, how you going to get anyon to by it, at gunpoint? Hey Vince, here's a news flash-- 15 year olds TALK TO EACH OTHER!! How the shit do you think we decid what games to buy, with a ouija board? Besides, only a 36K brain would lay out 40 or 50 bucks for a game with out downloading the demo and tryng it out first. So KIDS KNOW if its any good BEFORE we by it.

Anneke chuckled. Elliott held the high ground when it came to talking about fifteen-year-old boys. Elliott Washburn wrote like what he was—a fifteen-year-old hacker/ computer wonk/semi-genius who understood everything about games and nothing much about reality. Anneke wasn't sure if his parents deserved jail time for screwing him up, or canonization for not killing him in his sleep. Either way, she didn't envy them.

Elliott was self-taught, one of those intuitive programmers who could look at a blank monitor and effortlessly visualize the correct lines of code crawling down the screen. Unfortunately, he couldn't seem to visualize anything else; his high school grades hovered dangerously just above the magic 2.0, and people, it seemed, were a complete mystery to him. His postings were usually stream-of-consciousness affairs that might or might not have anything to do with the subject under discussion, beyond topic drift to the realm of total non sequitur. His spelling and grammar were so atrocious that Anneke would have considered the possibility of dyslexia if his code weren't so perfectly written.

He wrote about high school only rarely, and about local friends never, and Anneke had wondered occasionally if she should feel sorry for him. But his postings revealed a rich network of online friends, and a cheerful disposition that never seemed forced. Once he got beyond high school hell, she reasoned, he'd find face-to-face relationships that would work for him.

Elliott had never actually finished a game; he seemed more interested in creating endless modules featuring hand-to-hand battles, slavering monsters, and violent assassinations, all of them filtered through liberal gobs of splattered blood.

The flame war ended there for the moment, although Anneke had no doubt it would continue for a while. She wished both it and the next one would go away—the one headed "Wedding Bell Blues," in which Kell peppered her with daily questions.

<Kell>Anneke, how about some last-minute crises? I figure that the closer you get to the event, the more likely it is that something will go wrong, right? AND the more likely it is that whatever goes wrong will produce the greatest amount of trouble. Sort of a Murphy's Law of Weddings. :-)

I thought I'd program each crisis as a separate module, so that theoretically it's possible for the player to be hit by all of them either simultaneously or sequentially, and at almost any point in the game. But the later the crisis occurs, the more difficult it'll be to solve.

<Jesse>Just don't backload all the excitement, Kell. Remember, gamers deserve small payoffs as they go along, not just one

big one at the end. Not many players are going to stick with it to the very end, after all, and they shouldn't have to in order to enjoy playing it. "Life's the journey, not the destination."

<Elliott>Hey, Kell, how about having the bride kidnaped by a ninja attack squad? They culd be disgised as gests, see, and theyd snatch the brid and then the groom would get his own squad togethr and chase after them. It wuldnt have to be sexist either you could have the bride be an Amazon warrior and she culd be rescud by her own troops who are really an Amazon legion.

Anneke laughed out loud as she clicked Reply.

<Anneke>Hey, works for me, Kell. Sounds a lot more fun than dressing up like a Christmas tree and listening to people snicker. I might even have my Amazons kidnap Karl and force him to elope. As for last-minute crises, sorry to disappoint you but so far the only thing that's gone wrong is that Karl's best man had to cancel at the last minute, to go on a scouting trip to Seattle. I admit I'm really pissed about it, too, and I hope the Baltimore Ravens rot in last place. (Jay's a scout for them, and they're insisting he go on a scouting trip that he could easily put off a week.) But other than that, everything seems to be falling into place very nicely.

> *>BONNNNNGGGGGGGGG<*
>
> *A hollow voice says, "The Galloping Ghost Tortoise Express is now at your service!" With a swoosh and a swirl of water, a large tortoise rises to the surface of the reservoir and paddles over to the shore near you. The message, "I'm Darwin—ride me!" is inscribed on his back in ornate letters.*
>
> —Adventure: The Colossal Cave

The final subject heading, "See you at GameDev," was from Larry Markowitz, the nominal list owner. Larry was a senior programmer with Gallery3 Software, which produced, among other things, a graphics programming package loathed and loved almost equally by most game developers. They used it, they relied on it, and they railed against it, in almost equal proportions. Nothing else could do what Gallery3 did; why, developers screamed, couldn't it do it better?

<Larry>Wanted to remind everyone that we'll be a major player at GameDev this year. We've got a triple booth right at the front, and I HOPE we're going to be demoing the Gallery3 upgrade (if the Marketing mavens get their shit together in time). Anyway, I'll be at the booth nearly the whole weekend, so if any

26

of you folks are planning to attend, I'd love to have you drop by and chat for a while. In fact, I'm going alone, so if enough list members are around, maybe we could plan a pub crawl after hours Saturday night.

<Dani>You mean you're not bringing your wife, Larry? Ooh, count me in.

<Elliott> Shit, Id give anything to go to that, but my mother trets me like Im about six years old, you know? Larry, will the upgrade speed up the collision detection routines? because when I get my gladiators moving I really want to see those tridents whiping around, you know?

<Vince>I hope the upgrade is better than the piece of crap you've got now. Did anyone bother to fix the bug in the texture mapping module? Or did your marketing trolls tell you no one would notice?

<Anneke>What a shame. Larry finally on the loose and I don't get a shot at him. Sorry, gang, but I've got something ALMOST as important this weekend--my honeymoon.

As she typed the words she felt a pang of real regret. GameDev was a major event in the gaming world, a place to check out new developers' software, to learn about the latest in hardware advances, to meet and chat with other game programmers. She'd never gone before—until now, "Whitehart Station" had been too ephemeral for her to commit herself to it. This would have been the perfect year for her to attend.

With a sigh she quickly ran through the rest of the posts, pausing briefly at one headed "Lighting Call Question."

<Elliot> I wrote a function to calculate ligting intensity but I cant get it to work riht. Anyone know anything about how to do this?

27

<Vince>Shit, where did you learn programming, anyway, off the back of a cereal box? Besides, last time I looked this was a list about game DESIGN, not a tutorial for retards who've never even heard of the TestIntersectionS test. There's a whole set of formulas at http://www.csu.org/~lola/light.html where you can find what you need without bothering the rest of us.

<Elliott>Up yours, Vince. Big fat hairy deal-- just because you can find some freaking website, you think your some kind of genius.

Vince was presumably right about the Web site, though. It was why he was tolerated—because, wrapped inside the anger and vitriol, he nearly always had the answer to any question. Still, lately he seemed to be getting even nastier than usual, his act getting less amusing and more annoying. She wondered if even Larry Markowitz, the most laissez-faire of list mavens, would pull his plug one of these days.

With the thought in her mind, she saw the next thread with a start of surprise. It was also from Larry, and it was headed: "Vince Is Dead." So he'd finally kicked Vince off the list. She discovered that, in a weird way, she was going to miss him; he may have been a vicious jerk, but he brought a certain edge and energy to the conversation.

<Larry>I'm posting this to report that Vince Mattus was found dead in his apartment this morning. He was killed by a letter bomb that exploded when he opened it. Sorry, gang, I don't have any other details. I'll post more information as I get it.

It took her a second to shift mental gears, from list exile to actual death, and another moment to make the connection. Letter bomb . . . Vince lived in Ann Arbor . . . then *that* must have been the explosion Karl had been called out on. Quickly she clicked on the next posting.

<Dani>A letter bomb? Awesome. So someone finally found a useful function for snail mail.

<Jesse>Jesus, are you sure, Larry? Where'd you hear it?

<Seth>Are you kidding? You sure it was a letter bomb? Maybe he just got in the way when his personality exploded.

The responses came quickly, out of order, tripping over themselves as they shot through electronic relays.

<Larry>It's right off the AP. It showed up in my newswire mailbox just a couple of minutes ago.

<Kell>I'll be damned. Boy, some gamers are REALLY sore losers.

<Dani>Watch your backs, everyone. If there's a mad bomber out there targeting bad game programmers, get ready for a bloodbath.

Anneke laughed without guilt, accepting the culture of the Internet. You didn't find a whole lot of *nil nisi* hypocrisy in cyberspace, where black humor was more the norm than the exception. The Internet was where people said what they really thought, and what they really thought of Vince Mattus was that he'd been a vicious, nasty, self-absorbed prick.

More postings were pouring in even as she read the current ones. She scanned them all quickly, but there was no further information, only questions, expressions of amazement, and more one-liners.

And one last topic thread, arriving late to her mailbox

through who-knew-what stutter in the great system of relays that was the Internet. This one was headed: "Where Should I Start?" from a teenage newbie named Toby Weintraub.

<Toby>My problem is I've got all sorts of games in my head, and I can't decide what to do first. What's the best kind of game for a beginner to start with?

<Jesse>It's always a tough question, Toby. There are so many choices, aren't there? Card or board or RPG? Action or adventure or puzzle? Turn-based or real-time? 2D or isometric? Every decision changes the design parameters of every other decision--just like real life. You just have to do what feels right to you. Start with the kind of game YOU like to play, and go on from there.

<Vince>Oh shit, another one. Hey kid, if you send me a dime, I'll send you a clue, okay? This is a list for professional game developers, which you are not, because if you were you'd already know what you wanted to do. And no, we don't know how to get you a job with Electronic Arts--I assume that was going to be your next question, right?

<Toby>Up yours, Mattus. Thanks, Jesse. The trouble is, the kinds of games I like to play are the real complicated kind, you know? I suppose I could start with something simple, but that sounds so boring.

And that was the last of it. So that would be Vince Mattus's last word, on this or any other subject. Anneke reread the posting, thinking about Vince. What did she know about him? Hardly anything, she realized, and she'd been happy to keep it that way. She searched her memory for personal information he'd dropped into his postings, and came up empty. He lived in Ann Arbor; he had two games on the market; nothing else. She'd always assumed he was young, but only because most gamers were. She didn't even know if he was a Michigan student or not.

Well, was that so unusual, for someone she'd never met in person? Actually, yes. After being on the GameSpinners list for a little over a year, she considered most of the regular posters to be her friends, and she was pretty sure the others felt the same. True, their connection was only along a thin slice of each other's lives, but personal elements had a way of leaking through. Just as she'd chatted about her wedding plans, the others had chatted about their own daily lives. She'd heard about Elliott's sister's chicken pox; about Kell's apartment-hunting travails; about Dani's despised former employers. She knew that Larry's wife was an intellectual-property lawyer who was on the road far too much; she knew that Seth had just broken up with an aspiring actress; she knew that Jesse was suing a local rancher for diverting water from his New Mexico homestead.

About Vince, she knew nothing.

She returned to the "Vince Is Dead" thread and hit Reply.

<Anneke>Did anyone here ever meet Vince f2f? Larry, what do you know about him? How'd he come to join this list?

She clicked to send this and the other items in her outgoing mailbox, then clicked on the Netscape file menu. What was Vince's game company called? Gooseberry Software, that was it. She did a search, then clicked on "gooseberrygames.com."

Interesting. There seems to be something written on the underside of the oyster.

—ADVENTURE: THE COLOSSAL CAVE

An animated branch of mauve gooseberries waved gently over a logo reading GOOSEBERRY SOFTWARE, the letters sturdy but graceful against the dark, eggplant-colored background. Beneath the logo were the words "Irresistible Games." And below that, Vince had wisely gone directly to the product, the two games he offered for sale.

Neither game was even remotely what she'd have expected from the acerbic—no, just plain nasty—Vince Mattus.

An animated screen shot of "Tombs and Tokens" held pride of place near the top of the screen. Above the brightly colored octagonal game board, three crystalline bubbles floated back and forth, occasionally popping with small splats of sound. It was an attractive game, Anneke thought; colorful, well-executed graphics, and interesting if simple play, combining elements of chess, mah-jongg and Battleship. Blurbs from game reviewers beneath it indicated that others had also found it likable.

Vince's second game, an earlier effort called "Tanaka," was a derivative of the classic Tangrams, in which a series of shapes are combined to form a predetermined picture. Vince had added new shapes, and used multiple colors instead of the customary black, to create a series of surprisingly charming target pictures. Both games were light, bright, and cheerful.

Cheerful? Charming? Likable? Anneke couldn't imagine those adjectives in any sentence that included the name Vince Mattus.

She scrolled down the screen, examining the rest of the Web site. Instructions for downloading demos of each game. How to order the full, uncrippled versions. How to e-mail Gooseberry Software.

And that was pretty much it. There was no personal information at all about Vince—in fact, the name Vince Mattus never appeared. It was a company site, strictly business.

Did he have a separate personal Web site? She moved to AltaVista, typed "Vince Mattus" in the search box, and scanned the resulting seventeen hits. All of them seemed to be game-related—online game reviews, game download sites, and the like. She surfed through them but found nothing about Vince himself.

"Tombs and Tokens," however, looked to be a hit. Reviews and comments were almost universally positive— the Happy Beaver had given it four tails—and several of them were absolutely glowing.

She returned to AltaVista, reset it to search newsgroups rather than the Web, and clicked on Search once more. There were only three hits, all in rec.games.board, and all were about "Tombs and Tokens." There were no hits on postings by Vince himself. Well, not surprising; "Anneke Haagen" wouldn't have shown up on a search either.

She spared a sigh for the Good Old Days, before spammers and other forms of slimelife had made it necessary to maintain a level of anonymity. As she herself did, Vince probably posted to newsgroups using a nospam sig. She opened her newsreader, logged onto comp.games.programming, and dumped out the most recent one hundred postings. She ran her eye down the list of names, unsurprised to see no Vince Mattus among them. She tried comp.games.design with the same result.

Well, what about programming groups that didn't specifically concern games? She opened comp.programming.C++; still no Vince Mattus. She was about to move on when a name caught her eye.

There were half a dozen postings from someone named Matt Vincent.

She clicked on one at random. "It's like the Year 2000 bug," Matt Vincent had written. "You have to look beyond the immediate problem, try to see what the full result will be. Otherwise we create more problems than we solve."

That didn't sound much like her Vince. She clicked on another. "I used C-Side to compile, and I really didn't like the result. It ran slow AND it didn't compile as tightly as a couple of other packages." There was more, a spate of technical discussion that Anneke generally agreed with, but none of it told her anything about the writer himself. One more click.

Bingo.

"What you want," Matt Vincent wrote, "is a series of boilerplate formulae that you can use for various elements. Check out *http://csu.org/~lola/light.html*; there's a whole set of formulae that should give you what you want."

It was the identical Web site that Vince Mattus had recommended to Elliott.

It could be coincidence, Anneke thought, not believing it for a moment. The confluence of information and name was too obvious. Besides—she glanced at his sig—his e-mail address was posted as *2MLV3@nospam.umich.edu*. A University of Michigan address. Vince, she recalled, had a Netcom address, but that wasn't the point; both of them were located in Ann Arbor.

So that was that—Matt Vincent and Vince Mattus were the same person. Only . . . which was live, and which was virtual? Will the real murder victim please stand up?

She returned to AltaVista, typed "matt vincent," and scanned the resulting hits. There were half a dozen or so people with that name, but none of them seemed right. One was a college professor at the University of North Dakota; another was a tech writer in Virginia; a third was a Mormon missionary. None of them, she concluded, could possibly be Vince Mattus's alter ego.

Just to be absolutely sure, she logged on to Confer, the University's conferencing system, and browsed quickly through some of the programming conferences. She found postings from Matt Vincent in the Fortran conference, an engineering conference, and the Y2K conference. She checked a couple of the gaming conferences, but found no postings from either Matt Vincent or Vince Mattus.

She wondered if she should call Karl and let him know what she'd found, but then she thought: What exactly *have* I found? That his victim had two different online personas? So what? Lots of people did. For that matter, there was no reason even to assume that Vince's—or Matt's—computer activities had anything to do with his death; for all she knew, the bomb had been sent by a crazed ex-girlfriend who was even now under arrest. She'd better concentrate on her own work, not Karl's she scolded herself. She printed out the comp.games.programming postings, logged off, looked longingly at the "Whitehart" directory, and firmly opened the Loquat Café directory instead. "Whitehart" might have a future, but small-business operations were what kept Haagen/Scheede going at present.

She'd talk to Karl in the evening, she reasoned.

But in fact, she talked to him late in the afternoon, when he called to tell her he'd be home late.

"Bad one?" she asked sympathetically.

"Bad enough." He sounded grim. "Although, thank God, the damage was confined to the one apartment. But there are . . . ramifications."

"Oh?" She didn't ask him to clarify; instead, she asked merely: "The victim is Vince Mattus, isn't it?"

"Not exactly."

"Oh, of course—he was Matt Vincent, wasn't he?" The "real" persona, after all, had to be the one enrolled at the University.

"Not exactly." And what on earth did that mean? That there was yet a third persona? He didn't ask what or how she knew, and she didn't ask any more questions either; he must not be alone, she reasoned. "Don't wait up," he said. "It's going to be a long night around here."

"Phooey. You're probably doing this just to get out of dealing with wedding problems, aren't you?"

"Got it in one. See you in the morning."

But really, she thought when she arrived home, the wedding was fairly well under control—under Michael's control, anyway. There was a message from him on her answering machine, informing her that he'd arranged for another several dozen chrysanthemums for the museum rotunda. Informing rather than asking, she noted, not sure whether she felt relieved or annoyed. Some of both, but more of the former, she admitted to herself, putting a ham-and-cheese croissant into the toaster oven.

She put the croissant on a plate, added some raw carrots, and took the impromptu dinner into her office, a large, airy space that had once been the dining room of the big, old Burns Park house she and Karl had bought together the previous year. There she sat down in front of her computer and logged on to the Internet while she ate, a guilty pleasure that almost compensated for Karl's absence.

E-mail had poured in thick and fast over the course of the afternoon, especially when people had discovered, God knows how, that "Vince Mattus" and "Matt Vincent" were the same person.

<Elliott>I don't believe it. You mean "Vince Mattus" was just an avatar? What was he, some kind of schizo?

<Dani>You know, maybe that's exactly what he was. It would explain a lot, wouldn't it?

<Kell>You mean one of those multiple personality thingies? Wow, wouldn't THAT make a gonzo basis for a game?

<Seth>Oh, come on. Lots of people have more than one online persona.

<Jesse>That's one of the great charms of the Internet, isn't it? We can be different people in different places. In cyberspace we're not limited by what we "really" are. We can become whatever we want, even if it's just for a little while.

<Larry>And isn't that one of the joys of computer games, too? A really good game lets the player almost become the protagonist. That's what "virtual reality" is all about.

<Kell>For that matter, we do that in real time, too. I mean, we all have different personas for different situations. Like, we act one way with our mothers, and another way with our bosses, and we're someone else when we're with our friends.

<Elliott>Yeah, but Vince wasnt just goofing. I mean, why wold anyon invent a scumbag avatar like that? Unless you were playing the character in some game where you wanted to be the bad guy. gee, maybe thats it? He was like running a game?

<Jesse>The thing is, which was the real person, and which was the construct? Maybe "Vince Mattus" was the reality and "Matt Vincent" was the avatar. It's even possible that they were both avatars--that he was really someone else entirely.

<Larry> Well, the only one I knew about was Vince Mattus. At least, that's how he signed on to the list. He just said he'd written a couple of games, and he knew his stuff, so I plugged him in.

<Dani>It's funny how little we know about him. I mean, we all tend to talk about our personal lives, but I'm only just realizing that Vince never did. What about the Matt Vincent persona--did he ever talk about himself on comp.games.programming? (I don't read it, so I don't know.)

<Kell>I've got to admit, his games were more Matt Vincent than Vince Mattus. Do you suppose he may have written some other games we don't know about?

<Jesse>I think I came across him in comp.y2k last year, but I don't remember anything much about him except that he was very helpful and forthcoming, especially to newbies--and that's not so common, you know. I don't recall him saying anything personal, and I'm sure he never said anything about writing games. Seems to me he was working on some kind of large-system project, but I'm not sure of that either.

<Larry>Well, he couldn't, could he? Not if he wanted to keep the two personas secret.

<Dani> But why promote "Vince Mattus" as the writer of "Tombs and Tokens," unless that was his real persona?

<Kell>Maybe for the same reason authors use pen names. Privacy, keeping different aspects of your life separate, etc.

The thread ended there, leaving Anneke with more new questions than answers. She printed out the postings, added them to the stack from her newsgroup search, and set them aside to give to Karl in the morning.

Digging without a shovel is quite impractical. Even with a shovel progress is unlikely.

— ADVENTURE: THE COLOSSAL CAVE

He didn't want them.

Or rather: "Thanks, but I won't have any use for them." He glanced at the printouts over his coffee cup and shook his head. He looked tired and—not worried, exactly, but . . . bothered.

"I don't understand. Is something wrong?"

"Several things, I'm afraid." He took a last spoonful of cereal and pushed the bowl aside. "To begin with, I'm off the case."

"Why? What's happened?" She felt a trickle of dread.

"A couple of things." He sighed and leaned back in his chair. Behind him, the bright October morning sparkled through the bay window, leaves of red and brown and gold scintillant in the sun. A squirrel raced up the trunk of the big oak tree and disappeared from sight.

"First of all," Karl said, "it's a letter bomb. That makes it a case for the feds."

"Oh, hell." Anneke knew how badly cops hated having the FBI move in on their turf. "Still, they'll work with the department, won't they? Or at least . . ."

"Usually they do." He nodded, tightening his lips. "But there's something else. It seems that you are a suspect."

"I'm a— What did you say?"

"You're a suspect." He smiled slightly at her disbelief, but the smile didn't reach his eyes. "They found your name on a list next to his desk."

"On a list? What do you mean? What kind of list?"

"A list of names—they're checking the others now."

"But that must be . . . Look, what were the other names on the list?"

"Let me see." He thought for a second. "There were seven of them. Larry Markowitz. Kell Albright. Jesse Franklin. Seth Conroy. Elliot Washburn. Dani Noguchi. And you."

"That's what I thought," Anneke said. "There's nothing mysterious about it. That's just a list of some of the people on GameSpinners."

"GameSpinners?"

"It's an Internet mailing list, for game programmers. Vince was one of the people on the list. That's all it means." She felt a gust of relief until she realized that Karl's face didn't mirror her reaction. "Was there something else?"

"I'm afraid so. The list was titled 'The Blackmail Game.' "

It took her a minute to process the words, to understand their implication. "So they think he was blackmailing the people on that list?" She shook her head. "Uh-uh. If I'm on that list, then they're wrong." She looked at him directly. "I promise you, I am not being and never have been blackmailed."

"I believe you." Was there a flicker of relief on his face? Well, why not? They'd only known each other for two

40

years, after all; he couldn't know, for absolute fact, that there was nothing blackmail-worthy in her past. The important thing was that he believed her denial. Didn't he?

" 'The Blackmail Game.' " She repeated the words. "Well, he was a game programmer. Was it a real game? A computer game, I mean. Was there anything on his computer to indicate that he was actually writing a game with that title?"

"I don't know. And since I'm off the case, I can't find out."

"But— Oh, this is ridiculous. It must have been a game he was working on."

He shook his head. "It's not that simple, I'm afraid. If it was purely a fictional computer game, why did it include a list of real people?"

"I don't know. Maybe he planned to ask us gaming questions." Which, she knew even as she spoke the words, was ridiculous. The Vince Mattus she knew would never have asked GameSpinners members for advice about anything.

"Do you save all your e-mail?" Karl asked her.

"Not all of it. Only things I want to archive. Why?"

"Did you save the e-mail you received from Vince Mattus?"

"I never *did* receive any mail from Vince. Why would I?"

"But you were on the same mailing list."

"Oh. Yes, but that's different. The way a mailing list works is that everyone sends e-mail to a single list manager, and then that message is sent on to everyone who's a subscriber to the list. So yes, in that sense I got e-mail from Vince, but it wasn't to me personally, if you follow me."

"I see. And you never got any personal e-mail from him, sent only to you?"

"No, never."

"Did you ever meet him?"

"No. I never met him, never heard from him, and I know absolutely nothing about him, including why he had my name on a list." She heard the sharp impatience in her voice. "Sorry. It's just that I feel like I'm being interrogated."

"Consider it a practice session." His lips tightened. "The feds will be around with the same set of questions this morning. The difference is, *they* probably won't believe you."

She felt a sudden stab of anxiety. "An FBI interrogation?"

"I'm afraid so. I can be there with you if you like."

"You sound like you don't think that's a good idea."

"Unfortunately, I don't. It might look like I'm trying to get you special treatment. I think you'd be better off with Stanley."

"I suppose you're right, although criminal law isn't his field. Still, I'll call him. If he doesn't feel comfortable with it, he'll recommend someone else."

"And they'll show up with a search warrant, too," Karl warned her. "They're going to want to see everything on your computers."

"Good luck to them. Even I don't know what's on all of them." She struggled to remain matter-of-fact. "Karl, they're not really going to think I did this, are they? Just because I'm the only one on the list in Ann Arbor?"

"Actually, my guess is, you'll be at the bottom of their suspect list—although you will be on it. For one thing, since you do live in Ann Arbor, why bother to send a letter bomb?"

"Misdirection?" she suggested.

"Possibly." He grinned, more openly than he had until now. "But the major factor in your favor is that you're a middle-aged woman."

"And middle-aged women don't commit murder?" She laughed at her own resentment.

"Indeed they do. But they don't fit the profile of a mail bomber."

"Oh, right, I forgot. Women hate things that go boom, don't they? And besides, all that nasty, complicated wiring is *so* beyond us. Speaking of which," she went on, "what kind of device was it?"

"I don't know the details, I'm afraid." He took a sip of his now-cold coffee, made a face, and added more from the carafe on the table. "And of course I won't have access to the lab reports. All I can tell you is that it was in a square cardboard envelope, probably a disk mailer."

"Return address?"

He chuckled. "Microsoft. Redmond, Washington."

"Oh, great. I know he hated Windows, but isn't that a rather extreme reaction?" She wondered what the Internet comedians would do with that one when the news got out.

"Postmark?"

"Unreadable. The explosion destroyed that part of the package."

"Of course." She made a face. "Karl?" The question she should have asked first finally popped into her head. "Just exactly who *was* he?"

"His name was Matthius Vincent. Twenty years old, senior, in both computer engineering and finance, apparently."

"So Matt Vincent was the real person, and 'Vince Mattus' was the avatar," Anneke mused.

"Avatar?"

"It's a kind of representation of a person online." A thought struck her suddenly. "It just occurred to me—which of them was murdered?"

"That is the question, isn't it?" He nodded. "All I can tell you is that the bomb was addressed to Vince Mattus."

So a kid named Matt Vincent was dead because of the actions of a nasty slimebag named Vince Mattus. But that still didn't tell her which of them was real in the truest sense—which persona represented the true heart of the victim. Still, if he really were blackmailing people, that pretty much decided it.

"It's hard to imagine any of the people on the list as blackmail victims," she said. "They all seem so . . . I don't know, ordinary. For instance, what could a kid like Kell Albright have to be blackmailed about? She positively glories in being outrageous."

"Maybe she's actually a fifty-year-old bus driver."

"Or a member of the British royal family. Or a Chinese martial arts instructor." She laughed; Karl didn't.

"Have you met any of them in person?" he asked.

"No, but . . ." She started to protest, then stopped. Well, what did she know about any of them? "Okay, some of them are open to question, but at least a couple of them are known persons, if you know what I mean. Jesse Franklin is famous in the computer world. And Larry Markowitz is definitely head of software development at Gallery Three. I haven't met him, but I know Dani has. Which means," she realized, "that Dani's also a real person. Whatever the hell that means." She threw down the papers she'd been holding. "Oh, this is ridiculous. Of course they're real people. I mean, Elliott Washburn? If he turns out to be anything but a high school kid, I'll eat a bug. And anyway, we'll find out when they're questioned."

"No, we won't," Karl contradicted. "I can't be involved in this investigation at all. And in any case, the suspects are scattered all over the country. For the moment, I'm out of the loop entirely." He picked up the printouts and glanced at them. "All the same," he said, "I think I'll read through these."

"Good. And I'll see what I can find out about the others." She opened her palmtop and checked her schedule and to-do list. "I need to pick up that youth bed for Samantha." She glanced through the rest of her list, trying to shift mental gears from murder to wedding tasks. "Karl," she said suddenly, "is this going to affect the wedding? I mean, should we postpone it, do you think?"

"Nice try." He grinned openly at her. "But not a chance. In fact, maybe we ought to invite some of those nice men from the FBI. Michael could line them up along the aisle to make sure you don't make a break for it."

"Very funny. Well, if you want to risk marrying a mad bomber, I guess it's up to you."

You are in a debris room filled with stuff washed in from the surface. A low wide passage with cobbles becomes plugged with mud and debris here, but an awkward canyon leads upward and west. A note on the wall says: "Magic word XYZZY."

—ADVENTURE: THE COLOSSAL CAVE

The music was pounding once more when she reached her office. And Zoe was back at the computer, again surrounded by spectators. The monitor glowed molten gold; Anneke could see the metallic sheen of Whitehart Station's corridors, pierced by transparent bubbles beyond which iridescent creatures swam.

"What about the Game Room?" Max asked.

"Been there, done that." Zoe sounded frustrated. "Believe me, I picked up everything that wasn't nailed down."

"Maybe picking up things isn't all you can do there," Marcia suggested.

"What the hell do you expect me to do?" Zoe asked. "Roll dice with death, aka FOX?"

"Well, it *is* a Game Room," Calvin pointed out.

"Oh, jeez. Of course." Zoe swiveled to face him. "You mean I get to gamble with FOX for control of the area? Cool. Is it really dice? Does the player get a choice of games?"

46

"Hey, figuring it out for yourself is part of the challenge. You asking me to do your work for you?"

They were grinning at each other in a way that made Anneke reluctant to break up the party.

"How's it going?" she asked.

"Terrific." Zoe's face shone. "I've already gained control of the West Airlock and the Hydroponics Bay." She pointed to the screen, where a multicolored readout displayed game status details. "And the only thing I've lost is the South Airlock."

"Are you having fun?" That, regardless of Seth Conroy's position, still seemed to Anneke the most important point.

"If I weren't, I wouldn't be here." She grinned at Calvin as she saved out her game position and stood up. Well, true enough, Anneke conceded; but what exactly was she having fun *at*?

"I think it's great, really," Zoe said. "What do you do with it next?"

"Next we send it out for beta testing."

"You mean you have people try it and tell you what's wrong with it?"

"More or less, yes. Mostly we're concerned about technical issues—does it work with all the different video and sound cards, does it conflict with any other programs, do the commands work the way they're supposed to, that sort of thing."

"And when that's all taken care of, what then?" Zoe asked curiously. "I mean, are there publishers you send it to, like if you wrote a book?"

"Not exactly. There are game companies, but they generally produce and market games they've developed in-house. Some of them may occasionally buy a game from outside, but it's not likely, if only because it would conflict with their own titles."

47

"So you have to sell it yourself through computer stores?"

"We'll market it ourselves, yes, but computer stores are only a small portion of that—for one thing, there just aren't that many computer stores around any more." Again Anneke sighed over the Good Old Days, when you bought computers and software from actual stores, with actual, informed employees who could tell you what you were getting. "And it's difficult to get shelf space for a single game from a new company—the big software houses have so much of it locked up."

"Then how do you sell a game?"

"Actually, most software is sold mail-order these days. We can sell it ourselves, or we can sell it through catalogues and online companies. Or both, of course. The bigger issue is how to market it—how to get gamers to know about it. And most of that takes place on the Internet."

"You mean through chat rooms and stuff?"

"Oh, no. It's much more organized than that. To begin with, there are game zines and gamer Web sites and all sorts of game review outlets on the Net. And then there are a lot of demo sites—places where gamers can go to download a piece of the game, try it out and see if they like it. In fact, that's really our next step—developing a demo. And by the way," she said to Calvin, "I'd like to keep the demo under ten megs, okay? Lately some of them are running over forty megs and taking forever and a half to download, even at fifty-six K. I think that deters a lot of potential buyers."

"Yeah, I agree." He nodded. "Unless it's the latest block-buster from Electronic Arts, who's gonna bother with a three-hour download of something that's only a demo? Anyway, I'm gonna get started on it, but right now I'm stuck with that project for Your Closet."

"Huh?" Zoe looked at her. "You computerizing your clothes?"

"I wish." Anneke and Calvin both laughed aloud. "Your Closet is one of those self-storage places. We're doing a software package for them. But before you get started . . ." She paused. "Were you planning on working the full morning?" she asked Calvin. "Oh, and is Ken's office free?"

"Yeah, I think so," Calvin answered both questions. "What's up, boss-lady?"

She took a breath, keeping her voice as matter-of-fact as possible. "It's likely that the FBI will be here this morning, and they'll want access to all our computers."

"Are you kidding?" Marcia said. She looked interested; Max looked uneasy, but then Max always looked vaguely uneasy. Calvin looked . . . She couldn't read the expression on Calvin's face because she couldn't see his face. Instead, all she saw was his back, leaning over one of the Pentiums, his right hand dragging at the mouse in short, quick strokes.

"It's about that letter bomb yesterday." Anneke didn't comment on Calvin's activities. "The boy who died was a member of the gamers' mailing list that I'm on, that's all. But it might be just as well if you folks take today off."

"Yeah, I guess so," Max muttered.

"You're sure you won't need us?" Marcia looked like she'd rather stick around and watch.

Anneke shook her head. "Nope. Go have some fun—go to a movie or something."

"Some hope. I've got Parallel Algorithms this semester." She grabbed her purse, dislodging a (luckily empty) coffee cup from the top of the file cabinet. "See you tomorrow."

"I guess I'll go to the library," Max said. "I'm not really scheduled to work today anyway. I just came in to get a head start on the Wildstock database." He scuttled out the door.

"Calvin?" Anneke spoke to his back; his right hand

dragged and clicked for a minute before he finally shoved the mouse aside and stood up.

"I hear you. I'm outta here, too." He grabbed his jacket from the coatrack and picked up his bookbag. "See ya tomorrow." He was out the door before she could say anything more.

"Is that his computer?" Zoe was still there. She was pointing to the computer, but her eyes remained fixed on the door through which Calvin had made his abrupt exit.

"Not exactly, but it is the one he generally uses."

"He was deleting stuff, wasn't he? And then he took off like a scalded cat." Lines of worry dug furrows in Zoe's forehead. "What was he deleting?"

"I don't know. It could be something as simple as a piece of bootleg software."

"But then why would he take off like that?" Whatever her feelings, Zoe wasn't the type for self-deception. "Was he on this mailing list with you?"

"No. He said too much talking about games made him go stale. Honestly, I wouldn't worry too much about him leaving. Some people just get nervous about police. Believe me, I'm not exactly looking forward to this myself."

"Yeah, but . . . Maybe you're right." Zoe shrugged, affecting a nonchalance that Anneke didn't believe for an instant. "Hey, can I stick around and watch? You should have a witness anyway, shouldn't you?"

"Thanks, but my attorney's on call just down the hall."

"But I've never seen a full-scale FBI search." Zoe pouted, then laughed. "Okay, okay. But will you tell me all about it afterward?"

"Every detail. Now, out." She stood alone in the office finally, her eyes on Calvin's computer. What had he been deleting? And why?

The little bird attacks the green snake, and in an astounding flurry drives the snake away.

—ADVENTURE: THE COLOSSAL CAVE

They showed up before she could pursue the question, three men in dark suits, dark ties, and dark polished shoes, so stereotypically FBI that Anneke would have laughed if she hadn't been so nervous. Two of them carried large black cases. The third one introduced himself as Frederick Daheim and proffered a copy of the search warrant. Anneke took it and glanced at it and the man who handed it to her.

He was about thirty, good-looking in a yuppie sort of way, and shorter than she expected an FBI agent to be. His dark hair was shiny with gel, closely trimmed at the neck and brushed straight back from his forehead. The word that popped into her head was "dapper," and it wasn't a compliment. His suit was expensive but slightly too pinched at the waist, the paisley tie a little too bright, the Rolex watch a little too big. Portrait of a young man on the make. He probably wasn't in charge of the bombing investigation, but rather a field operative working under someone with more seniority.

"If you don't mind, I'd like my attorney to read this," she said.

"Sure." Daheim shrugged, but there was a shade of annoyance on his face. She wasn't what he'd expected. He looked her over openly, and she could see him trying out and discarding pigeonholes for her. He couldn't quite figure out what values to assign to a middle-aged woman with silver-and-brown hair, who wore not below-the-knee dresses but black jeans and a silk shirt and big, chunky silver jewelry. A woman who looked like his mother but didn't dress like her, and besides Mom couldn't even program her VCR and here was this one surrounded by a room full of sophisticated electronics that he couldn't even identify, let alone operate.

His uncertainty made him uncomfortable, which was probably not a good thing. She'd dealt with that kind of discomfort before, and in her experience, it generally led to hostility.

"You want your lawyer here, that's up to you," Daheim said. "But we're going to get started."

She picked up the phone and pressed four on the speed-dial. "Stan? It's Anneke. Good. Thanks." She replaced the receiver. "He'll be right in," she said to Daheim.

"Fine." He didn't seem to care. The other two agents were already seated in front of computers, their black cases open at their feet. One of them was tall and lanky, with curly brown hair; the other was a stocky Asian wearing silvered sunglasses. Both of them, to her relief, acted like they knew their way around computers.

Even so, she was suddenly uneasy. "Exactly how are they going to search?" she asked, worried about the pure mechanics of the problem. "These are computers, you know, not dresser drawers."

"They're going to copy everything onto tapes," Daheim said. "As far as I know, it won't hurt anything on your machines." He didn't sound like he cared very much about that, either.

"Yes, but . . ." Before she could pursue the question, the office door burst open.

"Okay, what's the story?" Stanley Bergman was everything Frederick Daheim wasn't—short, rotund, and sloppy. His suit, as usual, looked like he'd slept in it, and his thinning grayish hair, also as usual, was frizzed out around his head. It would have looked like a halo if there'd been the slightest hint of the angelic about him.

He slouched into the office and glanced casually at the three men in suits. "I hear you fellas have a search warrant?"

"Frederick Daheim, Federal Bureau of Investigation." Instead of replying to the question, Daheim held out his ID. "And you are . . . ?"

"Stan Bergman, attorney-at-law. How ya doin'?" He held out his hand. "I guess I better take a look at that warrant if I wanna earn my pay, right?" Daheim handed him the warrant without comment. Stan looked it over for a minute. "Judge Arthur Copeland Warren," he read aloud. "Good man." He beamed at Daheim. "So you got the right to search the lady's computers for anything relating to this Vince Mattus, or Matthius Vincent, both here and at her home." Anneke started; that hadn't occurred to her. "Okay, just so we know the parameters. And since this is the lady's bread and butter, you'll take real good care not to mess anything up, right?"

"We know how to conduct a computer search, Mr. Bergman."

"Come on, we both know the routine." Stan grinned amiably. "You're on a fishing expedition. Well, knock yourself out—but only with the computers, okay?"

"If your client is innocent, she doesn't have anything to worry about, Counselor."

"Right. I bet that's what you guys told Richard Jewell's lawyer, isn't it?" Daheim's lips tightened. Stan winked largely at Anneke. "I assume he's gonna want to put the thumbscrews to you, too; right, Freddy? No problem. Why don't the three of us adjourn to Anneke's office, and you can ask away while these guys do their thing." He didn't wait for Daheim to agree, but simply herded them toward her private office, where he waved Anneke to the chair behind her desk. Putting her on her own turf, and giving her a sense of control. Anneke understood and appreciated the strategy; Daheim clearly didn't. He'd been outmaneuvered, and he didn't like it. Sitting in one of the gray wool chairs in front of the desk, he pulled a notebook and pencil from his pocket and scowled at it.

"How well did you know Vince Mattus, Ms. Haagen?" he asked abruptly.

"I didn't know him at all."

"Then can you explain how your name came to appear on a list in his room?"

She hesitated. Damn, how much was she supposed to know? Should she admit that Karl had told her about the list, or would it cause trouble for him? Well, err on the side of caution; keep it simple.

"Vince was a participant on a computer mailing list that I was also on. I assume the list had something to do with that?" She made it a question, but Daheim didn't answer.

"But you just said you didn't know him," Daheim said.

"I didn't know him personally. I simply knew him as a member of the mailing list."

"So you did know him."

"I assume that depends on how you define your terms,

Mr. Daheim." She kept her annoyance in check with an effort. "As I said, I knew him only as an online presence. I would say more accurately that I knew of him." Stan nodded and jerked a thumbs-up at her.

"And what exactly did you know of him?"

"Practically nothing beyond the fact of his existence. He gave very little personal information in his posts."

"Such as?"

"Really, nothing at all. I knew he was a game programmer, and I knew he lived in Ann Arbor. That's about it."

"So you knew he lived in Ann Arbor." Daheim made a note, slowly and solemnly, as if the admission was hugely meaningful. "And you knew he was a University student."

"In fact, no, I didn't."

"He never mentioned classes, or teachers, or exams, or anything that would tell you he was a student?"

"Not that I can recall."

"So you only assumed he was a student."

"She didn't say that, Mr. Daheim." Stan had dropped his schtick when the questioning began; his voice was sharply businesslike.

"Did you know any of the other people on this mailing list?" Daheim proceeded as though Stan hadn't spoken.

"If you mean personally, no I didn't."

"But you had personal contact with some of them."

"No, never." She shook her head.

"You don't consider e-mail personal contact?"

"In fact, I don't," Anneke replied. "But even if I did, it wouldn't apply, because we're not talking about personal e-mail." She explained the mailing-list procedure, and Daheim's scowl deepened.

"I know how computer mailing lists work, Ms. Haagen." There was just the subtlest hint of sarcastic emphasis on the

Ms. "Are you saying you've never received any personal e-mail from anyone on the list?"

She was coming on too strong; maybe it was time to go into Nice Lady mode. She shifted in her chair, leaning her elbows on the desk. Stan's maneuver might also have been a mistake. Sitting behind her own desk put her in an authority position, and men like Daheim didn't like women in authority positions. Especially women who reminded them of their mothers.

"Occasionally I did, of course." Anneke tried a friendly smile. "Sometimes people want to talk about things that aren't really game-related, and you tend to take those off-list."

"Ah." Daheim seemed to pounce. "Such as?"

"Just ordinary things. You know." He didn't, of course. "Someone else's e-mail address. A question about hotels in some city. That sort of thing."

"And what sort of thing did Vince Mattus e-mail you about?"

"Nothing, truly." She poured simple innocence into her voice. "I never got a single piece of personal e-mail from Vince."

"You didn't like Vince Mattus, did you, Ms. Haagen?" Daheim switched attitude gears, affecting a conversational tone that didn't suit him.

"I suppose I didn't, really." She made herself sound almost sad.

"Why was that?"

"Well, much as I hate to say it, he really seemed like a very nasty person."

"In what way?"

"Well, he just went out of his way to insult everyone. I

56

think he was afraid to let people like him, poor thing." She sighed.

"Did he ever threaten people?"

"Threaten?" She cocked her head as if in thought. "No, I don't think so. I mean, poor Vince didn't really have anything to threaten people with, you know. He was just a kid working at being nasty."

"So he never threatened you, either on the list or by some other means?"

"No, never."

"But he did know something about you, didn't he?"

"I suppose so. I mean, he'd know the things I mentioned in my postings." She looked at Daheim and smiled. "I don't have any special secrets, after all."

"No secrets? That makes you a very unusual woman." There seemed no reasonable answer to that, so she made none. Daheim waited, staring at her, but she just shrugged and smiled. "Considering that you live in the same town as Vince Mattus," he said at last, "it would have been fairly easy for him to find out things about you that you might not have written in your e-mail, wouldn't it?"

"What kinds of things? I'm sorry, but I don't understand." Since he hadn't mentioned the word blackmail, she allowed herself to play dumb.

"Oh, come on, Ms. Haagen. Vince Mattus was blackmailing you, wasn't he?"

"Blackmailing me?" Anneke looked at him wide-eyed. "For heaven's sake, about what? Where did you ever get such an idea?"

"We'll find out about it, you know. Mattus will have left records somewhere, and we'll find it."

"Mr. Daheim, I assure you you're wrong. I truly don't

have a secret in the world worth blackmailing me for." Christ, now she sounded like Scarlett O'Hara; she'd be batting her eyelashes next.

Daheim seemed unimpressed by her protestations, but he did at least move on to other subjects. He asked more questions about the list, he asked about the other members of the list, and again and again he returned to Vince. Still, she had the sense that his heart was no longer in it. Once, out of the corner of her eye, she saw a flicker from the monitor of her computer, and realized the men in the other room were downloading its contents via network. And still the questions went on.

"Asked and answered," Stan said for the fourth time. "Unless you have some new ground to cover, Freddy, I think we're adjourned." He stood up. "You want to go check out her home computer now?"

"I don't think that's going to be necessary," Anneke said.

"Hey, don't worry about it," Stan said. "I'll be right there."

"No, that's not it." She smiled briefly. "My home computer's networked in to the office LAN. I think they've already downloaded everything on it, haven't they?" She addressed the question to Daheim, who shrugged and looked annoyed.

"Probably. If it's on a computer, they'll get it." She wondered if he even knew what a LAN was. "They'll want to get everything on that laptop, too."

"Of course." Anneke stood up, feeling cramped muscles protest, realizing how tense she'd been during the questioning and wondering if Daheim had picked up on it. Well, hell, who wouldn't be tense during an FBI interrogation? She looked at Stan, who winked once more.

"Pleasure doing business with you, Freddy." He clapped Daheim on the shoulder. "Now, let's go on out and see how those computer whizzes of yours are getting on."

The computer whizzes were finished. Anneke looked at her watch, amazed to see that the interrogation had lasted more than two hours. She stood next to Stan as they closed and latched their cases.

"You'll keep your client available for further questioning, Mr. Bergman?" It wasn't really a question.

"Sure will, Freddy." Stan grinned and slapped Daheim on the back. Anneke, suddenly remembering that she was supposed to leave for a honeymoon at the end of the week, swallowed her protest. Somehow she didn't think he would be real concerned about her wedding plans. Daheim and his computer wonks left, scowling.

Stan doubled over in laughter.

"Tell me something," he said between whoops. "Can all women do that, or do you have a special talent?"

"Do what?" she asked crossly, uneasily sure she knew what he meant.

"That 'little ol' me' routine." He laughed some more. "Too bad you didn't go into it from the beginning. As it is, you have him confused—he can't figure out if you're a dragon lady or just somebody's mum."

"Oh, shit." Anneke gave in and laughed as well. "That's my talking-my-way-out-of-traffic-tickets persona. Just don't tell the Women's Movement, okay? It's the most politically incorrect thing imaginable."

"Honey, your secret's safe with me. And speaking of secrets." He abruptly became serious. "Do you want to tell me any little thing about this Vince Mattus?"

"Stan, everything I told Daheim is absolutely true. I

59

really, truly, honestly, cross-my-heart-and-hope-to-die never had a single, solitary blackmail threat from Vince Mattus, or Matt Vincent, or anyone else in the world."

"I guess I believe you." Stan grinned at her. "Although after that performance with Daheim . . ." He left her office still laughing.

There is a message scrawled in the dust in a flowery script, reading: "This is not the maze where the pirate leaves his treasure chest."

—ADVENTURE: THE COLOSSAL CAVE

When she was finally alone, Anneke returned to her private office and went directly to the computer, where she accessed each of the office machines. All of them seemed to be in order; she could find no missing files, although it was impossible to be sure in a quick scan. She went to the fireproof safe, gathered up all the backup tapes, and moved them to a back shelf. She'd have today's backups done on a new set of tapes, and save these until she was sure everything was present and functioning. There was also a full off-site backup set at home, of course, but that was two days old. She didn't think of it as overkill; all sane computer people were belt-and-suspenders types.

Only when she'd completed her triple-redundancy check did she return to her machine, and as much out of curiosity as concern, access the computer Calvin had been working on. Nothing seemed missing or out of place that she could see, but of course she didn't know what to look for. Had he just been removing bootleg software? She checked for traces of a security delete, but found no sectors with zero overwrites. Had he been accessing the main server through the LAN? She checked it, too, for security deletes, with the same result. Well, what then?

All right, work from date and time stamps. She punched keys until her monitor displayed a list of recently accessed files across the network. Near the top of the screen was the company personnel file. She had an ugly premonition as she opened the file.

Calvin Streeter no longer existed.

She didn't bother to check the payroll files, or look for his personal directory or his name on "Whitehart Station" or elsewhere; if Calvin had set out to delete himself, he'd be deleted. Well, there could be any number of innocent reasons for it, she told herself, trying unsuccessfully to come up with even one. With a sigh, she put the problem of Calvin aside and logged on to download her e-mail.

She wasn't the only member of GameSpinners who'd been visited by the FBI. The mailing list erupted with reports of interrogations, searches, demands.

<Dani> What a pig. First he asked me all sorts of questions about what I used my computer for, like it was some kind of toy my daddy bought me, then he wanted to see my Web site, and what else I did online. And after he'd read through some of my columns for the GrrlPower Web site, he decided I was both a lesbian AND a hooker.

<Kell>Not that there's anything wrong with that. ;-)

<Elliott>Wow, it was SO awesome. They showd up at school and took me right out of class. You should have seen the other kids faces, they were like TOTALLY blown. Then they made me show them everything I ever accessed on the school computer (right, as if) and THEN they took me home and downloaded

everything on my machine there. They asked me about blackmail too, but I thought they wanted to know if I was blackmailing Vince, and i'm like yeah, right, like he had anything I want. My mothers gone postal of cours but everone else at school thinks its way cool.

<Dani>It's not that I mind them thinking I'm a lesbian, or a hooker either for that matter, but they seemed to think Vince was blackmailing me about it. Like I'd be ashamed of it or something, for shit's sake.

<Seth>Yeah, they mentioned blackmail to me, too. They kept asking me how well I knew Vince, and did Vince know I worked for a bank. And then a lot of shit about how I must resent the guys who run the place, and how I have access to all the accounts. And Christ, if they think I'm embezzling and go for a full audit, I may as well kiss my ass goodbye in this place. It doesn't matter that I didn't do anything, believe me. They'll be so pissed at having to put up with that shit that they'll can me just out of revenge.

<Kell>The one I got was real cute. I'd have come on to him, but I didn't think he'd be much of a dancer with that metal rod up his ass.;->

<Jesse>They asked me about blackmail, too. Anyone know where that's coming from? And why us? Not that there's anything to blackmail me about. I made my last blue box a lot of years ago, and Ma Bell wasn't even all that upset about it at the time. Especially after I gave them the schematics and showed their techies how it worked. God, I was a little shit, wasn't I?

<Larry>I wouldn't take this all TOO lightly, gang. These guys mean business. And remember, somebody DID murder Vince. I don't know where the blackmail thing came from, but if it's legit we could all be in for some very heavy investigation. So far, we know they've interrogated Seth, me, Dani, Elliot, Jesse, and Kell. Anyone else?

They'd know eventually anyway, Anneke thought. She hit Reply and typed:

<Anneke>They questioned me this morning, too. And yes, they mentioned blackmail. I had the feeling they didn't take me all that seriously, though; somehow a middle-aged woman involved in a mail bomb, let alone as the SOURCE of one, doesn't fit into their cosmology.

She hit Send and returned to the mail, where even lurkers and newbies were getting into the conversation.

<Toby>Shit, I haven't heard a word from them. It sounds like a trip; maybe they'll get around to me when they're done with the rest of you.

<Kevin>Yeah, how come some of you guys get to have all the fun and we don't? I guess I'll have to start posting more often.

<Larry>There's something else I want to mention to all of you. I was asked to give them a copy of the list archives, and I refused. The thing is, this kind of communication isn't like letter-writing, where you know going in that other people can see what you write. This is more like conversation, where most people just let it fly. You don't think in terms of permanence. So I don't think it's either fair or appropriate to give it to the police--it's kind of like ex post facto eavesdropping. I suppose maybe I shouldn't even have archived it at all, but there was some good technical stuff there that I thought I'd pull out someday and reproduce as a FAQ.

Anyway, it wasn't on my computer when they got here, and I refused to turn it over to them. My guess is it's going to wind up in court as an Internet privacy issue.

<Dani>If the guy who questioned me is a fair sample of their investigative prowess, I figure they'll have this solved about the time Windows stops crashing.

<Jesse>Good for you, Larry. We need to protect Internet privacy by any means possible, even though I'm afraid we're fighting a rearguard action. And BTW, one of the questions they asked me was, "Are you a member of any quasi-political organization?" Of course, I told them that I was the founding president of Programmers for a Fart-Free Society, but they didn't seem to be amused.

<Elliott>LOL Jesse. Right on Larry, this is the Internet you know? We got to protect it. No cops, no feds, no snoops, no controls, right? Don't give the bastards ANYTHING.

<Kell>I don't think they're allowed to be amused--it's in their contract or something. I told mine that if he'd lighten up a little he might have enough personality to make it as a crash test dummy, and for some reason he took offense. Jeez, some people are SO sensitive. :->

<Seth>Hey, gang, check out the Game Nazi Web site. It's got some great jokes. My favorite is "What do you get when you cross a game programmer and a bomb? Answer: Son of Mordor."

So the jokes were already starting. Well, it wasn't a bad line at that; "Son of Mordor," one of the most eagerly anticipated games in recent years, had turned out to be one of the worst. Still, it seemed to Anneke that everyone was taking this whole business—Vince's death, the FBI interrogation, the whisper of blackmail—with remarkable casualness, even cheerfulness.

If there were already a joke site, there must already be action on the Net, she reasoned, turning to Netscape. Sure enough, Yahoo headlined "Game Programmer Killed by Letter Bomb," offered the latest wire service reports, and provided nearly a full screen of links. It included Vince's own Web site, of course, as well as links to reviews of his games, to the FBI, and to several bomb sites, including the notorious—and preposterous—Anarchist's Cookbook.

(Anneke wondered briefly if anyone was really silly enough to try building a bomb to its specifications.)

Near the bottom of the list she found a link to Game Nazi, as well as a few oddities. She clicked on one called Parents Against Evil, and watched the screen fill with a line drawing of a cherubic tot chained to a computer, while snarling, snaggle-toothed demons flew leering around his head. "Learning Evil Early," the headline proclaimed, followed by: "The computer-game menace is seducing our children. YOU can stop them."

Below the sketch was the word NEW in letters of red flame. Next to it was the announcement: "Computer Games=Death." Vince Mattus, PAE exulted, had embraced evil and met the appropriate fate.

"Are we sorry he died?" the text went on. "No. Computer games are the equivalent of moral rape. Child molesters come in all forms. Maybe the animals who design these games will take this as a warning."

Anneke wondered if the FBI was taking any notice of this drooling mania. Wrinkling her nose, she returned to Yahoo and clicked on a site called Gamers Beware. This one had a black background on which large white letters proclaimed: "The Case the FBI Won't Solve." Below it was a dense block of text; skimming it, Anneke was informed that Vince Mattus was murdered by either a) a neo-anarchist militia group, b) a proto-Christian anti-game cabal, or c) Grey aliens from Zeta Reticula. In any case, the FBI, the CIA, and the Secret Service were all part of the plot. The major game companies, it continued, were beefing up security in expectation of further attacks.

Compared to this seriously weird craziness, Game Nazi was a breath of sanity if not compassion. The site's creator, tongue firmly in cheek, began by solemnly laying out the various "theories":

1) Vince Mattus was killed by an enraged gamer who, after six weeks of trying to get past level eight of "Tombs and Token," had encountered a bug that wiped out his scores on the first seven levels, thus sending him back to square one;

2) Vince Mattus was the target of Operation Wipeout, a government conspiracy to eliminate all independent programmers in order to prevent the development of an operational encryption program;

and finally;

3) Vince Mattus was killed by the Evil Empire because their version of "Tombs and Tokens" was vastly inferior to the original, and as usual, they decided to eliminate the competition.

Anneke, who much preferred the third theory, was already laughing when she scrolled down the page to the section that was headed: "Games are serious; death isn't." Below it was a full screen of jokes, most of them boringly scatological, or boringly juvenile, or just plain boring. The one Seth had quoted was the best of them, except for a line that made Anneke laugh aloud. "How many hackers does it take to send a letter bomb through the post office? Two; one to make the bomb, the other to explain what the post office is."

The Internet, she noted, was focusing on "Vince Mattus," rather than a UM student named Matthius Vincent.

Well, that was natural; it was Vince who was one of their own. And they were giving him the usual Internet send-off—conspiracy theories, black humor, and all the bad craziness they could muster. Not the worst epitaph for a hacker, she thought as she logged off.

This is a low room with a crude note on the wall. The note says, "You won't get it up the steps."

                                            —ADVENTURE: THE COLOSSAL CAVE

"If nothing else, it's giving me a chance to catch up on my paperwork." Karl finished the last bite of his hamburger. Anneke wasn't sure if the statement was meant to be humorous or not.

"I keep wanting to say it's ridiculous of them to keep you out of the investigation, but I guess from their viewpoint they have to consider me a suspect," she said gloomily.

They were dawdling over lunch in a wood-paneled booth at the Red Hawk, where Anneke had reported at length on her morning with the FBI. Karl's morning, by contrast, had been "eerily uneventful," he reported.

"It isn't just you, you know." He took a sip of coffee. "The fact is, I'm a suspect myself."

"You! But . . ."

"If you actually were being blackmailed, I could have killed him to protect you," he pointed out. "Or we could have been in it together."

"Now that is ridiculous." She shook her head. "So they're keeping you out of the loop entirely?"

"Oh, it's worse than that. They're keeping the whole AAPD out of the loop."

"What? But that's—"

"Ridiculous. I know." He smiled, the first time he'd smiled since they'd sat down to lunch. "But as long as I'm in the department, I'd have access to the case files. And so far, no one's prepared to talk suspension."

"My God." She put down the last of her chicken sandwich and stared at him in horror. "It couldn't possibly go that far, could it?"

"Oh, it could, certainly. The chief's in a real bind on this one. Right now, he's just hanging in there hoping they get it solved quickly."

"Oh sure, that'll happen," Anneke said bitterly. "Did you meet the precious Mister Daheim?"

"Yes." Karl grinned. "But remember, he's just one field operative. He's not in charge of the case."

"But whoever is in charge of the case has to depend on the information he gets from his field operatives. And from what I've seen, the others aren't any better than Daheim."

"What you've seen?"

"Here, look at this." She reached into her briefcase under her chair and withdrew a small sheaf of paper. "I printed out this morning's postings from the mailing list. Does this look to you like the feds have a clue what they're doing?"

He read through the pages quickly; when he handed them back to her he had an odd look on his face.

"Are they always like this?" he asked.

"The people on the list, you mean?" She grinned. "Pretty much. They're gamers at heart as well as by avocation, I'm afraid."

"I almost feel sorry for the FBI." There was a smile on his face. "Are these all the people on the mailing list?"

"Oh, no. There are thirty-some subscribers, I think, but most of them are generally lurkers. These are the people who do most of the posting."

"Lurkers?"

"People who read but never post. Actually, the term 'lurker' used to be a pejorative in the early newsgroup days; it meant people who used a newsgroup but never contributed anything to it. Nowadays, the vast majority of people are lurkers." She made a face. "Which is probably just as well, considering the kind of people you get on the Internet these days."

"What's the difference between a mailing list and a newsgroup?" he asked.

"Really, the biggest difference is privacy. Newsgroups are public; as long as an Internet provider carries a particular newsgroup, anyone using that provider can read it and post to it." She sighed. "Back in the Good Old Days," she tried to make the words humorous, "there were understood rules about newsgroup behavior. You didn't post your religious views on a newsgroup devoted to Unix programming; you didn't ask questions before reading the FAQ; and most of all, you absolutely, positively, *did not* use them for advertising." She heard her own voice rising, and took a deep breath. "Sorry. I'll tell you this, though. If you find some slimebag spammer murdered, then I really will be a suspect.

"Anyway," she went on, "as the scum began to take over newsgroups, more and more serious discussion moved to private mailing lists, where they can't get access."

"But can't spammers just send things to the list address?"

"No, because mailing lists are nearly always filtered. The GameSpinners list will only accept mail from previously approved e-mail addresses. If you want to participate, you have to send Larry a request, and he'll plug in your address. Anything from an unapproved address gets bounced."

"I see." Karl sipped his coffee thoughtfully. "And how does a list manager decide who to let in?"

"It varies. For a lot of them, of course, you have to be a True Believer."

"You mean religious lists?"

"Depends on how you define religion." She grinned. "Let's just say I don't think Charley Aarons would approve any Buckeyes on the GoBlue list. And it's not just sports. There are a lot of fan lists for TV shows, for movies, for individual actors, singers, that kind of thing. Someone who hated science fiction, for instance, wouldn't be allowed onto a *Star Trek* fan list."

"Well, they wouldn't want to anyway, would they?"

"You'd be surprised," she said bitterly. "There are far too many people who just like to use the Internet to cause an uproar. On *Star Trek* newsgroups, which are public, you get them posting just to complain about the show—to criticize the plots or the acting, to sneer at the people who do like it, that sort of thing. It's one of the things that's killing newsgroups."

"What about GameSpinners?" Karl asked. "How does Larry Markowitz screen applicants?"

"I'm not sure he does. When it's a technical subject, I imagine most list managers assume that anyone interested enough to bother might as well be accepted. And Larry's pretty laissez-faire about it all anyway. If he weren't, Vince Mattus would've been booted off a long time ago."

"That's something else that surprised me," Karl commented. "Is the level of hostility on GameSpinners customary on all mailing lists?"

"Not customary, but not unique, either. I guess every

Internet discussion group develops its own ethos—some are supportive, some are self-absorbed, and some can be very combative. There are some with strict rules against flaming other group members, for instance, and others that positively glory in it. It really depends on the dominant in-group."

"The ones who post regularly."

"Right. Newbies are generally either ignored or flamed until they show they're willing to conform to the dominant ethos. If they refuse, they're generally driven out."

"I'm guessing most newcomers don't last long on GameSpinners."

"I suppose that's true. I also think that's why we have as high a proportion of lurkers as we do. It's a tough crowd."

"I'm also guessing that Vince did more than his fair share of driving-out?"

"I suppose so." She thought about it. "On the other hand, he wasn't any more hostile to newbies than he was to anyone else. If someone bothered to read the postings for a couple of weeks before jumping in, I don't think they'd take it personally. And I certainly can't see it as a motive for murder."

"You can't imagine some of the motives for murder these days," Karl said. "Last year a kid in California shot up a carnival in an argument over a stuffed Tweety Bird."

"You're making that up." She didn't know whether to laugh or not.

"I wish I were. What's more, letter bombs are more often than not the weapon of choice for the truly deranged." He shook his head. "Still, there's nothing to suggest that that's the case here." He took a sip of his coffee. "You say that the majority of people on the list are what you call lurkers. If they don't participate in the conversation, what do they get out of it?"

"Oh, the arguments and the rest of it are only part of what the list is about. There are a lot of, I guess you'd call them functional postings. Information about conferences, new products, who's hiring, that sort of thing. Larry does a pretty good job of ferreting out news of the gaming world."

"He must spend a fair amount of time on it."

"Well, it's part of his job. He's a software engineer for Gallery Three, which produces a graphics library for game programmers. So in a way the list is a promotional tool for them."

"That would explain why he'd be reluctant to kick anyone off the list, no matter how obnoxious."

"Vince, you mean? I don't think he'd have been kicked off anyway. The thing about Vince is that he really was brilliant. If you had a tough question, the odds were pretty good that Vince would have the answer. You'd have to take a lot of abuse with it, but sometimes it's worth it. Besides . . ." She paused. "It's the Internet," she said finally, shrugging slightly. "Particularly among technical people, there's still a feeling that it's got to be open to anyone, even if you don't like them. Maybe even especially if you don't like them." She sighed. "There's no way people like Daheim are going to understand that, and if they don't, they'll never get Vince's murder solved."

"Well, if it was about blackmail, they will. That's exactly the sort of thing they're good at. For instance, have you withdrawn any significant amount of cash from your bank account lately?"

"Are you kidding? Would you like to know how much my wedding outfit cost?"

"But did you pay for it in cash?"

"Oh. No, I charged it. I see what you mean. But there wouldn't be a payoff, would there? I mean, why pay someone if you're going to kill him?"

"It happens, especially if the blackmailer makes multiple demands," Karl pointed out. "Besides, there are other investigative avenues. Right now they'll be digging into everyone's background looking for blackmail potential."

"I never thought of that. Ugh." She had a momentary feeling of nakedness, followed by a shiver of fear. "God, they can make our lives absolute hell, can't they? And the longer it drags on, the worse it's going to get. Look, what if you just . . ."

"I can't go near it," he reminded her forcefully.

"No, of course not," she agreed. "At least, not the usual way. But there's nothing to stop you from just taking a look through online sources, is there?"

"I can't imagine that it would do any good," he said. "Not now, well after the fact."

"Well, how about before the fact? Would reading through the archives be useful?" She smiled at his expression. "I just happen to have a full archive of GameSpinners for the last year. When I get home tonight you can at least take a look at it."

There is a very strange singing sword here—it is glowing and vibrating, and the eerie electronic notes of Charles Wuorinen's "Time's Encomium" issue from its blade and fill the air.

—ADVENTURE: THE COLOSSAL CAVE

When Anneke got home, earlier than usual because for once in her life she couldn't keep her mind on her work, the afternoon paper was lying on the porch. She wanted to read the report of the murder, but first she forced herself to the dining room table, where Helen, their three-times-a-week housekeeper, had stacked the latest batch of wedding presents. She opened each of them, removed the cards, and immediately wrote thank-you notes, feeling both self-congratulatory and impatient. Finally she shoved the last note into its envelope, went to the kitchen to pour herself a Diet Coke, and sat down at her desk to read the report of Vince Mattus's murder.

Or rather, Matthius Vincent's murder. Despite the fact that the letter bomb had been addressed to Vince Mattus, the local paper was clearly reporting on the death of a twenty-year-old University of Michigan student. Anneke, cut off from any official source of information, read it all carefully but with mental reservations.

Still, the prosaic facts of Vince's life were there. Matthius

Arnold Vincent: senior majoring in computer science and bus ad; originally from Muskegon; father a bus driver, mother a librarian; two siblings, a brother in the army, a high school–age sister still living at home. As to the person behind the facts . . .

"He was a brilliant programmer, one of the naturals"—from a computer science professor.

"Matt was pretty chill. He'd always help out when I had trouble with my computer, without making me feel like a dork"—from a tenant in his apartment building.

"He was kind of quiet, but real friendly and easy to talk to"—another neighboring tenant.

"He asked me out once and I turned him down, but he never acted like a jerk about it, y'know?"—a fellow bus ad student.

So Matt Vincent was the saintly Dr. Jekyll to Vince's Mr. Hyde. Anneke read further, but found only more of the same.

As to the "ongoing investigation," the feds were saying less than nothing. There was no mention of blackmail; no mention of GameSpinners; no mention of anything meaningful at all, in fact. Even the letter bomb was described simply as "powerful." Anneke was torn between annoyance at the lack of data, and relief that she herself wasn't a datum.

"Not very useful, is it?" Karl came up behind her and dropped a kiss on top of her head.

"Useful? Hell, it doesn't even focus on the right victim." Anneke tossed the paper aside. "Have you picked up *any* more information?"

"Only that Wes doesn't own a tuxedo, but does own a Marine dress uniform, and can he wear that instead of, and I quote, 'some damn rented monkey suit with somebody else's sweat all over it'?"

"Well, why not?" Anneke switched mental gears from

murder to wedding with an effort. "In fact, I kind of like the idea."

"Good. I'll tell him tomorrow, which should earn his life-long gratitude." He sank into the chair next to the desk, reached for Anneke's Coke, and drank half of it down.

"Just don't tell Michael. He's already bent out of shape because I won't carry a bouquet." She swiveled to face him directly. "Karl, are you still sure we should go ahead with everything?"

"Yes." He spoke seriously. "There's no reason in the world why this investigation should interfere with the wedding. Unfortunately, I'm less sure of the honeymoon."

"You mean they won't want us to leave town." Suddenly the honeymoon she hadn't wanted seemed infinitely precious. "But we're not leaving the country, after all. Or are we?"

"I suppose I can tell you that much, at least." He smiled, a shade sadly, Anneke thought. "No, we're not leaving the country. Still, they may want us where they can keep in contact with us at all times."

"Can they do that? Never mind." She shook her head, ideas chasing themselves through her mind. Damn Vince Mattus, or Matt Vincent, or whoever the hell he was. She mentally also damned GameSpinners, and the bomber, and the FBI, and everyone else who was making a hash of her— of Karl's—plans. She should have felt worried, she realized, but instead what she felt was angry. She reached into the cabinet behind her desk, pulled out a Zip disk, and shoved it into the drive.

"Let's start with this," she said, when the textfile filled the screen. She stood up. "That's the GameSpinner archives— everything that's been posted to the list in the last year. You take a look at it while I get you a Coke."

When she returned from the kitchen he was seated in her chair, his right hand on the mouse. She set the Coke next to him and withdrew, letting him browse the huge file on his own while she went upstairs to change clothes, then back to the kitchen to see about dinner. Helen had left a vegetable-rice casserole in the refrigerator, along with lamb chops marinating in a plastic container, but it was still too early to start things cooking. She wandered back upstairs and checked the spare bedrooms again. The youth bed for Samantha was already in place; did she have enough bedding for it? And should she get some more towels? And was it too late to call the Campus Inn and make reservations for four? Or maybe she should just grab Karl and run away from home.

She gave him an hour; when she returned to her office he was still where she'd left him, sitting in front of her computer scrolling through the archive.

"I'd like to pull out certain pieces of it," he said over his shoulder. "What's the easiest way to do that?"

"Save it under a different filename, and delete the things you don't want," she said. "Do you want me to do it for you?"

"No, thanks. I can't know what I want until I see it." He returned his attention to the screen. Feeling rootless without access to her own computer, she took her palmtop from her briefcase and sat down at the dining table at one end of the big living room, where she plugged the modem into the phone jack and logged on to the Internet.

<Seth>There's a website that's saying the bomb used ammonium nitrate.

<Jesse>How do they know?

<Dani>Wow, that's big-time stuff, isn't it? I mean, that's not something you have lying around your kitchen.

<Jesse>No, but it's not all that hard to get. Most farm supply stores have it.

Anneke clicked over to the Web site Seth had specified. BOMBS R US, the title read in flickering letters of flame, a cliché motif that Anneke found only marginally less annoying than crawling text. The self-described "bomb freak" offered links to dozens of bomb-related sites, from the Olympic bombing in Atlanta to the apparently ubiquitous Anarchist's Cookbook. There were whole screens of news stories about bombings, how-to articles, "The Bomb in History" as well as "The History of the Bomb," and a special section titled "Fun With Nukes."

The Web page, on the tiny palmtop screen, was even more annoying than it would have been at full size. It took her several minutes to locate what she wanted, under a flickering headline that read: "This Week's Bomb." The accompanying text was long on praise but short on details; the bomb was described as "beautifully crafted," using ammonium nitrate with a fuse created from the battery of a musical greeting card. It was, the bomb freak commented, a truly fine piece of work.

When she came to the end, she sat back and considered for a while, then went to AltaVista and entered the search terms "vince mattus" AND bomb AND "ammonium nitrate."

Examining the resultant six hits, she clicked on a site called BombNews, and searched through the badly designed welter of headlines and advertisements and self-promotion until she spotted: "Ann Arbor Letter Bomb Explosive Identified." It was a more sober and straightforward account, but the facts were roughly the same as those on Bombs R Us. She saved both stories to a file, logged off, and returned to her office.

Karl was still at her desk, but this time he was sitting back watching the laser printer spit out pages.

"What have you found?" she asked.

"That Vince Mattus was an exceptionally nasty piece of work." He reached for the thick stack of paper on top of the printer.

"I may have something useful." She plugged in the palmtop and printed out the file she'd saved. "Take a look at this."

He read it all the way through in silence. "Ammonium nitrate," he said, when he was done. "Not something you can pick up at your local supermarket, but not something that's all that difficult to come by, either."

"Neither of us would have access to it, though, would we?" Anneke asked hopefully.

"Any feed store out in Scio Township." He shook his head. "That won't get us off the hook, I'm afraid. On the other hand, this is the sort of thing the feds are good at. If one of the suspects bought it near his home, they may well find it."

"If any of this is true at all, of course," Anneke warned. "Remember, just because it's on the Internet doesn't make it true."

"Oh, I'm well aware of that." He picked up the printouts of the GameSpinner archives. "For that matter, it seems that just because someone is on the Internet doesn't make him a real person."

"No, I suppose not. But in this case, it wasn't the 'real person' who was murdered anyway; it was the avatar."

"We can't be sure of that," he cautioned. "I'll grant you that the bomb was mailed by someone who knew of the Vince Mattus persona, but that doesn't necessarily prove it was that persona that was the target." He looked down at the printouts, an expression of frustration on his face. "I wish there were a way to find out more about the real Matt Vincent."

"There might be," Anneke said thoughtfully.

"No. Don't even think about it. Neither one of us can go near anyone connected with this case."

"Oh, I know that." She smiled at him. "But Zoe can."

There is a delicate, precious, Ming vase here!
The vase is now resting, delicately, on a velvet pillow.
The Ming vase drops with a delicate crash.
The floor is covered with worthless shards of pottery.

—Adventure: The Colossal Cave

When Anneke got to her office Wednesday morning Calvin was already there, sitting in front of the computer and staring at a screen shot of a friendly-looking porpoise. She greeted him briefly and went directly to her own office, where she booted up the company database and checked the personnel files.

Calvin Streeter was back on the books.

She returned to the front office and looked over his shoulder. The porpoise had been replaced by lines of code crawling up the screen, disappearing off the top of the monitor like a receding tide.

"If they'd taken the backup tapes, you'd have been screwed," she said finally.

"Pretty sure they wouldn't." His finger clicked the mouse to halt the scrolling, but he didn't turn around.

"You want to tell me about it?" she asked.

"Not a lot." His shoulders were hunched, and the knuckles of his dark hand were tight on the mouse.

She sighed. "Calvin, you're one of the best programmers I've ever seen. Don't screw it up, okay?"

"Not to worry, boss-lady." He flung the words over his shoulder. "I haven't held up a gas station in, oh, a coupla months now."

"And I haven't hacked into a CIA computer since last Wednesday." She spoke sharply. "Look, Calvin, if there's something I ought to know, you'd better tell me. And if there's something you need to make right," she added more gently, "you have friends who can help. Okay?"

"I hear you." He still didn't turn around, but his voice sounded a shade less defensive.

"All right." It was the best she was going to get, at least for the moment. "Are you redesigning the porpoise?"

"Nah, just tightening up some code." They talked about "Whitehart Station" for a while. Max arrived then, and after discussing the database application he was working on, she returned to her own office. She didn't have any major projects herself—she'd cleared her schedule for the wedding and honeymoon—but she forced herself to spend an hour on necessary paperwork before finally logging on and downloading her e-mail.

<Seth>It's just all so stupid. Hell, if I offed every vicious bastard I came across online, there wouldn't be enough ammonium nitrate left in the world.

<Dani>Even if there WAS something to blackmail me about, what would be the point? It's not like I have any money. Now if you want to blackmail those bastards from Texonomy, give me a call and we'll talk.

84

<Jesse>It's possible, you know, that Vince wasn't doing it for the money. Vince was one of those people who really got off on making people squirm, and blackmail is sort of the ultimate power trip.

<Seth>That's true. Vince would've loved knowing bad shit about people, and having them know he knew (if you know what I mean.)

<Elliott>Shit, I always figurd he jerked other peopel around just to make himself feel important. He was like the school bully, you know?

It made sense, but there was another element they'd forgotten—"The Blackmail Game." Except they didn't know about it, Anneke realized, and she couldn't be the one to tell them. She probably shouldn't even know about it herself, after all, and it certainly wasn't something that should be broadcast on a public list. She shook her head and returned to the rest of the mail.

Although Vince's murder was Topic A, ordinary list business continued. There was more from Larry about GameDev; Elliott asked a question about TerminateWithError() functions; and Kell was still working on her "Wedding Game."

<Kell>Anneke, what exactly is the best man supposed to do? And how did Karl select a replacement when what's-his-name pulled out?

<Seth>"What's-his-name" is Jay Banning. He was a backup defensive end for the Steelers. Hey, is the new best man maybe Mean Joe Greene? If you get him, or Franco or someone like that there, I'll start angling for an invitation.

She hit Reply.

<Anneke>Sorry, Seth. Karl's new best man is a Lowly Cop. I guess he figured we really didn't absolutely need someone to block for the bride.

There was one more post from Kell, with an attached file for download, under the heading: "First game module— check it out!"

<Kell>Hey, guys, I've actually got a piece of this magnum opus under construction, and I was hoping some of you would take a look at it. There's a design-your-own-wedding-dress module, and a maid-of-honor module. It's still rough, but if some of you could check it out and give me some feedback I'd really, really appreciate it.

So she was actually putting real effort into the game. Despite herself, Anneke conceded that Kell might be on to something. She clicked to start downloading the file, and was about to move on to the next post when there was a knock on the door.

"Do you have a moment?" To her surprise, it was Karl who stepped into the office. He'd left the house in the morning wearing his usual impeccable dark suit, but now he wore khakis and a suede jacket over a brown patterned shirt open at the neck.

"Did they suspend you?" She asked the question without preamble, out of pure dismay.

"Not exactly." He sat down in one of the gray chairs and stretched his legs out in front of him. "I'd already arranged for two weeks' comp time starting Friday, and the chief 'suggested' that I take it a couple of days early, that's all." His voice was utterly impassive, devoid of either humor or resentment. His expression was utterly blank. This was his linebacker persona, she realized suddenly, cold and focused and filled with such disciplined, implacable anger that she had to make an effort not to flinch away from him.

He shifted in the chair, and the image shifted with him. "Sorry," he said, as though reading her mind.

"Don't be." She felt her own anger rise. "What are you going to do?" She wasn't sure what she meant by the question, exactly.

"Do?" He seemed to consider for a moment. "Well, first I'm going to do another close reading of that mailing-list archive."

"Good." She spit out the word savagely. "And while you do that, I'll gather all the information I can find about the people on Vince's blackmail list."

"Stick to indirect sources," he warned her. "At least for the moment."

"All right. And Zoe should be dropping by shortly."

He hesitated. "I'm not sure we should involve her."

"When she finds out you've been suspended—all right, all right, 'put on vacation'—you won't be able to stop her," Anneke pointed out. "It's better for you to control her than to let her go haring off on her own."

"I suppose you're right. But let me be the one to talk to her, please."

"Absolutely. Would you like to use Ken's office? He's out of town. That'll also give you computer access so you won't have to look over my shoulder—I'll forward everything I come across to your own account."

"It would probably be better to give it to me on disk," he said. "You have to assume that the FBI is reading all your e-mail."

"Not unless I want them to." She laughed aloud. "You're talking about the guys who can't even keep a teenage hacker from trashing their own Web site. Believe me, there are ways to keep e-mail private. Actually, though, I wasn't talking about e-mail. It's easier to redirect everything to your computer via network." A thought struck her. "Tell you what. Let's see if the feds really are as clueless as everyone thinks they are."

Because she did occasional consulting for the police department, she had an account on their system. Now she turned to her computer and keyed in her access code. "Well, they did at least think to shut down my account." She tapped again on the keyboard. "Bingo! They left the back door wide open and swinging." She quickly cut the connection. "If I root around in there they might find traces," she said. "But if at some point we do need access to department files, I can get them. Now, let's go see if Zoe's here for her daily dose of gamesmanship."

I respectfully suggest you go across the bridge instead of jumping.

— ADVENTURE: THE COLOSSAL CAVE

What she liked about him most, Zoe decided, was his intensity. Whatever he was doing, he did it with such total concentration that he made it exciting, even if it was something that should have been ordinary, or even boring. She'd always thought computer games were for male adolescent mouth-breathers, but Calvin had sucked her in somehow.

"Got it!" She clicked the mouse and grinned at him. On screen, a kelp forest glowed, fronds waving gently. Tiny fish swam in and out, beautiful in the half-light. "Let's see FOX break *that* entry code."

"You're right. Can't be done." There was something funny in Calvin's expression, like he was waiting for something to happen. She turned back to the screen.

"Oh, shit." A small reddish device drifted out from behind a kelp frond. She grabbed the mouse and clicked on the control panel at the side of the screen to zoom in on the kelp forest's computer terminal, but she was too late. The seabot had already hit Reset. The monitor went to black.

"Son of a bitch." She clicked on a corner of the screen,

and the Windows wallpaper appeared, a simple A/H logo on a moiré background. FOX's creature had shut down its program. "How much did I lose?" she asked.

"Everything since your last save." Calvin laughed unsympathetically. "You're up against a computer, remember? You've got to learn to protect yourself."

"Yeah, just like real life." She snorted. "Figure anything Windows can do to fuck up your life, it will."

"Now you're starting to get it." He leaned around her to scribble something on a scrap of paper next to the keyboard.

"Got end-played by one of the seabots again?" Anneke spoke from the doorway.

"Yeah. How am I supposed to know when there's one of them around, anyway?" Zoe complained. "I mean, it wasn't visible while I was setting the entry code, and believe me, I checked out that kelp tank from top to bottom as soon as I broke in."

"There's a way to detect them," Anneke said. "Do you really want me to tell you what it is?"

"I guess not." Zoe sighed. "I mean, what's the point of playing if you already know the solution?" She glanced at Calvin, but he was seated at the next desk, scribbling away on a yellow pad and muttering to himself. She sighed again and turned the glance toward Anneke, who shrugged and smiled.

"Zoe, have you got a minute?" she asked.

"Sure. What's up?"

"We'd like to ask you about something."

"Are you kidding me?" Zoe was outraged. "They can't be serious."

To her surprise, Anneke had led her not to her own office, but to Ken Scheede's, a room decorated chiefly with contemporary movie posters. To her even greater surprise, Genesko was sitting behind the blond Thirties desk, under a larger-than-life-size blowup of Tom Hanks in *Saving Private Ryan*. But surprise turned to shock and anger as he explained that he'd been suspended. Well, not suspended exactly, but the next thing to.

"I'm afraid they are." Genesko laid his hands flat on the desk in front of him. "I can't even seriously quarrel with them—you can't run an investigation under the eyes of a suspect."

"Oh, please. Suspect? What bullshit." Zoe snorted. "If you were any more of a straight-arrow you wouldn't be able to sit down." Anneke laughed aloud. Genesko smiled and shook his head.

"They don't know me as well as you do," he said solemnly.

"They also don't know you won't just slither away and wait under a rock for them to screw it up, do they?" Zoe cocked her head. "What've you got in mind, and tell me if I can help."

"I think perhaps you can." He looked at her consideringly. "What I need," he said at last, "is information."

"Whatever it is, it's out there," she said. "What do you need and where do I go to get it?"

"What I need is anything you can find out about Matthius Vincent."

"That's all? Hell, that's easy. Actually . . ." She thought for a minute. "Wouldn't the AAPD have some sort of liaison with the feds?"

"Yes, in fact they do." Genesko glanced over at Anneke, looking kind of amused. "Eleanor Albertson."

"Oh, shit." Anneke made a face, and Genesko laughed.

Zoe looked from one to the other of them. "What am I missing?" she asked. "Old girlfriend?"

"She wishes," Anneke said. "Let's just say, failed effort, and leave it at that."

"Got it." Zoe grinned. "So do you want me to interview her, too?"

"Absolutely not," Genesko answered at once. "I don't want you going anywhere near the police, or the FBI, or even the University administration. What I want you to do, if you're willing, is to interview anyone who knew Matthius Vincent personally. That includes housemates, professors, fellow students, even hometown friends, if you can."

"No problem." Zoe thought about it for a minute. "Do you want the story to actually run, or would it be better if it didn't?" Normally, she'd have cut off an arm before voluntarily passing up a good byline, but there was nothing normal about this situation.

"Let me think about that," Genesko said.

"Okay, whatever you decide." In her head, Zoe was already mapping it out: "Portrait of a victim: Why Matt Vincent had to die." Even if Genesko didn't want it to run now, he might okay it once they'd solved the crime. She didn't have a doubt in the world that they'd solve it. "Do you have particular questions, or should I just follow my nose?" she asked.

"These are the specifics I'd like you to focus on." He passed a sheet of paper across the desk. "But you needn't be absolutely limited by them. By all means follow up on anything that seems promising or revealing."

"Got it," Zoe looked at the sheet of paper, containing a list of questions in Genesko's precise handwriting. "There's a couple of things here I never would have thought of," she said, tapping the paper.

"That's because it's not the kind of information you'd want for a newspaper story. Zoe, remember, you're *not* actually interviewing for publication."

"No, I see what you mean." She read through Genesko's questions again, visions of a great profile story rapidly evaporating. "Okay, Chief." She stood up and saluted smartly. "Zoe Kaplan, of the State Street Irregulars, ready for duty."

"Zoe—"

"Hey, don't worry. I know how serious this is." She turned to Anneke. "I guess this means my career as a game-tester is on hold for a while." Despite herself, she glanced toward the front office.

"Actually, I'll have something new for you when you're done with these interviews."

"Oh, goody. Do I get to fight a giant squid bare-handed?"

"No, it's not about 'Whitehart Station' at all. It's a module of a game being written by a friend of mine." She had a funny look on her face. "It's called 'The Wedding Game.'"

"Urk." Zoe made a face. "Boy, are you yanking the wrong chain." Zoe couldn't imagine anything she was less interested in. It was one thing to be happy for Anneke, but a wedding for herself? Not with the things she had planned for her life.

"You mean you don't have a burning desire to design your wedding dress and select a pattern for pickle forks?"

"Yeah, sure. And while you're at it, why not sign me up for the picket fence and the golden retriever?" She stood and picked up her bookbag. "I'd better get out of here before you have me in a Lamaze class."

"What now?" Only when Zoe was gone did Anneke fully realize what was happening. "Karl, do you think you can really do it? I mean, solve this thing without being able to investigate personally? And without any of the department's resources?"

"I don't know." He shook his head. "Damn it, I don't have any choice." He grinned at her suddenly. "I promised you a honeymoon, and by God you're going to get one you won't forget in a hurry."

"I don't need—"

"Oh, yes you do. Besides," he added, his grin widening, "if Nero Wolfe can do it, don't you think I can?" There was something in his expression Anneke had never seen before, a kind of tense awareness, a suppressed anticipation of . . . something. She identified it suddenly as the pre-game face of every great football player, the mental preparation for combat. Only this time the opponent wasn't the Dallas Cowboys.

"It's the FBI, isn't it?" she said.

"It's Matt Vincent, and Vince Mattus, and the bomber, and the AAPD, and yes, it's the fucking FBI." He looked almost exuberant. "Now, you wanted to know what we do next."

"Right." She noted with pleasure his use of the word "we."

"Well, Zoe is getting us information about the victim. The next thing we need is information about the primary suspects."

"The people on Vince's blackmail list, you mean." Despite knowing his actual identity, she still thought of him as Vince Mattus. "And of course without any direct contact."

"For the moment, no direct contact. I want to know them better first. So let's find out if this great and wonderful Internet is everything it thinks it is."

"Aha. A challenge. All right, Lieutenant, you've got it. And while I'm slogging through cyberspace, what exactly is the great detective going to be doing?"

"What all great detectives do." His grin was positively wolfish. "Thinking."

She returned to her own office, and as always, started at the Alta Vista search screen. She'd simply take them alphabetically, she decided, typing "Kell Albright" into the search box. First search the Web, then she'd move on to Usenet. Some of them might be using other UIDs for different newsgroups, too; she'd have to work on that. Maybe using domain names and fuzzy-logic searches for alternative e-mail addresses . . .

When she finally came up for air it was nearly mid-afternoon, and she was starved. She plucked the thick stack of paper from her printer and crossed the hall to Ken's office. Karl was sitting at the computer, leaning back and staring at a screen full of text. As she stood in the doorway, he reached for the mouse, clicked, and dragged a selection up to the top of the file. He leaned back in the chair and examined the result thoughtfully.

"Is that the GameSpinners archive?" she asked.

"Yes." His eyes remained on the screen.

"Anything?"

"Maybe." He swiveled the chair finally to face her.

"What?" She felt a surge of excitement. "No, wait," she said as her stomach growled its complaint. "Let's talk about it over lunch. I may've found some useful data, too." She waved the sheaf of papers.

"Way ahead of you. There's a Cottage Inn pizza on its way right now."

"Double mushrooms?"

"Would the Great Detective forget something that important?"

"All right, give." Anneke bit into hot mushrooms and sausage and thick, gooey cheese. "What did you find?"

"Read the first few pages." He motioned at the screen with a folded slice of pizza, sliding his chair aside to give her room.

He had isolated a series of exchanges between Vince and the others—some of Vince's nastier ones, she noted. But they didn't seem to have anything else in common, certainly not the subject matter. She read through them carefully, searching for the common thread Karl had apparently found.

<Seth>Sports games are another genre that's gone Holly-wood. Don't even bother unless you can pay huge bucks to put some fucking celebrity on the box. Shit, even that Vegas creep Danny Mollick is raking in the bucks on "Beat the Spread," like he actually knows anything about computer games.

<Vince>Poor Seth--bitching again because someone else in the world is making money and he isn't. I'm BETTING you'd like to get a piece of what Mollick's got, wouldn't you? Just think, there you are working in a BANK, with ACCESS to all that MONEY, and I'll BET you never even get to see the MONEY, do you? Or maybe you DO?

<Elliott>I mean like who gives a shit about grades anyway?

<Vince>Yeah, who gives a shit about GRADES, eh, Elliott? Especially when they're so EASY to UPGRADE, right? Especially for you--you're such a genius you don't even have to study to RAISE your GRADES, do you, Elliott? Why, I'll bet you're so good you can even help OTHER kids raise their GRADES, maybe even SHOW them how to do it without even studying.

<Kell>There's no way guys are gonna like any game I'd write anyway, so why worry about it? The poor things won't know what they're missing, of course, but that's their loss, not mine.;-)

<Vince>How about taking the guy-bashing to alt.don't. give.a.shit? You want to CHEAT yourself out of two-thirds of the gamers in the world, that's your BUSINESS, okay? But then, you chicks only know how to FAKE it anyway, don't you? Like PRE-TENDING to be a programmer when you don't know the difference between a sprite and a FAIRY?

<Jesse>I didn't write Mordona to make money anyway. Hell, back then there weren't enough computers to get rich off of even if every single user bought a copy.

<Vince>Good old Jesse, last of the POPULISTS--even if you are sitting on a dozen acres of New Mexico real estate. Do you still buy into that old HACKER'S cliche, "Information wants to be FREE?" It sure isn't FREE anymore, is it, Jesse? Nowadays it's called DATA and it comes with a PRICE TAG as big as that ranch of yours.

<Larry>Yes, the new version will be a little more expensive--I think they're talking about $695 for the complete package. But the upgrade will only cost $115, which is what most of you guys will be paying.

97

<Vince>Gee, wouldn't it be nice to be one of those folks who think of a hundred bucks as "only?" Of course, we don't all have the same SOURCE of capital that Larry does, let alone the goodies--the two-million-dollar house, the Range Rover, and then there's that collection of classic cars. Not bad for someone with a company that just floated out a RED-INK quarterly earnings report. Of course, we don't know what kind of DEAL Larry got for himself, now that he's on the INSIDE. Hey, Larry, how do you get on the Silicon Valley STOCK merry-go-round, anyway?

<Dani>Venture capitalists? Are you kidding? Those are the guys who walked away from Texonomy Systems and hung the rest of us out to dry.

<Vince>It's called SLEEPING WITH THE ENEMY, sweetheart, and if you don't have the stomach for it you're not going anywhere in this business. But then you're more interested in blaming other people for your problems--especially MEN. Of course, you could have BLOWN the whistle on them while you were still on the INSIDE, but you didn't, did you? Now why was that, I wonder?

<Anneke>Right about now I wouldn't mind a paycheck job. At least it would mean I could spend my time hacking code instead of hunched over my desk grinding out government paperwork.

<Vince>But a paycheck job wouldn't be as CREATIVE, wouldn't it? I mean, even filling out GOVERNMENT forms can be creative if you just look at it from the right angle. And then there are all those nasty rules and regulations to get AROUND--must be a real drag, especially for a small ENTREPRENEUR. Maybe women just aren't cut out for the big, bad world of business.

The uppercase words jumped out at her, of course, but did they mean anything? Since you couldn't underline in most e-mail, people generally used uppercase for emphasis, and in the normal reading of GameSpinner postings she wouldn't even have noticed them. Still, as she reread the text Karl had selected, she realized that these particular capitalized words didn't make sense as emphasis. But they didn't seem to make sense as anything else, either.

"I don't get it," she said finally.

"Read yours again." He waited, and when she looked up from the screen and shook her head, he said: "Now, suppose you were fudging on your taxes, or paying some of your programmers under the counter to avoid making worker's comp or social security payments. How would you react to Vince's comments then?"

"But that's silly," she protested. "For one thing, I don't do any of those things, and for another, even if I did, how could Vince know about it?"

"He couldn't, of course. Any more than he could *know* anything damaging about any of the others." He dropped the crust of pizza into the box and leaned back in his chair, his eyes on the monitor. "What I think," he said slowly, "is that Vince Mattus was playing an advanced game of 'I Know What You Did.' "

"Good God. Could he have been that stupid?"

"Remember, he may have been a brilliant programmer, but he was basically a kid." He took another slice of pizza from the box.

"Do you think he was really planning blackmail?" she asked. "Or was he doing it as background, or a trial run or something, for a computer game?"

"I have no idea, and without access to his computer, I doubt that we could find out. But in fact, I don't think it matters. Whatever his reasons for doing it, I think Vince struck a nerve with someone on that list."

"It's so scattershot, though." Anneke nibbled the edge of her pizza and dropped the crust into the box. "I mean, apparently he was accusing me of some sort of tax evasion and I didn't even realize it."

"That's because you were innocent. But suppose Jesse Franklin really is in the business of selling illegal data? Or suppose Seth Conroy has been embezzling from his bank to pay gambling debts?"

"And the others?" She leaned past him and scanned the screen again. "He's accusing Larry of some kind of stock fraud, I guess. He capitalized the word *inside*—insider trading? And accusing Kell of being gay? That isn't all that blackmail-worthy these days—certainly not worth killing over. And Elliott . . . he's accusing him of changing grades, probably by hacking into the high school computer. I don't quite follow the post to Dani, though. It seems to mix sex and business, but it isn't very clear."

"No, but it might be to Dani. Remember, there's no evidence that Vince actually knew anything concrete about anyone—in fact, the posting to you is evidence that he didn't. I think he was simply blasting away at whatever target he could think of, hoping to hit something."

"Which apparently he did." She reached for another piece of pizza, changed her mind, and picked up her Coke instead, trying to wash the taste of Vince's game out of her mouth.

"Yes. And apparently it hit back."

"So where do we go from here? Do we try to figure out which one of the accusations is true?"

"You can't be sure that only one of them is true." He looked at her over his pizza. "Now," he said briskly, "what can you tell me about these people?"

"More than I expected." She reached across him for the mouse. "Take a look."

Blasting requires dynamite.

—ADVENTURE: THE COLOSSAL CAVE

Kell

Kell's Web site—a charmer. On the main page, dancing figures swooped and whirled. Abba's "Dancing Queen" provided background music, segueing into Cyndi Lauper's "Girls Just Want to Have Fun."

Other pages: An homage to "the mother of all game programmers," the great Roberta Williams, whose "Wizard and Princess" virtually invented the graphic adventure game. "The seminal (you should pardon the expression:-) computer game," Kell described it.

A page devoted to "Girl Groups," singing groups past and present, including a spirited defense of the Spice Girls. Complete with photographs and RealAudio buttons that played musical clips of each group.

A page titled "Boy Toys," with beefcake pictures of Leonardo DiCaprio, Matthew Perry, and other smooth-faced boys, most of whom Anneke had never heard of.

Links: To fan sites for the Supremes, the Shirelles, and other female singing groups. To girl-games sites. To sites about the *Ally McBeal* television show. To a collection of

"Post-Feminist" sites (Kell's term) that included online zines, post-punk fashion, and what-to-do-about-guys pages.

Kell's newsgroup postings--more of the same.

<alt.music.girlgroups>No, of course the Spice Girls aren't going to make anyone's Top Ten list. So what? They're fun, and as far as I'm concerned that qualifies as a major survival skill (and not just in music!:-) I never said they were the second coming of the Shangri-las. All I said was that I enjoy watching them.

<rec.tv.ally-mcbeal>But that doctor was SO hot--I mean, absolutely drop-dead gorgeous. I just about cried when she screwed that one up, because it meant I wouldn't get to look at him anymore. {:-(

<rec.games.frp.misc>The trouble with fantasy-role-playing games is that they're based on GUYS' fantasies. What I mean is, character attributes are always male-oriented, even if you're playing a female character. When I write the Great American FRP Game, it's going to have a sex-appeal attribute, because that's a very powerful tool for women--if they know how to use it. (And no, Appearance or Beauty are NOT equivalent attributes, fellas. You just THINK they are. ;-)

Seth

Seth's Web site—a mess. Seth designed on the principle: If you can do it, you should do it. His homepage was an eye-assaulting welter of flickering colors, jerky animation, crawling text, bandwidth-busting graphics, unreadable dirty-typewriter fonts. There were buttons to push, and drop-down menus to select, and imagemaps to play with.

Other pages: A fan page devoted to the Oakland Raiders, with large, uncompressed pictures of Charles Woodson and Tim Brown that took forever to download. A fan page for the Los Angeles Lakers, heavy on Shaquille O'Neal. A surprisingly sophisticated page devoted to beer, with historical notes, an article titled "The Best of the New Microbrews," and a reprint of a technical treatise on brewing techniques. A page headed, with no originality, "Babes of *Baywatch*," containing even more, and even bigger, uncompressed graphics. A page containing Seth's résumé.

The résumé: Born 1971; B.A. in computer science, California State Sacramento; current job—programmer, Management Information Systems division, Bank of Los Angeles. Photograph included, showing a round, pudgy face with little expression, pale blue eyes, and blond hair already visibly thinning.

Links: To beer-related pages, including several scholarly articles. To "The Hottest New Games on the Net," heavy on sports-related games. To more *Baywatch* sites, as well as other soft-porn pages. To football pages, including other Raider pages and several oddsmakers' sites.

Seth's newsgroup postings:

<rec.nfl.cowboys>Gimme a break. Aikman is such a fucking loser without Emmitt to carry him. Face it, he chokes when the pressure's on, and then he yells that he's "injured." Yeah, sure he is. And we all know that Emmitt's all washed up. Face it, you guys are dog meat.

<rec.nfl.raiders>Shit, at least if he'd made the fucking field goal they'd have beaten the spread. Dumb son of a bitch cost me plenty.

<rec.nfl.raiders>You read it here first--no way we're gonna

lose to the Chargers. Leaf's a total phony. Our linebackers will be in his face all day.

    <rec.tv.baywatch>Anybody know who's got the rights to a Baywatch computer game? Probably Hasselhoff's already optioned it to EA or one of the other biggies. As if they'd know how to work the jiggle factor.

    <rec.tv.baywatch>Didn't someone say there was a site with naked pictures of Yasmine Bleeth? Anyone know the url?

Other Internet references—Seth's beer page was linked from three or four other beer-related pages, and his Raiders page from one other football page.

Elliott

Elliott's Web site—all about games, games, and more games. Bright, busy, and surprisingly well-structured. "The Cutting Edge," it was headed, in bold green lettering under an arch of scimitars. Spatters of blood dropped from each swordpoint onto a row of fantasy figures, each figure a link to additional pages. At the bottom, the blue-ribbon logo of the Internet Freedom Foundation.

Other pages: Reviews of the latest games, most with screen shots. Each review gave a body count, a "Catharsis Quotient," and a rating system of one to four blood spatters. "Carmageddon," for instance, received four spatters and a Catharsis Quotient of 160 for "revenge against every idiot who ever cut you off in traffic."

A page of news from the gaming world, including reports of new hardware, company mergers, and a schedule of anticipated new releases. Two upcoming games were illustrated with screen shots flagged "Exclusive Preview!"

A page of commentary, headed by a piece titled "In

Defense of Games," badly written but cogently argued. Another essay, bylined by someone else (and probably pirated off some other Web page), titled "Why People Play."

Surprisingly for a fifteen-year-old, Elliott's Web site contained neither personal information nor anything about school.

Links—an endless string of game sites, game companies, and game development tools. Links to sites about mythology and folklore, including Asian myth and the Finnish *Kalevala*. Links to sites about warfare and weapons.

Elliott's newsgroup postings:

<rec.games.action>Face it, Mortal Kombat wasnt relly all that good the action was jerky and the graphics sucked. But the adrenalin rush was awsome thats why it was so popular. But a lot of other games give you the same rush now and they do it a LOT better. Lots of bloodshed isn't enough anymore.

<rec.games.frp>Their new 3D engine really rocks. You relly feel like your IN that dungeon and when you chop off the trolls head and the blood sprays out you feel like you want to duck its so relistic.

<comp.games>Yeh but if they start sensoring games where do they stop? Its like now they want to sensor porno stuf but next itll be violence and then who knows what. And anyway who gets to decide whats okay and what isnt? Why should some old fart in Washington get to tell me what to do? Shit if everone who played Mortal Kombat went out and killed someone there wouldnt be anyone left.

Jesse

Jesse's Web site—beautiful, playful, serious, deceptively simple. Across the top, a photograph of a desert sunset, glowing colors stretching across the screen. Beneath, another desert photo, of cactus and some small animals, serving as an imagemap leading to other pages. Prominent along the side, the blue-ribbon logo of the IFF—the Internet Freedom Foundation.

Other pages: A montage of desert photographs, each small thumbnail linking to full-screen versions big enough to serve as Windows wallpaper. A page that provided an online playable version of "Mordona," as well as a free download of the original game, and an Apple][emulator to allow it to run on a PC. A full-page essay on Internet freedom, complete with legal references.

Aside from the IFF logo, no links to other Web sites.

Jesse's newsgroup postings:

<alt.internet.freedom>Wasn't it Thomas Jefferson who said that the best government is the least government? But if you say that today, they consider you a threat to society. Which you are, of course.

<alt.internet.freedom>The Internet ran very smoothly as a self-regulating community, perhaps the best example of a successful anarchy in history. The trouble was, it didn't have any means to defend itself against invaders. When the army of newbies poured over the borders in the early '90s, we were overrun before we even recognized the threat for what it was. We simply didn't have the resources to repel the attack.

<rec.games.computer>The line between learning and play is entirely artificial. Play IS learning. So when you design a game, you're really designing an educational syllabus. That's important-- it means you have to think about what you're teaching when you design a game. No, you can't wiggle out of it by saying you're just "giving people what they want." If you design a game that teaches

106

racism, and cruelty, and barbarism, at least have the guts to accept responsibility for it. Don't, for God's sake, try to hide behind that "it's only a game" crap, because you know better.

<alt.urban.legends>Nope, that one's real. You can try it yourself. In WinWord, type "I'd like to see Bill Gates dead," select the text, and click on the Thesaurus. It really does suggest "I'll drink to that." At least it does in Word 97; they may have removed it in later versions.

Internet references to Jesse: Too many to count.

Dani

Dani's Web site—angry but funny. Or maybe, funny but angry. Like Kell's site, Dani's featured dancing figures. Except it wasn't girls dancing across Dani's page, but cucumbers, dipping and swirling in astonishingly suggestive poses. Beneath the cavorting vegetables, Dani wrote: "We already know that cucumbers are better than men. Click on the chorus line of studly cucumbers for the Interactive Cucumber Page, and tell us YOUR reasons why."

Other pages: The cucumber page itself, line after line beginning: "Cucumbers are better than men because . . ." (The best of them: "A Cucumber will never make a scene because there are other cucumbers in the refrigerator.") Along the side, a series of odd and hilarious and scatalogical cucumber graphics. A page of original computer art, dark and risky, better than much else in the genre. And a page for "Grendel," the game she was working on. Screen shots and a synopsis showed that it was surprisingly far along. "Grendel" was dark, murky, and highly original—a revisionist *Beowulf* with Grendel as the heroine protecting her home. And finally, a page advertising her Web design business, with links to sites she'd created, but no résumé or personal information.

Links: Under the heading "Pop Culture for Women," links to sites featuring Wonder Woman, *The Avengers* ("the TV show, NOT the sucky movie"), and the "Death to Ally McBeal" page. Other links to Grrrl Gamer sites, to online feminist zines, and to sites about revenge, including the alt.revenge newsgroup.

Dani's newsgroup postings:

<alt.art.newart>Okay, here's a test. Throw a party, and when it's really rocking, you come out and stroll through the room naked. If you're uncomfortable, or embarrassed, or ashamed, you're not an artist.

<IceQueen>Did you do it? What happened?

<Dani>Sure I did. It was cool. After a couple of minutes a lot of other people started taking their clothes off, too, and we got into body painting.

<BlueGirl>Oh, come on, that's a crock. Look, if you get off on exhibitionism, that's cool. But don't tell us every artist has to be on the same wavelength.

<Dani>Hey, if you're hung up about it, that's your problem. The thing is, if you're too uptight to expose your body, how can you be willing to expose your soul? Because that's what a real artist does.

<rec.art.computer>Think of a great computer game as partici-patory art. Like those things Vasarely did back in the sixties--pieces of plastic that could be moved around, so the person could do his own riff on Vasarely's basic idea, you know? In a game, you drag the viewer INSIDE the work of art, force her to view multiple perspectives. It's a way of dragging people out of the mindset that considers art to be static, you know?

<alt.revenge>Good, Gracie. Remember--every woman thinks

all men are scum except hers. At least you've taken the first step by realizing that yours is scum, too.

Other Internet references: A column by Dani on the BadGrrrl site, extrapolating violence-on-television research studies to violence in video games. Her thesis seemed to be that women needed violent games of their own. A review of a computer game titled "Black Tide Rising," in which Dani did her best to rip the designer a new asshole. Also, two computer art sites featuring some of Dani's works.

Larry

Larry's Web site—strictly business. In fact, there was no Web site for "Larry Markowitz;" there was only a complex multipage site for Gallery3, for which Larry was webmaster. The corporate level offered product information, press releases, and stockholder data. Another level offered upgrades, patches, technical support, hints and tips, and technical specs. A third level contained a gallery of work done with the product. There was no personal information for anyone named "Larry Markowitz."

Larry's newsgroup postings:

<comp.games.programming>, <comp.graphics>The latest upgrade to Gallery3, Version 4.0, will be demoing at GameDev next week. It's got a whole new set of subroutines to automate a lot of movement algorithms. We're also offering a competitive upgrade, so if you're using another graphics library, you can get Gallery3 for only $129. If you'd like to see it in action, drop by Booth 39–42 at GameDev.

<alt.collecting.cars>I'm having a hell of a time locating a front grill for a 1939 Pontiac. Anyone know anyplace I could find one?

There is no way to get past the bear to unlock the chain, which is probably just as well.

—ADVENTURE: THE COLOSSAL CAVE

"These are just from a quick first search, of course," Anneke pointed out. "I can poke around for more material later, but this will give you some basic information about everyone."

"What, no credit reports and DMV records? What kind of a hacker are you?"

"No kind at all." She waved a hand in protest. "People seem to think that every programmer can instantly hack into any system in the world. The truth is, most programmers, myself included, couldn't begin to break into secured sites. That kind of hacking is a specialized skill I've never bothered to learn. Calvin probably could," she added reluctantly, "but I don't really want to ask him unless . . ."

"Absolutely not. For half a dozen reasons, not the least of which is that the FBI is undoubtedly keeping a close watch on everyone on that list, including you. What you've come up with is a good start, at least, although it's a little spotty." He leaned back in Ken's desk chair and regarded the monitor screen. "I wish there were more personal information on them. What do you know about the others besides what's here?"

"Well, start with Jesse because he's the easy one—he's one of the most famous names in computer history. He was one of the original 'blue box' kids back in the seventies." She smiled at his quizzical expression. "Blue boxes were mechanisms that bypassed Ma Bell's circuits and allowed people to make phone calls without paying for them."

"And I assume that instead of having him arrested, they gave him a job?"

"They offered him one, but he wouldn't take it. He gave them the box, explained the circuitry, and showed them how to prevent it. Then he went out and wrote 'Mordona.' "

" 'Mordona'?"

"One of the first great RPGs—role-playing games. That's the kind where you design your own character before you start playing. You select various attributes, like strength or wisdom or magic-using, and that determines the kinds of resources your character will have. If it's done well it can be the most involving kind of game there is—and 'Mordona' was done very well."

"Did he make a lot of money with it?"

"I have no idea." She shook her head. "He certainly couldn't have made the kind of money big-name games do nowadays, but it was wildly successful for its time."

"That would have been when?"

"Early eighties. Which is practically Jurassic, in the computer timeline."

"And what has he been doing since then?"

"I have no idea." She rummaged through her memory but came up empty. "Probably consulting, I suppose."

"Which could mean anything, of course." Karl picked up one of the printouts. "What about Larry Markowitz?"

"I don't know anything about his background, but I believe he's been with Gallery Three since its startup. That would be about six years ago."

"Is the company successful?"

"I should think so. Gallery Three itself is a major package for game programmers, and they have several other products for software developers."

"What about their stock? If Larry was part of the startup group, I assume that most of his payoff came as stock options."

"I don't know, but stock information is the sort of thing I can find out easily enough." She scribbled a note to herself.

"What else do you know about him?"

"Not much, I suppose. If I remember correctly, he was with a small game company before joining Gallery Three—TerraNova Games? I think that was it. Whatever it was, it went belly-up at the time Larry left. He seems happy enough with Gallery Three, anyway. I can't remember him ever complaining about the company."

"Not on your mailing list, at least. From those archives, he comes across as the perfect company man."

"I suppose he does, doesn't he? Of course, he's head of software development, which would have to be upper management, so in a sense you could say he is the company. As for personal information, the only things I know about him are that he lives in Silicon Valley—Sunnyvale, I think—and that his wife is a lawyer. I'm pretty sure there are no kids."

"Do you know how old he is?"

"No. I've always assumed he was early thirties, but that's

probably because I assume that everyone in this business is young."

"All right." Karl sounded dissatisfied. "Seth includes a résumé, which is helpful, and there's a fair amount of information about Dani. I'll take Elliott at face value for the moment. But what about Kell?"

"Our resident party girl." Anneke smiled. "She's a student at Wisconsin, I think."

"Do you know that for sure?"

"Well, no, I guess not. I do know she's in Madison. I guess I just assumed she's a student."

"What else do you know about her?"

"Well . . ." Anneke repeated, then stopped. "Not a lot, I guess. Just that she likes music, and dancing, and . . ." She stopped again and looked at him. "I don't know anything about her at all, do I?"

"Not from the mailing list, certainly. She doesn't seem to have mentioned a single personal detail in anything she wrote."

"And that's unusual," Anneke noted. "I mean, all of us drop occasional references. About birthdays, or family events, or exams, or complaints about work—something, at least. I can't imagine—is she hiding something?"

"Well, of course, everyone's hiding something, but Kell does seem to have been remarkably secretive."

"And without anyone even realizing she *was* secretive. Which is no small trick."

"No. Whoever Kell Albright is, she's clever. Dammit." He brought his fist down on the desk, pulling back at the last minute so that it made a small thump. "I'd give a lot for ten minutes with the FBI files on this case."

"Well, we'll just have to approach it another way." She

forced herself to sound cheerful, only to discover that she really was. "I've got a couple of ideas I can follow up on. And if all else fails, you know," she grinned at him, "we can always just ask her. I can't believe the Kell I know is some sort of master criminal or something."

"You could be right." He shrugged. "But let's hold off for the moment. I'm not ready for direct questioning of people yet. Let's wait to see what Zoe turns up."

Aaaaaaaaaaaaaaaaaaaaahhhhhhhhhhhhhhhhhhhh.......>squish<

—ADVENTURE: THE COLOSSAL CAVE

Being a cop wasn't all that different from being a reporter, Zoe decided. You just collected up all the information you could find, and then you wove it into a pattern that made sense.

Not that the word *just* really belonged in that sentence. For either reporter or cop, the collecting part of the equation was a pain in the ass. And she had a sneaking suspicion that the weaving part wasn't going to be any walk in the park either.

Still, she wasn't too unhappy with what she'd gotten so far. She'd tried to focus on the information Genesko wanted: Did Matt Vincent seem to have money? Did he ask a lot of questions about people? Did he ever talk about writing computer games? When was the last time you saw him? And, in and around the nuts and bolts, to get some sense of who Matt Vincent was.

"Matt was okay, I guess." Jack Eichhorn contemplated the Budweiser can in his hand. He could have been musing over

115

mortality and the meaning of life, but Zoe was pretty sure he was deciding whether to get himself another beer. "I mean, he wasn't a lot of fun or anything, but he was okay."

"Tell me some things about him. What'd you guys talk about?"

Instead of answering, Jack looked over to the other end of the ratty sofa, where his roommate sprawled with his own can of Bud in his hand.

"He was a nice guy, he just wasn't very, well, social." Warren Cochran put his bare feet on the battered coffee table, pushing aside a blackened banana peel with an almost equally blackened big toe. Zoe suppressed a shudder. At least the stuff littering the floor in her dorm room was clean. Well, mostly. This place was a kind of caricature of a student slum, filled with molting furniture and moldy food and filthy piles of unidentifiable things she didn't want to think too much about. She had the feeling there was something living in that pile of fabric—dirty T-shirts? used underwear?—in the corner.

"We talked about classes and exams, that sort of thing," Warren went on, "but he wasn't interested in the important stuff, like girls and basketball and movies." Warren's face was owlishly solemn, but Zoe thought she detected a flicker of amusement in his eyes behind the wire-rimmed glasses.

"Well, if he didn't care about girls or basketball or movies," Zoe asked, "what *was* he interested in?"

"Fucking computers," Jack said. "That was about it."

"Computer games?" she asked innocently.

"Nah." Jack shook his head. "He didn't even have a PlayStation. He had this humongous computer system, but all he ever did with it was work."

"You must have been surprised, then, to find out he was a game programmer."

"Yeah." Jack seemed unimpressed by the contradiction.

"It does explain the money," Warren said.

"He had a lot of money?" Zoe followed up the comment quickly; money was one of the big things Genesko wanted her to find out about.

"I don't know that he had a *lot* of money," Warren said thoughtfully, "but he had money. I mean, he never complained about tuition or rent, he bought all his books new, and he always had some cash in his pocket for when he wanted a pizza or something. He wasn't a cheapskate, either. If you needed ten bucks to pay the pizza delivery, for instance, Matt'd lend it to you without making a big deal out of it."

"Did it seem like he was trying to buy friends?"

"No, nothing like that." Warren shook his head. "He didn't brag about having money, and he didn't offer to buy us things or stuff like that. The thing is, Matt wasn't one of those lonely, pathetic, poor-little-computer-nerd types. He wasn't a whole lot of fun, but he wasn't one of those guys who didn't have a life, either." He crumpled his empty Bud can and dropped it on the floor under the coffee table. "In fact, he seems to've had two of them."

"And he never said anything to you about his other life."

"Nope." Warren's eyes were serious behind his glasses. "Never."

"What did you talk about the last time you saw him?"

"Actually, except for passing him on the stairs a couple of times, I hadn't seen him for several days," Warren said thoughtfully.

"Me, neither." Jack had discovered an unopened can of Bud under the sofa cushion. He popped the tab and drank noisily. "And he was acting kind of weird, too."

"Weird? How?"

117

"Relax." Warren grinned at her too-obvious eagerness. "Jack's idea of weird is a guy who turns down a chance to watch *Naked and Naughty* three times."

"Yeah, well, I even offered to bring it over to his place," Jack said. "He always bitched when he came over here, like he was some kind of neat freak, so I figured I'd do him a favor. Turned me down flat. Something wrong with that boy," Jack opined.

"You think he didn't like girls?"

"Not exactly." Jack hesitated. "I mean, I don't think he was, you know, one of them, but he sure didn't talk much about girls. Maybe he was just scared shitless of them."

"He went out with Dee Wadsworth, didn't he?" Warren said.

"According to him." Jack shook his head darkly. "But he never said a word about it afterward, even when I asked. And if he couldn't get anywhere with Wadsworth, well . . ." He raised the beer can to his mouth and chugged. "Wanna call out for a pizza?" he asked the room.

"Sure." Warren looked at Zoe. "Want to hang around and join us?"

"Sorry, but I've got to get back to the *Daily*." The idea of ingesting food in this room was totally sick-making. She turned off her tape recorder, shoved it in her bookbag, and stood up. "Thanks, guys."

Warren dropped his feet to the floor and stood also. "Look, why don't you give me your phone number, and if we think of anything else useful we'll call you."

"Sure." She pulled out a *Michigan Daily* business card and handed it to him. "You can always reach me through the *Daily*."

"Okay." He grinned knowingly. She grinned back. He wouldn't be too bad-looking if it weren't for the stained white T-shirt and the ratty jeans, not to mention the filthy feet. "I clean up real good," he said.

"Then why don't you?" she retorted as she left.

"I mean, he did have Stones tickets." Dee Wadsworth was slim and blond and tanned, with rich, full breasts pushing against her white shirt, and the best nose money could buy. Gold hoops gleamed at her ears, and gold bangles adorned her wrists.

"And that's why you went out with him?"

"Well, sure. I mean, he was a nice guy and all, but it's not like he was the kind of guy I'd really *date*, you know? And I was sure right about that." Her voice took on an aggrieved tone. "Because I never actually did get to see the Stones."

"How come?"

"Well, it's not like I wasn't up front with him, you know? I mean, that wouldn't be fair, would it? When he came to pick me up, I was like, it's just two friends going to a concert, you know? I mean, I didn't want him to get the wrong idea." With a graceful finger, she smoothed her immaculate cap of gleaming golden hair.

"No, of course not." Zoe hoped the irony in her voice went unnoticed. "What happened then?"

"He just sort of went apeshit." Dee cocked her pretty head. "He took out the concert tickets, and he waved them in front of my face, and he was like, this was the only reason you agreed to go out with me, isn't it, and I was like, well, yeah, come on, and then he's like, okay, see what you can do with this. And then," her voice rose in anger, "he tears the tickets into little pieces, and grabs a handful of the pieces, and shoves them down my front. He nearly tore my dress, too, and it was a Calvin Klein. And when I tried to put the pieces together I couldn't, because they weren't all from the same ticket, so I never did get to see the Stones."

Way to go, Matt! Zoe cheered silently. Aloud, she said: "What happened the next time you saw him?"

"I never did see him again, luckily for him," Dee said. "After all, it's not like we moved in the same social strata."

"Stratum," Zoe said.

"Huh?"

"Stratum. It's the singular. Strata is the plural."

"Of what?"

"Never mind. Thanks for your time." Zoe turned off her tape recorder, thinking dark thoughts about the University's admissions office.

"He wasn't really around the department all that much." Professor Robert Turling didn't sound sorry. He didn't sound glad, either. Mostly, he just sounded annoyed. He sat behind his gray metal desk before banks of gray metal bookcases filled with loose-leaf binders and stacks of wide green-striped printouts. It was a curiously plain-vanilla office; apparently, Turling couldn't be bothered adding personal touches to his work environment.

"Was he having trouble with his classes?"

"Oh, no. He was pulling A's in everything. In fact, I offered him an assistantship at the end of last year."

"And he turned it down?" Zoe allowed herself to sound surprised, although given what she already knew about Matt Vincent, she wasn't.

"Yes," Turling said shortly.

"Did he say why?"

"No."

"I take it he wasn't very popular around here," Zoe said. What she really meant was: I take it you didn't like him

120

much, but she knew no faculty member would say that aloud about a student—especially a student who'd just been murdered. To her surprise, Turling shook his head in disagreement.

"I'd say people liked him well enough. He was a nice kid. He even went out of his way to help some of the newer students with class problems."

"Did he ever talk about what he wanted to do after he graduated? Was he planning to go on to grad school?"

"No." Turling pressed his lips together. "He couldn't wait to get out of school and 'start living,' as he put it." So that was the source of Turling's annoyance; what Matt Vincent—what most students—saw as freedom, Turling, like many faculty, saw as intellectual waste.

"Sometimes I know the feeling." Zoe grinned at him. "So he seemed bored?"

"Actually, no." Again Turling contradicted her. "In fact, in the last couple of weeks he seemed almost . . . excited. A bit hyper, perhaps. I think he was seeing the light at the end of his senior tunnel." He sighed. "He'd have made a fine teacher."

"I guess he already was a pretty good game programmer."

"So it seems." Once more Turling sounded annoyed.

"Nobody around the department knew he was writing games?"

"Not as far as I know." Turling shrugged. "I can't imagine why he was so secretive about it."

Sheesh, I can, Zoe thought. Aloud, she said: "Thanks for your time, Professor Turling."

"I really didn't know him that well." Sandra Coulbert's eyes drifted back to the thick textbook open on her desk.

"Sure, but since you lived in the same house I thought

you'd be able to tell me something about him." Zoe glanced toward the window of the long, narrow attic room. Not because there was anything much to see outside, but because there was even less to see inside. Sandra Coulbert's apartment was the emptiest room she'd ever seen. Besides the minuscule kitchen at the far end, there was a bed, a desk and chair, and two three-foot-wide bookcases filled with neat rows of books, a small radio, and an old TV set. That was it. No table, no sofa, not even a dresser. She must keep all her clothes in the closet, Zoe deduced. Or maybe under the bed? The question fascinated her, but she couldn't figure out how to ask it without antagonizing the girl. She knew she wasn't going to have much time to squeeze in her questions.

"Not really." Sandra shrugged. "I mean, I liked him okay, he was a nice guy, but I don't have time for socializing."

"I know how that is." Zoe grinned, one overburdened student to another. "But you must have shared a pizza or something now and then."

"Yes, but he knew I'd pay him back," Sandra said angrily. "And it's not like I ever asked him for anything—he'd just show up occasionally with a pizza or some Chinese or something."

So that was it. "He *was* a nice guy, wasn't he?" Zoe said quietly.

"Yeah." Sandra's eyes glittered with defiantly unshed tears. "Look, I've got to get back to work."

"What are you in?" Zoe asked out of sheer curiousity.

"Pre-med, but what I really want is to go to vet school. You know how tough that is? There are more candidates for veterinary colleges than there are for med schools. And they've *all* got straight A's."

Okay, no time for anything but quick, straightforward

questions. Sandra Coulbert was too obsessed with her own problems to wonder about her questions anyway.

"Did Matt ever tell you about the games he'd written?"

"No."

"So he never mentioned the name Vince Mattus?"

"No. Mostly we just talked about classes, and exams and stuff. Is that it?"

"Just one more question. When did you see Matt last?"

"The morning he—the morning it happened. I passed him on the stairs on my way to class."

"Did he seem any different?"

"No, of course not." Sandra stood up, crossed the room and opened the door. "That's all I can tell you," she said. "I've got to get back to my books."

I'm game. Would you care to explain how?

—ADVENTURE: THE COLOSSAL CAVE

"My God, this day feels like it's lasted about a week and half." Anneke dropped her briefcase on the kitchen counter and opened the refrigerator.

"I had a feeling it might. Top shelf, behind the Coke." Helen spoke over the sound of running water.

"What is it?" Anneke reached behind the Coke and withdrew a white plastic pitcher.

"Old family recipe." Helen grinned. "Just add vodka. Or rum. I've always been partial to rum, myself."

"I don't think we have any." Anneke lifted the fluted lid of the pitcher and sniffed the liquid inside. It smelled slightly fruity but not sweet. "What's in it?"

"I told you—it's an old family recipe. And there's a bottle of rum in the liquor cabinet in the living room." Helen finished scrubbing the sink and turned off the water. "There's a kedgeree in the oven on low—you can leave it there until you're ready for it. And I've stacked today's mail on the coffee table, and today's wedding presents on the dining table."

"Oh, Lord. Thanks, Helen. You're not going to be here tomorrow, are you?"

"No, sorry." Helen shook her head, gray curls bobbing. "I've got an early midterm." Helen had raised three children alone working as a housekeeper, put them all through Michigan, and then decided to follow them. "But I'm giving you the whole weekend, just the way we arranged it. I'll be here Friday, and Saturday of course, and then I'll come back Sunday to clean up after your kids."

"And here I thought those days were finally over." Anneke grimaced. "But I couldn't very well ask them to leave Saturday night after the wedding, and I didn't like the idea of just letting them close up the house on their own." She sighed. "I wish everything weren't so damned *complicated*."

"It's called living a rich, full life." Helen grinned at her. "Don't worry. I'll take care of the house; you just go enjoy your honeymoon." As she spoke, Helen was taking a tray from a cupboard, putting two glasses on it, and pouring the contents of the pitcher into a multicolored glass decanter. "I'll put this in the living room. The ice bucket's full. Go."

"Thanks, Helen," she said again. "I think first I'll slip into something more comfortable, to coin a phrase."

"Not a bad idea." Helen's blue eyes crinkled. "You might also want to follow through with what that phrase usually implies."

"I might at that." She picked up her briefcase, laughing.

By the time she came back downstairs, wearing a loose lime-green lounging outfit, Karl had arrived and was standing next to the dining table examining the latest stack of gift-wrapped packages.

"Oh, good, you're home." She joined him in contemplation of the pile of boxes. "You know, I've always believed 'registering' for wedding presents was the tackiest thing in the world, but now I'm beginning to wonder. I think we'd have done our friends a favor—it's not easy buying gifts for people who already have two of everything." She picked up a large, square package in shiny blue wrapping paper and shook it experimentally. "If we get one more bread-maker I swear to you I won't be responsible for my actions."

He wasn't listening; instead, he was looking at a small, flat package wrapped in brown paper. "Who do you know in El Paso?" he asked.

"El Paso? Good God, nobody. Who's it from?" She reached for the package but he grabbed her hand before she could pick it up.

"No. Don't touch it."

"Why? What . . . Do you think it's . . . ?" She backed away from the table.

"I don't know." He continued to look down at the package.

"But that's silly," she protested. "I mean . . . isn't it? *I'm* not blackmailing anyone."

"We don't know for sure that that's the motive," he reminded her.

"But . . ." She shook her head, trying to focus. "Why this package?"

"No name. A post-office-box return address. Six stamps in odd denominations—probably more than needed. Everything printed in block capitals. FRAGILE printed in three places." He recited the litany as though he were reading from a list. "And neither of us knows anyone in El Paso."

She backed further away from the table. "What do we do now? Call the bomb squad?"

"No. I don't think so. If I'm wrong . . ." He stood and thought for a moment. "Do we still have that old tree-trimmer?"

"Do we still have what?"

"It's a long pole—eight feet or so, I think, with a pruning-shear arrangement at the end. It's for trimming high branches. I found it in the garage attic when we bought the house."

"Then I imagine it's still there. What are you going to do?"

"And the twin beds in the guest room have foam-rubber mattresses, don't they?"

"Oh, no. Don't even think about it. No. Not. *Nada*." She realized with horror what he planned to do. "There is *no way* you're going to blow up those mattresses the day before a houseful of guests arrives."

He laughed aloud. "Now I know where I stand in this week's hierarchy of values."

"Oh, please." Anneke felt her face redden. "This is— Look, why don't you just take the damn thing out in the back yard and shoot it?"

"Even if I did—and I'd rather not attract that much attention if I can avoid it—I'd still need the mattresses for protection. Besides," he grinned at her, "suppose it's a Venini vase?"

"I don't care if it's a Keith Haring sculpture." She threw up her hands. "Oh, this is ridiculous. Go ahead—take the damn mattresses. If you blow them up, we'll put Rachel and Marshall in our bed and *you* can sleep on the sofa. Alone."

It was Helen who stripped the guest-room beds and helped Karl drag the mattresses out to the backyard, over-riding Anneke's attempt to send her home.

"Are you kidding? I wouldn't miss this for the world. You know how often I've wished I could blow up bedding?"

They propped the mattresses against the big maple tree behind the house. Karl found half a dozen concrete blocks, which he arranged at right angles to the garage. Finally he brought out the tree-trimmer, a clever arrangement of blades and levers on an eight-foot pole.

"I'd rather have a ten-foot pole not to touch it with," Anneke said edgily.

"This is a safe distance out in the open," he said. "Still, I want you and Helen inside when I open it."

"Not a chance." She wanted to be crouched behind the mattresses about as much as she wanted to swing from a tree, but she was damned if she'd run off like a frightened cat.

"You can't stay here," he said. "There isn't enough room. I need to be able to maneuver and still be behind the mattresses."

"Have you ever done this before?" The question, she realized, should have occurred to her before.

"I did a course in explosives when I was with the Pittsburgh PD."

"Wonderful. Should I ask what your grade was?"

He grinned. "Don't worry. I'm not trying to defuse it, remember. And if it is the same type of bomb that killed Matt Vincent, it isn't nearly powerful enough to do any damage from this distance."

"Promises, promises."

"How about if we watch from the back porch?" Helen suggested. "We might bring a handful of peanuts, too."

"Swannee!" She'd forgotten all about the squirrel who'd become a family pet. "We need to make sure he's out of the way, too, don't we? All right." She sighed and looked at the mattresses, at the tree-trimmer, at the concrete blocks. "Why do I feel like I'm in an episode of *Mission: Impossible*?"

It was too weird, she thought, as Karl emerged from the house carrying the package carefully in both hands. He set it down at the side of the garage, inside the formation of concrete blocks. Anneke and Helen stood on the back porch, about thirty feet away. On the porch rail, Swannee chittered eagerly and flicked his tail as Helen held a peanut aloft. Only when she felt her fingernails dig into her palms did Anneke realize how tense she was.

Karl crouched behind the bunker of mattresses and extended the tree-trimmer. Its blade cut through the coarse twine tied around the package. Carefully he maneuvered the pole, slicing through the brown paper wrapping to expose a flat white box about the size of a sheet of paper, perhaps two inches deep. Settling himself lower behind the mattresses, he slipped the edge of the pole under the lid of the box, and as Anneke held her breath, flipped the top off and onto the ground.

Nothing happened.

After what seemed like a year, Karl stood up and gazed toward the box, and then finally stepped out from behind the mattresses.

"Is it all right?" Anneke called out.

"I think so." He took several steps forward, stopped and peered at the box, and then strode to it and looked directly down at its contents. At which point, to Anneke's dumbfounded astonishment, he sat down hard on the ground and remained there, laughing uproariously.

"What on earth—" She looked at Helen, who raised her eyebrows and shrugged. Anneke stepped off the porch and trotted over toward Karl, who was still on the ground, still laughing. Wordlessly, he pointed to the box.

Lying face up, in a cheap metal frame, was a photograph of Karl. He was standing in front of his locker in the Steelers' locker room, one foot propped on the wooden bench, adjusting his cleats. Aside from the cleats and heavy socks, he wore absolutely nothing else.

"What on earth . . . Blackmail?" She couldn't imagine

any other reason for sending someone a naked picture of himself, but the word only made Karl laugh harder.

"No," he said finally. He handed her a small square card. "Not blackmail—a wedding present."

"A *what*?" She looked at the card.

"So the G-Man's trying again," it read. "Here's something that should give it a jump start." It was signed "Your Friend, Bumper."

She searched her memory of things Steeler and came up empty. "Who is he?"

"Bumper MacReavey." Karl wiped his eyes with the heel of his hand. "One of the assistant coaches when I first broke in. The last of a dying breed."

"And not a moment too soon. It's kind of a rotten joke, isn't it?"

"Oh, I don't think it's a joke." Karl shook his head, grinning. "Knowing Bumper, I'd guess he really thought you'd appreciate it."

"Hmm." She leaned over and picked up the picture. "Now that you mention it . . ."

"It's hard to believe I ever looked that young." Karl pulled himself to his feet and looked over her shoulder.

"Young? Oh, you mean the face. Sorry, I hadn't gotten to that part yet."

130

Good try, but that is an old worn-out magic word.

               —ADVENTURE: THE COLOSSAL CAVE

"There's still time to put them up in a hotel, you know." Karl finished the last of his kedgeree and took a sip of Corona.

"I know." Anneke pushed curried rice and fish around on her plate.

"You think they'd be offended?"

"No, not really. It's just . . ." She stopped, thinking about it for the first time. Why *was* she so determined that Emma and Rachel and her family should stay in the house with them? Karl said nothing, waiting for her to work it out. "All right, two connected reasons. First, I seem to want to prove that I'm still a good mother, whatever the hell that is. There's some sort of traditional-role engram stuck in my brain, and it's telling me that mothers always have room for their kids."

"And the second reason?" he prompted when she hesitated.

"I seem to be worried that they'll feel the same way, and blame you."

"Is that a legitimate concern?" The question was straightforward, asking for information.

"I'm honestly not sure." With her fork, she drew a pattern in the rice on her plate. "Maybe, especially for Emma." Emma, her unregenerate radical daughter, had been a tough sell, horrified when her mother took up with a man who was not only an ex-football player, but even worse, a cop. It had been Zoe, in fact, who'd finally brought her around; Anneke never knew how, and was smart enough not to ask. "The thing is, Emma wouldn't see the problem. 'Hey, I'll just crash in the spare room—what's the big deal?' And in a way she'd be right, if it were just her. It's when you add Rachel and Marshall and a three-year-old that it gets to be a big deal. But I can't have Emma here and put Rachel and her family in a hotel, because Rachel *would* resent that. So . . ." She looked down at her plate, which now had a nearly perfect circle of rice around its perimeter. "Oh, bloody hell." She threw down her fork and pushed away the plate.

"You know, I don't really have any family, barring a couple of cousins somewhere," Karl said.

"Oh, sure, go ahead and rub in your good luck." She looked up at him and grinned suddenly. "Wait'll you find out what you've been missing all these years."

He grinned back. "I'm looking forward to it."

And that was the third reason, she thought—because he meant it. Karl wanted to be part of a family, and this was the only one she could ever give him. "All right then, we carry on." She held up her glass of Corona in a salute. "Just don't say I didn't warn you."

She cleared the table and cleaned up the kitchen—since Karl did more of the cooking, it seemed only fair that she do more of the cleaning—and then went into the living room, where he was once more reading through the various printouts. She stood watching for a few moments. Every now and then he made a note in the margin; more often he would read a section and then lean back in thought. Concluding finally that detecting wasn't much of a spectator sport, she left him to it and went to her office to check the latest e-mail from GameSpinners.

<Seth>Isn't it true that if a case isn't solved within 48 hours, it's probably never going to be?

<Dani>If the guys who questioned me are what the feds have to work with, you can drag this one to the Recycle bin right now. Shit, we've got a better chance of solving it ourselves than they do.

<Jesse>We probably do at that. After all, crime-solving's really a lot like game-playing. You have to follow up on each clue until it leads you to the treasure, but more important, you have to be able to recognize what IS a clue.

<Elliott>You can forget the feds, then. They wouldn't recognize a clue if it jumped up in the air and bit them on the ass.

<Kell>Hey, that's not a bad idea, you know? Why DON'T we solve it ourselves? We'd have to be better at it than the feds. And we already know a lot more than they do, because we know each other.

<Seth>Why are we assuming it's one of us? Isn't it more likely that it was someone Vince knew personally?

<Jesse>No, probably not, because the bomb was addressed to "Vince Mattus," and his real name was Matt Vincent.

<Larry>But he used the name Vince Mattus for his game company, too. It could have been someone connected with that.

<Dani>I don't think there WAS anyone else. It wasn't really a company, you know. Vince just wrote a couple of games and sold them online as shareware. Unless you really do think he was offed by an enraged gamer, it pretty much has to be one of us. And if it isn't ever solved, we're going to be suspects for the rest of our lives.

<Seth>I never thought of that, but she's right.

<Kell>Okay, so is everybody game (so to speak? :-) What do we do first? Don't the cops always start with means/motive/opportunity?

<Jesse>I don't think that'll do us much good in this case. You can write off opportunity because we don't know where it was mailed from. And we don't have the resources to consider means--there's no way we can track down the source of the ammonium nitrate, and anyway that's the sort of thing the feds ARE good at. If it can be solved that way, they'll solve it. So that only leaves motive.

<Dani>Based on the questions we were all asked, the feds apparently think Vince was blackmailing one of us. So maybe that's where we should start looking for motive.

<Jesse>I wish we knew WHY the feds are thinking blackmail. They must have a reason, and I have a feeling that reason is an important clue.

<Larry>Not necessarily. We can't even be sure they HAVE a reason. They could just be on a fishing expedition.

<Kell>Well, let's think about it for a bit, and then come back and see what we've got. I make it seven people--me, Dani, Larry, Jesse, Seth, Elliot, and Anneke. Anneke, are you in?

Anneke read through the postings, not sure whether to laugh, cheer, or throw a fit. She hit Reply, then aborted and hit Print, logged off, and took the printout into the living room.

"You'd better take a look at this." She handed the printout to Karl. "Well?" she asked when he didn't say anything immediately. "How the hell should I handle this?"

"Oh, join in by all means." He nodded, almost to himself.

"Well, but what should I—" She stopped when the doorbell rang. "I'll get it," she said, and then: "You don't suppose it's . . ."

"I don't know." He shuffled the printouts together and stood up. "Why don't you answer the door while I put these away. There's no reason to shove it in their faces if it isn't necessary."

"All right." She headed toward the front door, unconsciously stiffening her shoulders and then shaking herself loose angrily. Being afraid of the police in her own home was ridiculous. She threw open the door in full attack mode.

"Michael! What the hell are you doing here?" Michael's perfectly shaped eyebrows rose. "Sorry." Anneke laughed, both at his expression and at herself. "Misdirected anger. Come on in."

"I'd hate to be the real target," he said. "You looked like you were about to spring at my throat."

"Wrong throat. Come have a drink." She led him into the living room, where Karl was sitting in a corner of the big brown velvet sofa. He put down the paperback book he'd been holding and stood up.

"Hello, Michael. Can I get you a brandy?"

"Possibly a double." Michael sank into the dark orange chair across from the sofa.

"What's the matter?" Anneke refused to be drawn into his gloom and doom; it if were a true crisis, he'd be more matter-of-fact. "The caterer run out of shrimp?"

"You make jokes, while I suffer." He took the snifter from Karl's hand. "Shrimp can be replaced. The Minstrel Trio, I'm afraid, cannot."

"The band canceled." Anneke decoded his words. "Well, the hell with it, get a CD player and some discs."

"A CD player. Some discs." Michael regarded her as if she were an errant child, then switched his gaze to Karl. "And you're really planning to marry this . . . this philistine."

"Well, I imagine I can civilize her eventually."

"Very funny, both of you." Anneke made a face at them and took a sip of brandy. "Well, then," she said to Michael, "what's your solution?"

"I have here—" he shoved his hand inside his jacket pocket "—tapes of two other groups. Would you both listen to them, please, so we can hire a replacement?"

"I'll be glad to listen," Anneke said, "but you know perfectly well I trust your taste. Better than mine, if it comes to that—music is one of those things that seems to have passed me by."

"Let's see what you've got." Karl took the tapes and glanced at them as he crossed the room and popped one into the tape player. Rich, string-filled music filled the room. Karl stopped the tape and replaced it with Michael's second offering. More rich, string-filled music. As far as Anneke could tell, they sounded identical.

"Yes." Karl nodded. "Not much question, is there?"

"No, I didn't think so." Michael nodded in agreement. "But I wanted to be sure you agreed."

"Which one?" Anneke asked.

"Oh, the first one, definitely," Michael said. "They're young, but they have a fine sound."

"We agreed they wouldn't play that dreadful wedding march, remember," she warned him.

"Absolutely," Michael agreed. "They'll play the 'Ode to Joy.' That's Beethoven, not chamber, in case you didn't know."

Anneke, who didn't, nodded with what she hoped was an intelligent expression and sipped her brandy. As far as she was concerned, both chamber trios (at least, she assumed they were all trios) made moderately pretty sounds, and that was about it. She wished, as she often did, that she could share the love of music so many people obviously had, but she seemed destined never to understand what it was they got from it.

"Don't worry. It'll be fine." Michael took a last sip of brandy and stood. "I'm off. There's no rest for the maid of honor."

"Thank you, Michael." She stood and walked him to the door. "Have I told you that I adore you?"

"Frequently." He grinned. "Ah, I wish I'd thought to marry you before you met Karl."

"Wouldn't have worked." Anneke laughed, knowing he didn't mean it. "You'd never survive monogamy."

"Monogamy?" Michael contrived to look horrified. "You mean neither of you will ever . . . with anyone else? Ever? Oh, the horror of it."

"Good night, Michael." Laughing, she returned to the living room. "Now, where were we?" she said to Karl, and then: "Oh, God, what now?" as the phone rang from her office.

"Mom? I forgot to ask about something," her daughter Rachel's voice said.

"Ask away." Anneke hoped her voice didn't reflect the trepidation she felt.

"Do you have outlet covers in your house?"

"Outlet covers?"

"Plastic coverings for unused electrical outlets," Rachel explained. "To keep babies from sticking something into the outlet and electrocuting themselves."

"No, I don't, sorry." She hoped her voice indicated that she wasn't about to go out and buy them, either.

"Well, would you get some, please?" So much for voice inflections. "And I assume all your drugs and things are in childproof containers? And that the kitchen cabinets lock?"

"Rachel . . ." She stopped just short of saying what she was thinking. "You know, you did that once."

"Did what?"

"Stuck a fork into an electric outlet."

"I did?" Rachel's voice spiked. "My God, what happened?"

"What happened? You got a shock." Anneke laughed at her daughter's reaction. "And you yelled for a couple of minutes, and I gave you a lollipop."

"Oh, that's something else," Rachel said. "Samantha doesn't eat sugary sweets, so would you have some fruit around?"

"Right." Anneke sighed.

"Thanks, Mom. I can't wait for you to see Samantha."

"Me, too. Bye, dear."

"Honestly," she said to Karl when she returned to the living room, "they live in a state of such perpetual fear that I don't know how they stand it."

"They're bludgeoned with terrors," he said. "Fear sells, after all, especially on television. Any time a news show promos something for people to be afraid of, their ratings go up. A new disease, a product recall, something else linked to cancer—it's all just grist for the media mill."

"I don't know how they stand it," Anneke said again. She looked down at the printouts in Karl's hand. "Now, about this murder game."

"The first piece of real luck we've gotten."

"You *want* them playing games with this?"

"I want them talking. About Vince, about each other, about anything." He picked up his pen, looked at it, put it down, as though discharging energy through the metal shaft. "And once they get going, it shouldn't be too hard to steer the conversation."

"I'm not so sure about that," she warned him. "Trying to manipulate these people is going to be a lot like herding squirrels."

"I never said it was going to be easy. But at least now we have a game plan."

"We do?"

"Oh, absolutely." He stretched, working his shoulders, and leaned back. "Why don't you log on and tell them you're in the game."

"All right." She sighed. "And what is the Great Detective going to be doing while I'm online?"

"The Great Detective," he said, "is going to be relaxing with a good book." He picked up the paperback, an old Nero Wolfe mystery entitled *The Doorbell Rang*.

It is now pitch dark. If you proceed you will likely fall into a pit.

ADVENTURE: THE COLOSSAL CAVE

"He seems so . . . I don't know, ordinary." Anneke looked disappointed, but Genesko just looked thoughtful. Zoe popped the tape out of her recorder and set it down on Anneke's desk.

"Sorry there were no great revelations," she said. "Is it worth anything at all?" She'd been pleased with her interviews, but now she realized she'd been thinking in journalistic terms. She might have material for a kind of victim profile, but there sure didn't seem to be anything useful for a murder investigation.

"Absolutely," Genesko answered her question. "First, it clears out some underbrush. In the absence of any apparent motive against Matt Vincent, we can at least take it as a working hypothesis that Vince Mattus was the intended victim. So we know which group of suspects to concentrate on."

"Hell, we already knew that," Zoe said.

"No, we only supposed it." Genesko smiled. "This is what most police work is like, you know—more a matter of elimination than discovery."

"Bo-o-oring. And anyway," Zoe said, "any of these people—" she jerked her head at the tape "—could have been lying, couldn't they?"

"Yes, they could. But in all those interviews, I didn't hear even a hint of any strong feeling about Matt Vincent, good or bad. I'd guess he was the sort of person who simply didn't generate strong feelings. Whereas Vince Mattus clearly did, which makes him a much more likely target for murder."

"Poor Vince," Anneke said. "Or poor Matt. You get the feeling that the 'Vince Mattus' persona was a cry for attention."

"It was also a way to vent a lot of hostility," Genesko pointed out. "The scene with the Wadsworth girl shows he had a lot of anger in him."

"Poor Vince," Anneke said again. "What an odd kind of secret to be walking around with."

"Speaking of secrets . . ." Zoe kept her tone light. "Did you happen to talk to Calvin?"

"Not really."

"So you still don't know what he was doing at the computer?" When Anneke remained silent, she persisted. "He didn't want them to know about him, did he?" She wished suddenly that she were the kind of person who'd be better off not knowing.

"Something like that." Anneke sighed.

"Is there a problem with Calvin?" Genesko asked.

"Not really," Anneke repeated. "At least . . ." She threw up her hands. "I don't know. Just before the FBI got here, he erased all references to Calvin Streeter from the computers. It could be he just . . ."

"Look, he grew up in the Detroit projects," Zoe pointed out. "Kids with that kind of background maybe just don't like cops." She grinned at Genesko. "No offense."

"None taken. And you're right—it may be nothing more than that."

Now how come I don't believe that? Zoe thought. "Okay. So what do we do now, Lieutenant?" she changed the subject.

Genesko stood. "Now I think I want to talk to Wes."

"How about me?"

"At the moment, there's nothing for you to do."

"I could work on the other suspects," she offered. "How about if I did phone interviews with them?"

"Absolutely not," he said at once. "You're not even supposed to know who the other suspects are, remember?"

"Right. Sorry." He looked so severe she felt a flutter in her stomach. "I won't do a thing unless you tell me to. Scout's honor."

"Good." To Anneke, he said: "I'll meet you back here around lunchtime."

"I want to spend some time with 'Whitehart,'" Zoe said when he'd gone.

"Instead of that," Anneke replied, "how about taking a look at this?" She clicked mouse buttons, then stood up and moved away from her desk. "It's Kell's wedding game."

"Yuck." Zoe made a face as she sat down in front of the monitor. The screen displayed an amazingly realistic living room, complete with furniture, wallpaper, and decorative objects. There were five women in the room. Three of them sat in a row on the green sofa; the other two stood on opposite sides of the room. All five of them glared out at Zoe in peevish anger.

"Yikes." Zoe peered at the screen. "Who are they, and where'd they leave their cauldron?"

"Click on one of them," Anneke suggested. Zoe did so, choosing the least repellent-looking of the women, a blond figure on the sofa who wore a very short, very tight black dress.

"Remember, you were *my* maid of honor." The high, vaguely southern voice that emerged from the speaker made Zoe jump. At the same time, the words appeared in a balloon above the figure's head. "So of course I'll be yours, won't I? After all, you *did* promise." The head bobbed, and the lips moved as she spoke. It wasn't exactly realistic, but it was lively and amusing.

Zoe clicked on the middle figure on the sofa, a large, homely woman with frizzy hair and an ugly flowered dress.

"We may just be cousins, but we *are* family," the voice simpered. "And your mother will be *very* angry if her favorite sister's daughter isn't your maid of honor."

"Oh, yuck." Zoe was beginning to get it. She clicked on the third figure on the sofa, a girl with magenta-and-black hair shaved to the scalp along one side. She had two rings in her pierced eyebrow, a nose ring, and a long, dangling skeleton hanging from one ear. A studded dog collar encircled her neck, above a T-shirt that read: "What're you looking at, asshole?" She was also very pregnant.

"Yeah, right, like I really want to be a maid of honor," the voice from the speaker sneered. "Just because I'm your fiancé's sister? Don't make me laugh. But if I don't, my mother's going to kick my boyfriend out of the house. So you *better* pick me, or else." The figure raised an ominous fist in the air, and Zoe saw that a thick chain was woven between its fingers.

"Wow." They both laughed. "It's the wedding from hell, isn't it? What happens if I choose one of these horrors?"

"I don't know." Anneke shook her head. "I haven't run it yet myself."

"Let's go with the one semi-human in the group." She double-clicked on the blonde, who instantly jumped to her feet and began twirling around the room in a dance of triumph. The other two remained on the sofa, glaring. It was the two standing women who moved, jumping forward to the center of the screen and shaking their fists at Zoe.

"I didn't think you were good enough for my son anyway," the hag on the right shouted. "If you think we're going to pay his law school tuition now, you've got another think coming. And believe me, when he finds out there's no money he'll change his mind about marrying you."

"Tell your mother I'm never speaking to her again," the hag on the left snarled. "As far as I'm concerned, I don't have a sister anymore. What's more, I'm going to make sure Daddy disowns her."

"Y'know," Zoe said, "the one on the left reminds me of my Aunt Susan." She laughed. "This is really evil, isn't it? What happens next?"

"I don't know," Anneke said. "Try one of the doors."

Zoe clicked on a door at the back of the living room. A box popped up: "Kitchen under construction. Caterer still to come." Another door responded: "Bedroom under construction. Sorry, no sex yet." And when she clicked on the heavy front door, it read: "Outside world under construction. Travel agency, department store registry, dressmaker, limo service, florist, and other elements still to come."

"I get it," Zoe said, pleased. "You move from room to room, and each room gives you a different part of the wedding to deal with—picking the menu, the wedding dress, like that. Not bad."

"And presumably each time you make a decision the other elements shift to adapt to it. It's really good. The only thing is, I'm not sure it's exactly for twelve-year-olds."

"It is if you want them to stay unmarried for life." Zoe laughed. "Maybe this game is for me after all. Is there any more of it?"

"There's one more module. It isn't connected yet, but it's the wedding dress selector." Anneke leaned around Zoe and clicked the mouse. This time the screen displayed a graphic of a young woman in frothy white underwear, against a background of soft blue draperies. Along both sides were a series of icons.

"Oh, great." Zoe glared at the Barbie-doll contours of the on-screen figure. "Even if I were interested in weddings, what good would it do me to select a wedding dress for some tall, skinny blonde?"

"Click on that button there." Anneke pointed to a small icon labeled "Bride." Reluctantly, Zoe did as she was told. Instantly a new set of icons appeared. Zoe clicked on one labeled "Hair," and a color bar appeared, white at one end, black at the other. She clicked a point on the bar; the bride's hair darkened from ash blond to light brown.

"Hey, cool." Zoe was impressed in spite of herself. She clicked all the way to the right, until the bride's hair was as black as her own. She clicked on another bar, and the hair lengthened; a third bar added curl. "What about the body, though? Oh, there." She clicked on a button labeled "Shape," and played with choices until the bride was shorter and fuller-figured. There was another button labeled "Coloring," and she played with that, too, making herself darkly African American and looking at the image with interest before bringing the skin tones back to her own olive complexion.

"It's fun, isn't it?" Anneke was grinning at her.

"Yeah, it is," Zoe admitted, "but not because it's about weddings. It would be fun to use for selecting clothes, you know?"

"It would, wouldn't it? Go back to the wedding-dress screen," Anneke suggested. Zoe did so; now the bride—

short and full-figured, with dark, curly hair—was surrounded by icons labeled with clothing and parts of clothing. There was "Bodice," and "Sleeves," and "Skirt," "Shoes," and "Veil," even one for "Pants." She clicked at random, playing with colors and styles, laughing at the various effects.

"I think I'll go for the hippie blue-jeans style," she said finally, examining her effort.

"It's a definite fashion statement, anyway." Anneke laughed.

"Better than this, at least." She clicked rapidly, dressing the on-screen simulacrum in a long, full-skirted white dress with flowing train and waist-length veil. "I mean, can you see me in that getup?"

"Well, not this week." There was something in Anneke's voice that made Zoe nervous.

"Not this *lifetime*," she retorted. "You know what it really is?" she said suddenly. "High-tech paper dolls."

"You know, you're right. That's another possibility. I think I'll suggest that to Kell. It really is good, though, isn't it?"

"Yeah, it is," Zoe admitted. "But I'd like it a lot better if it were about dressing for work instead of weddings. And I'd still rather match wits with FOX than worry about seed pearls and freaking stephanotis." In fact, she concluded as she left Anneke's private office heading for "Whitehart Station," she'd rather go one-on-one with an enraged alligator. Sure, it was all right for Anneke, but . . . She saw Calvin leaning over the keyboard and felt a little flutter that had nothing to do with undersea exploits.

She wanted to ask him about his vanishing act yesterday, but she couldn't figure out how to phrase it. Instead, she said: "Jeez, this place is becoming wedding central."

"You checked out that game module?" Calvin looked interested. "What'd you think of it?"

"It's kind of fun to poke around in, I guess. The trouble is, I have zero interest in weddings. Except Anneke's, of course." An idea formed in her head. "You all set for the big event?"

"Not going." Calvin mumbled the words, his head bent over his keyboard.

"What? What do you mean, you're not going?"

"What I said."

"Why not?"

"Just not my sort of thing, that's all."

"Not your . . . Calvin, tell me you're just yanking my chain, right?"

"What's the big deal?" He twitched his shoulders. "Anneke won't care—she spends half her time complaining about the damn wedding anyway. And I don't feel like buying a suit just to stand around like a dweeb with a bunch of strangers."

"Jesus, Calvin, I knew you were self-absorbed, but I never figured you for a totally selfish pig. This isn't about what *you* want, it's about Anneke, who damn well *will* care if you don't show." Zoe's voice rose in anger. "For reasons that escape me, she thinks of you as a friend as well as an employee, and she has this funny attitude about friends, y'know? She thinks they should actually *be* there for each other. Besides . . ." His final comment penetrated at last. "Besides," she changed direction, "who said anything about a suit?"

"You think I oughta show up in these?" He waved a hand to indicate his clothes, the usual student uniform of battered blue jeans, battered tennis shoes, worn and faded T-shirt, clothes not much different from Zoe's own.

Except I've got plenty of other things in my closet, Zoe

reminded herself. And I can go out and put a three-hundred-dollar dress on my dad's Visa card. She changed direction again.

"Sheesh, I don't believe it. How can guys *be* so helpless about clothes?" She shook her head. "Calvin, come with me."

"Look, I don't . . ."

"I *said*, come with me. You've got your bike outside, right?"

"Yeah, but . . ."

"No. No buts. Come on."

"All right, let's start with the jackets."

"I'm damned if I will." Calvin stood in the doorway and glowered. Above his head, the red shield of the Salvation Army overlooked a cavernous room filled with racks and racks of clothing. "I'm not gonna show up at Anneke's wedding wearing other folks' old garbage."

"Garbage?" Zoe laughed. "You see that guy?" She pointed to a short, stocky customer pushing a shopping cart piled high with clothes.

"What about him?"

"He owns three vintage clothing stores. This is where all his high-priced, chic, terminally hip stock comes from. Now, you can pay his markup, or you can buy from the same place he does, but you are going to that wedding and you are going to look great. Now come on." She grabbed his hand and dragged him forward.

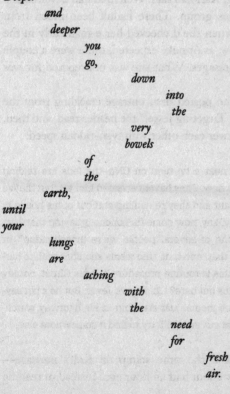

You plunge into the stream and are carried down into total blackness.
Deeper
  and
    deeper
      you
        go,
          down
            into
              the
            very
          bowels
        of
        the
      earth,
until
your
    lungs
    are
      aching
        with
        the
              need
              for
                    fresh
                    air.

149

Suddenly,
with
a
violent

>*splash!!*<

you find yourself sitting on the edge of a pool of water in a vast cham-
ber lit by dozens of flaring torches.

—ADVENTURE: THE COLOSSAL CAVE

Get them talking, Karl had said. Well, that had never been a problem with this group. There hadn't been much from GameSpinners when she'd checked her e-mail early in the morning, but now, as Anneke expected, there were a couple of dozen new messages. What she was unprepared for was the topic.

It was Kell who posted first, outrage crackling from the screen. "They're Targeting Jesse!" the header read, and then, words tumbling over each other with typo-ridden speed:

<Kell>If youre near a tv, tuen on CNn--the feds are raiding jesse's house right now. They havent arrested him yet, but theyve got a search warrant and they're hauling stuf out of his house in cartons and bags. Okay, now some fbi honcho is saying that "mr. Franklin is just one of several people we're investigating" or some bullshit like that, and that "the media shouldnt rush to jugment" and that "this is routine procedure." Jesus Christ, dothey think we're all feebs out here? Oh, there's Jesse. But he's not saying anything to the media, just standing in his doorway watching. Dmn, CNN just cut away. I'll try to find it somewhere else.

Anneke checked the time stamp on Kell's message—10:13 EDT, only about half an hour ago. Instead of reading further postings, she quickly opened a TV window on her monitor and switched to CNN, but as Kell had said, they'd moved on, to some kind of talking-heads show. She closed the TV window, thought for a moment, then turned to Yahoo.

Bingo. FBI FOCUSES ON JESSE FRANKLIN IN MAIL BOMB CASE, read the headline in their news listing, and underneath: "View the search LIVE on Channel 6, Albuquerque." Four mouse-clicks later, a RealPlayer window popped open to show a long, low house set against a breathtaking desert landscape. Several vehicles were drawn up haphazardly at the front door, and as Anneke watched, two men in dark coveralls emerged carrying stacks of cardboard boxes.

"Tom, do you have any idea what's in those boxes?" a woman's voice asked.

"No, we don't, Lorraine." The RealPlayer view shifted to a dark-haired man holding a microphone. "Special Agent Winstead will only say that they're looking for evidence, but he hasn't revealed what specific items they're searching for. We're hoping to get an interview with him later, and maybe he'll have something to tell us then. Oh, wait a minute. I think they're bringing out computer equipment."

The view switched abruptly back to the house. Two overall-clad men emerged, one of them carrying two computer CPUs stacked atop each other, the other struggling under the weight of what looked like a twenty-five-inch monitor. As they wrestled their loads into one of the black vans, Anneke noticed a small crowd of people in the background, most of them with cameras and sound booms and microphones. The search of Jesse's house had become a full-scale media event.

But how? Were suspect searches usually conducted under

the glare of cameras? How had the media even found out about it? And besides, why Jesse, for heaven's sake? It *couldn't* be Jesse, dammit. And did they really have the right to confiscate his computer equipment?

Too many questions, not enough answers. Anneke opened a mail window and messaged the GameSpinners list, giving them the URL of the Albuquerque TV station. Then she picked up the phone and started to call Karl's office before remembering that he wasn't there. Instead, she punched in the number for his cell phone, and when he answered, quickly told him what was happening on the other side of the country.

"Where are you?" she asked finally.

"Just down the block," he said. "I'm having coffee with Wes. Is it still on?"

"Yes." She glanced at her monitor. "They're still going in and out of the house. And the announcer said a few minutes ago that they were hoping to get the agent in charge to talk to them."

"I'm on my way."

The first thing he said, when he sat down in Anneke's chair and looked at the scene from Albuquerque, was: "Hal Winstead."

"You know him?" She perched on a corner of her desk, looking at the monitor over his shoulder.

"I met him once. He's not local to New Mexico, he's out of Washington."

"Then he's the one heading up the whole investigation?"

"Mmm." Karl nodded, most of his attention fixed on the screen.

"Which means this has to be more than a local office's fishing expedition."

"Yes. Can you make this bigger?" He pointed to the RealPlayer window, a small square only a few inches across.

"Sorry, no. That's as big as it gets. This is still infant technology, I'm afraid."

"So, unfortunately, is that." He gestured at the window, where miniature figures continued to move back and forth.

"So is what?" Anneke asked, confused.

"Profiling." He leaned back in the desk chair, his eyes still on the screen.

"Is that . . ." It was her turn to stare at the computer screen. "You think *that's* why they zeroed in on Jesse?"

"I'd lay long odds on it. Of the available suspects, he's one of two with several of the characteristics of this kind of criminal."

"Such as?" Anneke challenged.

"I'm no expert on profiling, of course, but for this kind of crime what they'd probably look for is someone technologically sophisticated, anti-authority, with a previous history of technologically oriented crime, and a loner." He ticked off each element on his fingers. "There are other characteristics, of course, but I'm guessing those are the ones that turned them toward Jesse."

"That's ridiculous," she argued. "To begin with, all the suspects are technologically sophisticated—we're computer programmers, for heaven's sake. And where did you ever get the idea that Jesse is a loner?"

"Anyone who lives alone in an isolated setting is presumed to be a loner. My guess is that they see Jesse as a bitter, aging loner who thinks he's unappreciated and who's resentful of younger people who've gone beyond his early work."

"What nonsense," she said angrily. "Jesse is the most giving person I know. And as for being a 'loner,' he's probably more involved with other people than I am. The fact that his friends don't live next door doesn't mean he has none. Or is this one of those hacker prejudices?" She glared at the monitor. "You know, the one about how anyone who spends a lot of time online is by definition emotionally crippled? Honestly, if I spent a couple of hours a day writing snail-mail letters to friends I'd be considered beautifully grounded, but if I spend the same amount of time writing electronic letters I'm obviously incapable of healthy relationships. When are these people going to get a clue, for God's sake?" She transferred her glare to him and he held up his hands.

"Don't shoot the messenger," he protested.

"Well, I feel like shooting somebody. Besides, you said there were two people who might fit the profile. Who's the other one?"

"I am."

"What?"

"Oh, not exactly the same characteristics—which is one of the problems with profiling. But as a former football player, and for that matter as a cop, I'm accustomed to using violence to solve problems. And both professions often either attract or produce people who are emotionally rigid and have problems with anger management."

"Oh, for . . ." Anneke sputtered to a halt. "But what about technologically sophisticated? Not that you're incompetent, but you're not exactly an electronics whiz."

"No, I'm not." He cocked his head at her. "But you are."

"My God." She drew a deep breath. "Together we'd make a perfect mad bomber, wouldn't we? You'd have the will, and I'd have the way." Suddenly she laughed aloud, struck by the absurdity of it. "Karl, this is too silly for words. Besides," a thought struck her, "if you can draw up a profile to fit two people as different as you and Jesse Franklin, what on earth is the good of it?"

"Oh, in some cases it's very good indeed. Sexually oriented crimes, for instance, where there's a great deal of available psychological data to back up the analyses. Or serial crimes, because as the number of events increases, so does the amount of information you have to work with. The trouble comes when you try to extrapolate from previous profiles to a single event, because you simply don't have enough data. And in a case like this, where the murderer wasn't even at the crime scene, you really have nothing to work with except the package itself."

"What exactly did the package look like?"

"Like a disk mailer—which is what it was. Four inches square, with preprinted lines for the address and return address—both of which were block-printed in ballpoint ink. Ordinary stamps. I'd guess it was just under the weight limit to be dropped into a mailbox."

"Weight limit?"

"Since the Unabomber business, the postal service won't deliver any package over one pound unless it's been handed in over the counter. Creating a lethal letter bomb under that weight limit is a very sophisticated problem."

"Hmm. I see what you mean." She pondered briefly. "I think I could probably manage the detonator, but I don't know a thing about explosives."

"No, but I do." He grinned. "See what I mean?"

She returned his grin. "You've got a point. Maybe we should start our own company. Genesko and Haagen, Discreet Exterminations." A movement in the RealPlayer window caught her eye. "They're setting up for an interview. Is that Winstead?"

"Yes."

Anneke increased the volume and leaned forward, squinting at the small picture.

The bucket flies through the air and thoroughly drenches the dwarves. They shake themselves off and curse violently; they *REALLY* look angry!

— ADVENTURE: THE COLOSSAL CAVE

"This is Special Agent Harold Winstead of the FBI, who is heading the investigation into the letter bomb that killed a computer programmer three days ago in Ann Arbor, Michigan." The reporter held out a microphone. "Mr. Winstead, can you tell us why you're searching Jesse Franklin's house and exactly what you're hoping to find?"

"Jesse Franklin is one of several people who were involved with the victim, Matthius Vincent." Winstead was tall and thin, wearing the regulation FBI dark suit. His narrow face was dominated by a beak of a nose that directed attention away from the small, tight mouth. Anneke loathed him on sight. "We have evidence to suggest that one or more of them had reason to want Mr. Vincent dead."

"Is Jesse Franklin under arrest?" the reporter asked.

"No." Winstead shook his head. "Mr. Franklin is one of several suspects."

"Are you conducting this kind of full-scale search of any of the other suspects?"

"No." Winstead bit off the word, his tight mouth even tighter.

"Can you tell us exactly what you're searching for here?"

"We are looking for any evidence that Mr. Franklin was or was not involved in this crime."

"Can you give us an example? Are you searching for bomb-making components, for instance?"

"That would certainly be one form of evidence, yes." Winstead made the statement sound like a major admission.

"Can you tell us if you've found anything relevant yet?"

Winstead shook his head. "It's too early to answer that question."

"But you've removed a great deal of material from the house," the reporter pressed. "Can you tell us what sorts of things are in those cartons your men are carrying out?"

"I'm afraid not at this time. We'll need time for analysis before we can make any statement to the press."

"But it's clear at least that you are focusing on Jesse Franklin. Are you planning to arrest him?"

"As I said, Mr. Franklin is one of several suspects, and it would be premature to label him in any way." Winstead fixed his reptilian gaze on the reporter. "We still have a long way to go, and I would hope the media would not rush to judgment in this matter, regardless of Mr. Franklin's previous, um, background."

"You mean his activities as a hacker?" The reporter jumped on the statement. "He was arrested in 1978 for using a so-called blue box to defraud the telephone company, wasn't he?"

"Yes, that's true." Was there a gleam of satisfaction in Winstead's eyes? "But that is only one element of our investigation."

"My God." Anneke glared at the monitor with loathing.

"Of all the nasty, vicious, hypocritical *toads*. How he *dares* lecture *them* about a rush to judgment." She turned to Karl, suspicion suddenly rising. "For that matter, how did the media happen to be there in the first place? How did they find out that there was going to be a search?"

"Probably because Winstead had it leaked to them." Karl nodded agreement with her suspicions. "I've seen this tactic now in two or three high-profile cases."

"But why, for heaven's sake? Just to keep the media happy?"

"No. Sometimes it's simply to get the public involved, so that if anyone has seen anything, or knows anything, the additional publicity will jar it loose. But occasionally they do it in the hope that the media spotlight will put pressure on the subject, and that with enough pressure, he'll break."

"Do they ever bother to consider what that kind of pressure would do to someone who's actually innocent?" she demanded. "Or do they just figure anyone they target has to be guilty? No, never mind." She swallowed her anger. "Sorry. I'm shooting the messenger again, aren't I?" She looked back at the screen. Winstead was gone, having said nothing at all in the most damning way possible. As she watched, Jesse emerged from the house, walking calmly between two men in dark suits.

She'd seen one or two photographs of him, but none of them recent. He looked much older than her mind had pictured him, with a deeply lined face behind tinted eyeglasses and long gray hair pulled back in a ponytail. How old was he, anyway? she wondered. If he'd been in his late twenties when he pulled the blue box scam, he couldn't be much more than fifty, yet he looked much older. He wore blue jeans, a gray shirt with a bolo tie, and what appeared to be cowboy boots, although in the small RealPlayer window it was hard to be sure. It was even harder to judge his expression, but Anneke had the vague impression he was smiling gently. She felt tears spring up behind her eyes.

"What's going to happen to him now?" she asked.

"They'll take him in for questioning," Karl replied. His eyes were fixed on the screen.

"But they already questioned him, didn't they?"

"That was just preliminary. Now they start playing hardball."

"My God." She stared at the screen, watching Jesse being handed into a dark car, watching the car drive away, out of the frame. Wondering how Jesse would hold up under intense pressure. She had the sudden thought that there was something fragile about Jesse Franklin. "Karl, we've got to do something. We've got to help him."

"Are you so sure he's innocent?" It was a serious question, not a challenge, and Anneke thought about it for a moment before answering.

"Yes. In fact, I am. There's something fundamentally *gentle* about Jesse, an enormously high level of empathy, for want of a better term. Jesse is one of those people who seems to really feel the pain of others. I think maybe that's why he lives apart the way he does—as a kind of self-protection."

"Aren't you reaching a bit? After all, you've never even met him personally."

"Maybe." She shrugged. "You asked me what I thought. Besides, look at it this way," she argued. "If I'm right, and the feds are wrong, eventually they'll drop the case against Jesse and go looking again. And next time they may decide to focus on me. On us. So we *can't* drop it."

"Oh, I never intended to drop it." He smiled. "Have you gotten your crew working on their 'Murder Game' yet?"

"No. I was about to when I got the news about Jesse."

She looked back at the screen. The search was apparently over; with Jesse's departure, the Albuquerque TV station had signed off the Internet, and the RealPlayer window was blank. She closed it and turned to her e-mail. "I'm afraid that right now everyone's going to be so outraged about Jesse it's going to be hard to get them to focus."

Outrage was almost an understatement; foaming at the mouth was more like it. And not just on GameSpinners. The entire Internet, it seemed, had exploded in Jesse's defense.

<Dani>Do you believe that prick? And probably 90 percent of the country is going to believe that a kid who made some illegal phone calls is obviously capable of murder.

<Larry>Unfortunately, all you have to do is say the word "hacker" and you can get people to believe just about anything. And this was, what? 25 years ago?

<Kell>Yeah. But after all, he was just experimenting with it, and at least he didn't inhale. :-)

<Elliott>LOL. I found this on the Net--How many feds does it take to change a lightbulb? Six--five to buy five different kinds of bulbs, and one to file down one of them until it fits the socket.

<Setb>This was crossposted to half a dozen comp news-groups. I thought you all should see it.

>>JESSE FRANKLIN DEFENSE FUND

>>A group of hackers (yes, they're using the word purposely) have established

>>a Defense Fund for Jesse Franklin. It's being administered by the First Federal Bank of

>>Albuquerque to be used for both Jesse's legal expenses AND to replace the

>>computer equipment that the feds confiscated. The Open-Internet Consortium

>>has already provided him with a fully equipped Thinkpad so he can continue to

>>communicate, but he also needs a Unix system so he can keep his business going.

>>The feds would like nothing better than to destroy Jesse even though he's innocent

>>--in fact, they don't care if he's innocent or not, as far as they're concerned any

>>time you can remove a force for Internet freedom they consider it work well done.

>>You can contribute financially online, via either the Free Jesse Web site or

>>through the Albuquerque bank's site, both of which can take contributions via

>>credit card. If you have computer equipment you can lend, contact the OIC at their

>>Web site.

>>DON'T LET THEM GET AWAY WITH HARASS-MENT!!!

<Dani>Good deal! Larry, Gallery3 ought to have some high-powered equipment you can loan out, don't you?

<Seth>Yeah, Larry, that's a great idea. It'd be good PR for you, too--I mean, Jesse's a hero to game programmers, and that's who your customers are, right? Think how good you'd look if you jumped in to help him out.

<Elliott>Besides, it's the right thing to do. Jesse's a good guy. Come on, Larry, you know Jesse couldnt do anthing like that--not the guy who wrote Mordona.

<Dani>Larry? How about it?

<Larry>Give me time, Dani. I'd love to help Jesse, but remember, I don't own Gallery3, I just work here. I'll take the idea upstairs and I'll let you know as soon as there's a decision. It's also possible that this will all work itself out soon.

<Dani>What exactly do you mean, "work itself out"? You sound like you think Jesse's guilty.

<Elliott>Do you? Hey, you don't relly think Jesse did this, do you, Larry?

<Seth>Well, he's not exactly leaping to his defense. Maybe he's afraid Jesse'll turn out to be guilty and his precious company might have to eat dirt or something.

<Larry>Hey, when did I become the devil here? I SAID I'm trying to find equipment for him, and that's what I'm doing. For the record: No, I do NOT think Jesse's a mad bomber. Yes, I DO want to help him. And I really don't appreciate being the target for your anger just because you can't find anyone else to yell at.

<Kell>Sorry, Larry. He's right, gang. Let's not go off on Larry just because we can't go off on the feds.

<Dani>I'd like to send them something that would REALLY go off on them. Right about now I wish I did know how to make a mail bomb.

<Elliott>Hey, theres an idea. If someone else got a bomb while Jesse was in jail, that would get him off the hook, wouldn't it? (Note to feds evesdropping on my e-mail: kidding, kiding.)

<Dani>Jeez, I never thought of that--they probably are reading our mail, aren't they?

<Larry>If they're intercepting your mail through your own ISP, they may be. But I'll guarantee you that they're not intercepting the mailing list at this end.

<Seth>Doesn't matter. If they can intercept incoming mail from anyone on the list, then they have it all anyway.

It was true, Anneke realized. Since every posting went to every list subscriber, the feds merely needed to tap into the e-mail of any single subscriber. So it didn't matter how good her own firewall was; anything she sent to GameSpinners was wide open.

<Dani>Well, why don't we give them something interesting to read, then? Hey guys, if Jesse Franklin sent that bomb, I'll walk naked through the White House at high noon.

<Seth>Big deal. Like a naked woman in the White House would be unusual?

<Kell>LOL, Seth. I've got a better idea anyway. If they're reading this stuff, why don't we make it worth their while and actually solve the case for them. We talked about it being like an adventure game, remember? And we've GOT to be better at it than those clowns.

<Dani>If I'm not, I'll turn in my computer and go scrub floors for a living. Count me in.

<Elliott>Me, too. Anything we can do to help Jesse is fine with me. Where do we start?

<Seth>Well, we could start with the victim. What do we know about Vince?

<Kell>Not a lot, actually. Anneke lives in Ann Arbor--maybe she knows something about him?

Bingo. Anneke leaned back in her chair and regarded the screen. She didn't even have to nudge them in the right direction. But what now? She realized she didn't have the slightest idea how to proceed. Well, she could post the local newspaper stories; at least it would give them Vince's background. After that, it was up to Karl.

There is a tiny little plant in the pit, murmuring "Water, water, . . ."
WATER PLANT
The plant spurts into furious growth for a few seconds. There is a 12-foot-tall beanstalk stretching up out of the pit, bellowing "WATER!! WATER!!"
WATER PLANT
The plant grows explosively, almost filling the bottom of the pit. There is a gigantic beanstalk stretching all the way up to the hole.
WATER PLANT
You've over-watered the plant! It's shriveling up! It's, it's . . .

—ADVENTURE: THE COLOSSAL CAVE

"They're really feeling the heat." Karl returned shortly after noon, bearing two warm gyros, Greek salads, and scuttlebutt about the FBI investigation, courtesy of Wes Kramer. "Rumor is, the higher-ups are hoping to use this case as a wedge to increase their investigatory powers over the Internet."

"Why doesn't that surprise me?" Anneke took a savage bite of her gyro. "The Internet must drive them crazy. All those people saying whatever they please, doing whatever they please—it's a control addict's nightmare."

"The trouble is," Karl went on, "this isn't the usual letter bomb case. For one thing, they're pretty sure it has no political component, which means their expertise in that area is useless. For another, although they have a finite list of suspects, every one of them has more or less equal means, motive, and opportunity—as well as technical ability. So really, all they have to fall back on is psychology."

"Psychology? Oh, please. You'd get a better analysis from the Psychic Friends Network." Anneke dumped the uneaten remains of her gyro into the takeout bag and swiveled to the computer. "They should've had a chance to read the newspaper stories by now."

<Elliott>Wow, Vince had like this whole other life, didn't he? Kind of like Beltrana in High Capricorn, where hes 2 whole different people depending on which planetary phase hes in.

<Larry>I feel sorry for his family. Maybe we should write them a letter of condolence from all of us on the list?

<Seth>Oh, come on. What would we say? Sorry your scum-sucking son was offed? Whatever this Matthius Vincent was like, the Vince Mattus we knew and loathed was a 14-karat dickhead.

<Kell>You know, that's what struck me about it, too. It really does seem like he was two different people.

<Dani>Yeah, that's what I thought, too. And what that means is that background about Vince isn't worth shit, because "Vince" doesn't HAVE any background.

<Larry>I don't know that that's true. The seeds of "Vince Mattus" have to be in Matt Vincent somewhere.

<Dani>Maybe so, but it doesn't really matter, does it? I mean, we pretty much know why he was killed, so what good will character analysis do?

<Seth>The blackmail scenario, you mean? I've been wonder-

ing about that. Just because the feds say that blackmail was the motive doesn't make it true, you know. Why couldn't there have been a different motive entirely?

"You know, he's got a point," Anneke said.

"Well, at least it's not a bad way to get them talking about themselves," Karl replied. "Why don't you ask them to suggest other motives?"

"All right." She typed rapidly.

"And while we're waiting for responses, I want to go back over some of the earlier postings. Should I use Ken's office again?"

"I think—no, wait." There was a sound outside her office door, followed by a rapid rat-tat-tat, followed by Ken himself bursting through the door. His cheerful Howdy Doody face wore a grin that didn't conceal his worry.

"I'm back," he said needlessly. "And not a minute too soon, apparently. Boy, you give some people a postage meter."

Anneke laughed, cheered by his irreverence. "I take it you know about the bombing?"

"That, and the full-body-cavity computer search, and the raid on Jesse Franklin, *and* the fact that you're one of the suspects?" He made it a question.

"Where did my name come up?"

"Oh, I have my sources. Besides, the feds don't search offices just to keep in practice." He frowned. "Did they screw anything up?"

"No, not as far as I can tell."

"Did they plant anything?"

"Oh shit, I never thought of that."

"Do you want me to run a check?" Ken offered.

"Would you, please?" Anneke thought for a moment. "If

you find anything, though, don't erase it. Just let me know about it."

"Will do." He grinned and raised his voice to a falsetto. "And how was your session with StatFinder, Mr. Scheede?" He dropped his voice to an artificial baritone and answered his own question. "It went very well, Madame Haagen. Remind me to tell you about it some day."

"Oh, hell." She laughed. "I forgot all about it. How *did* it go?"

"Like I said, very well. Don't worry about it, there's nothing we have to deal with until you get back from your honeymoon." He stopped and looked at her closely. "There isn't any problem about the wedding, is there? I better not have rented a tux for nothing."

"No, the wedding's going ahead as planned." She didn't mention the honeymoon. "I can't wait to see you in something besides ratty old blue jeans."

"I just hope the shock doesn't do you in." He grinned again. "I'd better get to work. I'll let you know if I find anything."

When Ken had left, she turned back to the computer and downloaded the latest batch of mail. There were more than she expected; the GameSpinners people were apparently staying online, replying almost in real time.

<Anneke>But if not blackmail, then what? (Remember, the bomb was addressed to "Vince Mattus," not to Matt Vincent.)

<Kell>Okay, let's be organized about this. The classic motives for murder are money and sex, right? Everything else is just a subset of one of those two. So let's focus on money, because even seeing the words "sex" and "Vince" in the same sentence makes me want to crawl into my CPU and reboot.

Anyway, how about this for subsets of a money motive--(1) someone had money Vince wanted, or (2) Vince had money someone else wanted. <Note: "money" doesn't necessarily mean cash here, it's just a code word for any particular thing of value>

<Elliott>But number one doesnt make sense, does it? If someone had something Vince wanted, then wouldn't Vince have killed him instead of the other way around?

<Dani>Not necessarily. In fact, blackmail fits into that category. Say someone had something Vince wanted, and Vince had found a way to get it from him, like by blackmail. So then he killed Vince to keep him from doing it.

<Larry>It could also be about something Vince had ALREADY gotten. For instance, suppose he'd plagiarized the code for one of his games, and the real programmer found out about it?

<Elliott>So? he culd just sue, culdnt he?

<Larry> Not if he didn't have any proof. And sometimes people who feel they've been wronged just go into a rage and want to strike back.

<Dani>Revenge as a motive. Not bad, Larry.

<Seth>Maybe we're making it too complicated. Suppose he was just plain killed for his money? Those games of his may not have been blockbusters, but they were bringing in something. Maybe it's as simple as a brother or someone killing him for the inheritance. I doubt that Vince had a will, so probably his estate goes to his family.

<Kell>Maybe he was about to blow the whistle on someone, like at the university? You know, academic plagiarism, or a prof fooling around with a student, or something like that? Vince would really have gotten off on bringing someone else down.

"Damn, they're going off on a tangent." Karl, reading over Anneke's shoulder, shook his head.

"Half a dozen of them." Anneke shrugged, grinning slightly. "These people could raise topic drift to the status of an art form."

"We need to get them to focus. Especially, we need to get them talking about themselves and each other, not imaginary plagiarists or randy professors."

"In other words, we need to convince them that they themselves are the main suspects," she said. "I don't know any way to do that except to tell them about Vince's 'Blackmail Game' list, which I assume I'm not even supposed to know about. Besides, if I put it online, even on a private mailing list, I guarantee you it'll be all over the Internet in about a minute and a half."

"I know." He sighed. "What about sending them all private messages?"

"I could do that. But of course, once they start discussing it on-list it probably won't stay secret even if they intend it to."

"Would it be possible to start a separate mailing list of just you seven people?"

"Oh hell, of course. I should have thought of it right away."

"That's why they pay me the big bucks."

"Really? And all this time I thought it was for your body." She laughed as she began tapping keys. "Let's see—Larry, Seth, Elliott, Kell, Dani, and me. Oh, and Jesse. I'll send them all encrypted e-mail telling them how to access it, and then I'll post the 'Blackmail Game' information. Oh, and should I tell them what you deduced from the archives?"

"Yes, but not immediately. Let them deal with the list

first. I want to get them talking about their roles as suspects before they move on to specifics."

"I'll do my best, but with this crew it's just as likely to turn into a game of charades. Or a round-robin poetry contest."

"I'm beginning to see that." He sighed. "Also, could you print out today's list postings for me?"

"Sure. But why don't I also download them to my laptop and turn that over to you? I don't really need it this week. For that matter, it's probably time for you to get your own laptop anyway. A Thinkpad with a full docking station would give you all the computing power you need, either at home or at the office." She swiveled to pick up the laptop, then swiveled back as she heard the office door open.

"Hi, Mom. Where do you want me to dump my stuff?"

With a loud "zap" a bolt of lightning springs out of midair and strikes your lamp, which immediately and violently explodes. You narrowly miss being torn to shreds by the flying metal.

—ADVENTURE: THE COLOSSAL CAVE

"Emma!" Anneke turned toward the door and held out her hands. "You're early. I didn't expect you until tonight."

"Caught an earlier flight on standby. Even wound up in first class. Thought there might be someone interesting there, but it was all fat, boring businessmen and people with frequent-flyer upgrades." She dropped a khaki duffel bag on the floor with a thud. "So you're Karl Genesko."

"Yes." Karl had stood when she entered. The two of them regarded each other, Emma's head thrown back, on her face an expression of—what? Challenge? Distrust? Curiosity?

Anneke had forgotten how much Emma resembled her father. The same long, lean figure, the same pale complexion, the same thick, straight hair (although Tim would have blanched at the mixture of blond and acid green that adorned Emma's head). She had her father's blue eyes and small, almost bow-shaped mouth as well. In a sudden flash of memory, Anneke remembered Tim's mouth, tight with disapproval or twisted in sneering superiority. She shook off the memory; on Emma's face, the same features expressed generosity and a kind of cheerfulness Tim never achieved. It occurred to Anneke suddenly, with enormous pleasure, that her daughter was happy.

"Is that a Super Bowl ring?" It was the last thing Anneke could have imagined Emma saying. She was surprised that Emma even knew what a Super Bowl was.

Karl looked down at the ugly, diamond-encrusted ring on his right hand. "Yes, it is."

"You were good at it, weren't you?"

"Yes, in fact I was." Karl nodded, taking Emma's question seriously, as though he understood the point of it. Which was more than Anneke did. "I also enjoyed it enormously."

"Right," Emma said obscurely. "Glad to meet you." She held out her hand. "What should I call you?"

Karl shook her hand, smiling for the first time. "Why don't you call me Karl?"

"Good." Emma poked the duffel bag with the toe of her dirty white running shoe and turned to her mother. "Can I just leave this here? I want to catch up with some people."

"Of course." Anneke nodded. "We'll take it back to the house with us. Will you be joining us for dinner?"

"Don't know yet. I'll let you know."

"Well, let me give you a key to the house." Anneke removed an extra key from the office safe and handed it to her daughter.

"Good." Emma shoved the key into the pocket of her jeans. "See you later."

Anneke took a deep breath as the door closed behind her. "Am I wrong, or did that go pretty well?"

"I think it did." Karl was looking at the duffel bag with a quizzical expression on his face. "Just one question—I take it she usually flies in and out this way?"

"The dump-and-run, you mean?" Anneke laughed. "All adult offspring do that—it's practically a law of nature."

"That's more or less what I concluded." He grinned. "In that case, why don't we get back to work?"

"Fine. I figure we have about four hours before the next wave of the invasion blows in."

"Yes, but remember that I've already met Rachel and her family."

"True." Anneke didn't point out that he hadn't met all of them together at one time. Emma and Rachel got along well with each other, but they were . . . different when they were together. Or, no, not different, rather the reverse. Together they seemed somehow *more*, more of what each was separately. Well, it would work itself out, she told herself, turning back to the computer with the relief she always felt at putting aside messy emotions. She downloaded the messages sent to the new mailing list.

"I take it that's encrypted?" Karl looked over her shoulder at the screen full of garbage characters.

"Right. In my setup message, I told everyone to use PGP on all postings. I'm comfortable enough with my own firewall, but I don't trust other people's if I don't have to."

"What does PGP stand for?"

"Pretty Good Privacy." She laughed at the expression on his face. "Truly, that's its real name. It was developed by a guy who gave it away free via the Internet—and believe me, the feds just about went ballistic over it. It's not absolutely unbreakable, of course—there's no such thing, given enough time and resources—but close enough." She was tapping keys as she spoke; now she slid her chair sideways, and Karl pulled his closer to the screen to read the decrypted postings.

<Anneke>I'm taking this off-list because I think we're at the point where we need privacy, not only from the feds but from the rest of the Internet. I've set up a private mailing list on my

own system, open only to seven of us--myself, Larry, Kell, Dani, Seth, Elliott, and of course Jesse. I believe my system is secure, but I'd rather not take any chances, so I'm asking all of you to please use PGP encryption for all messages. Send all postings to *murdergame@haagen.com*.

Some of you may think I'm overreacting, but please read the next posting before hauling out the flamethrowers.

"Murdergame?" Karl cocked his head.

"Well, it sounded funny at the time. Internet humor," Anneke said guiltily. "Besides, it's the sort of thing that will get their juices flowing, and that's what we want, isn't it?"

"Oh, I'm not criticizing. What's in the next posting you refer to?"

She clicked the mouse. "That's where we hit them with Vince's blackmail list."

<Anneke>Okay, here's the piece of information that nobody knows--although how (or why) the feds kept it from leaking I don't know. When Vince was found, there was a list of names on his desk. Our names--the seven of us here. And the list was headed "The Blackmail Game." Now, that's all the information I have. I don't know if he was actually writing such a game, whether it was some sort of joke, or anything else about it. But that's why the feds have been questioning us all about blackmail. And that's why the seven of us are the prime suspects in Vince's murder.

<Elliott>Wow, what an awesome idea for a game. Wonder if Vince was going adventure or rpg?

<Dani>Knowing Vince, he was probably developing a black-mailer superhero.

<Kell>That's not a bad idea. You could make the blackmailer the sympathetic figure--he's out to squeeze money from polluters, or religious hypocrites, people like that, and then he gives the money to Planned Parenthood clinics and homeless shelters.

<Larry>So that's where the blackmail notion came from. But isn't that a little ridiculous? He couldn't have been blackmailing all of us. It's much more likely that he really was writing a game, and he was just using us as models for the characters.

<Seth>But why us? He didn't even really know us.

<Dani>He didn't really know anybody. This is Vince we're talking about--it's not like he had friends. I always pictured him living alone in an underground cave, like a troll.

<Larry>Maybe he used us BECAUSE he didn't know us. That way he could make up any fantasy he wanted.

<Kell>Nice try, people, but I can only believe six impossible things before breakfast, and this isn't one of them. I'm afraid we have to figure it was one of our happy little group who did the deed.

<Larry>Except, as Seth pointed out, he didn't even know us. How could he know anything that damaging about people he'd never even met?

<Dani>Are we sure he never met any of us?

<Kell>Well, why don't we start there--did anyone ever meet Vince in person, or get private e-mail from him, or snail mail, or any kind of communication off-list? I'll even start off by saying that I did. Vince e-mailed me a couple of months ago asking if I knew of a cheap motel in Madison where he could stay for some conference he was attending.

<Larry>Did he actually stay there? And did you ever meet him f2f?

<Dani>I never had ANY interaction with Vince. Unless you count sticking pins in a voodoo doll.

<Kell>I don't know if he came to Madison or not. In fact, I never heard from him again--hell, after I sent him the names of a couple of motels he never even mailed back to say thank you. Did anyone here ever meet him in person? Anneke, are you sure you didn't run across him in Ann Arbor?

<Seth>I never had anything to do with him off-list either. Larry, did he ever contact you directly about anything to do with Gallery3?

<Elliott>I nevr heard from him either.

<Anneke>As far as I know, I never laid eyes on Vince, even though we both lived in Ann Arbor. Of course, he could have been stalking me around State Street, I suppose, but if so he never bothered to introduce himself.

<Larry>He did e-mail me two or three times with bug reports, but there was never anything personal in it.

<Dani>Sorry, but this is dumb. I just don't see this whole blackmail shit. For one thing, most of us don't have enough money to be worth blackmailing. For another, why reach for an off-the-wall motive like that when there were so many other reasons to kill the little shit?

<Seth>Well, not really, you know. I mean, not real reasons to commit a real murder. People say things like, I could kill him for that, but they don't really mean it.

<Larry>Dani's got a point, though. Vince did a lot of damage to a lot of people.

<Anneke>But the damage Vince did was almost entirely on GameSpinners. Remember, this is the only place outside his Gooseberry Software Web site where the "Vince Mattus" avatar manifested itself.

<Kell>That's true. So even if the motive is different, the circle of suspects doesn't change much. Let's look at that, though. What motive besides blackmail did any of us have for killing Vince?

<Dani>I thought about doing it as a public service--does that count?

<Larry>The truth is, Seth's got a point. Hell, if everyone who behaved like a prick online got himself murdered, there wouldn't be enough people left to run a newsgroup.

<Dani>Except for thee and me, of course, and I'm not so sure about thee. Wasn't Vince agitating to get GameSpinners out from under Gallery3?

<Larry>Oh, come on, Dani. Are you seriously suggesting I'd kill someone for the dubious pleasure of running a mailing list?

<Seth>Except, wasn't he sending complaints to your bosses, Larry? Maybe he was causing you real trouble at work.

<Dani>Is that why you didn't throw him off the list, Larry? Because he threatened to cause trouble if you did?

<Larry>Hey, when did someone paint a bull's-eye on my back? What about you, Dani? I seem to remember you going postal when you saw that nude picture of yourself circulating all over the Net.

<Dani>I wondered how long it would take for someone to bring that up. For the record, as all of you fucking well know, it wasn't a nude picture of ME, it was my head pasted on someone else's body. And it was such a shitty job that everyone knew it was a phony--it wasn't even an Asian body, for Christ sake. The truth is, that stunt of his got me a lot of sympathy, AND a lot of publicity. I got half a dozen projects from people who never would have heard of me otherwise. Besides, that was last year. If I was going to take him out over that, why would I wait so long?

<Seth>Hell, he fucked over all of us at one time or another. Remember when he got Elliott in trouble over that bootleg screen shot of "Forever Plane"?

<Elliott>Oh puh-leez. Like, big fat hairy deal. So I borowed a graphic from the Game Nazi website and put it on mine. So freaking what?

<Seth>So the Game Nazi people paid good money for an exclusive preview of the hottest new game of the year, that's what, and they weren't happy when it turned up on your site.

<Elliott>I repeat--big fat hairy deal. So they tell me to take it down, and I take it down and thats the end of it. <insert massive shrug>

<Dani>What about you, Seth? Didn't Vince catch you plagiarizing a chunk of code for your football-pool game?

<Seth>It wasn't plagiarizing, for shit's sake. Just because he found a couple of similar subroutines, Vince thought he could

yank my chain. I mean, how many ways are there to write a recursive descent parser? Anyway, all we've proved is that Vince was a vicious piece of shit who trashed everyone here.

<Elliott>That's true, you know. He even dug up Jesse's arrest and claimed he turned in some other hackers in order to get himself off the hook.

<Seth>Yeah. You do have to wonder why Parker and Caminetti got jail time while Jesse got a job offer.

<Anneke>Because they were SELLING their blue boxes and Jesse wasn't, that's why. Parker and Caminetti weren't hackers; they were crooks. They didn't develop the blue box technology, they just stole it from other hackers and used it to make themselves some money. So do yourself a favor and don't go there, Seth.

<Larry>You know, it wasn't just us. Vince targeted other people on GameSpinners, too. Including a few he drove off the list completely. Remember that kid Bruce Beasley? He got into a flame war with Vince, and Vince supposedly e-mailed his English teacher about the Web site where Beasley got his term paper.

<Dani>They never proved that was Vince--Beasley had some enemies right there in his high school, didn't he? And IIRC, he deserved them. Still, you've got a point, Larry. There were some others who left GameSpinners because of Vince, too-- I remember Hal Bacon, and Jeannie Chang, and some kid named George (who I always thought was actually a girl, BTW).

<Seth>I remember George. Wasn't (s)he some kind of obsessed Trekkie?

<Kell>Right. I think (s)he left in a huff after Vince accused Kirk and McCoy of having a homosexual relationship. ;-) I don't know about gender, but George was definitely brewed from the shallow end of the gene pool.

You are in a maze of twisting little passages, all different.
You are in a little maze of twisty passages, all different.
You are in a twisting maze of little passages, all different.
You are in a twisting little maze of passages, all different.
You are in a twisty little maze of passages, all different.
You are in a twisty maze of little passages, all different.
You are in a little twisty maze of passages, all different.
You are in a maze of little twisting passages, all different.
You are in a maze of little twisty passages, all different.
You are in a maze of twisty little passages, all different. You're at Witt's End.
You are at Witt's End. Passages lead off in *all* directions.

—ADVENTURE: THE COLOSSAL CAVE

"They're still busy denying reality." Anneke shook her head as the postings came to an end.

"That's not particularly unusual among a group of suspects," Karl said. "They'll almost always start out by looking outside their own group, trying to distance themselves from the crime. I will admit, though, you don't usually get them this . . . creative."

"No, I imagine not. Still, in Vince's case it's harder to find people without motives than with them."

"Well, I did notice the absence of two people in that litany of loathing."

"I figured you would." Anneke grinned. "Vince tried it on me once, and I do mean once. He suggested that I'd purposely screwed up a project in order to squeeze more money out of a client. I immediately sent him private e-mail informing him that I would sue his assets off if he ever said another word. And he never did."

"I thought you told the FBI that you'd never had any contact with Vince except on the list," Karl pointed out.

"No, I didn't," Anneke contradicted him. "I told them I'd never *received* private e-mail from Vince, and I never did. He didn't answer me, he just shut up and moved on."

"To someone more easily intimidated, apparently. So that leaves Kell."

"Kell. Yes. I can't remember any confrontation between her and Vince. Oh, they quarreled a lot, but it was always over game issues, or programming, things like that. It was never over anything personal."

"Which suggests that Vince didn't know any more about Kell personally than you did. I wonder if he actually went to Madison after asking Kell about motels."

"Or if he ever intended to in the first place. Considering the way Vince operated, he might have intended the whole exchange as a subtle threat of exposure." Anneke stared at the monitor screen. "But exposure of *what*? Who the hell *is* Kell?"

"Well, let's put that aside for the moment," Karl said. "Are there any more postings?"

"Probably. I think everyone's more or less sitting online." Anneke downloaded the messages that had arrived while they'd been going through the previous batch. They read through the latest ones, occasionally adding responses of their own under Anneke's name.

<Kell>Okay, listen up, people. Instead of just spinning our wheels, why don't we approach this the way we'd approach a real game--think of it as a Murder Game. The way I see it, it's basically an rpg, only we're not just role-playing the characters, we ARE the characters.

<Elliott>Hey, cool. Its like we wander through the scenario as a group, kind of like a wizards party on a quest. Only one of the party is a traiter, and we have to figur out which one.

<Seth>But we don't know what kinds of clues we're looking for. How will we even recognize one when we see it? Hell, we don't even know that there ARE clues.

<Kell>Oh, there are always clues. Otherwise, what would be the point of the game? <(:-)

<Seth>Come on, Kell. Much as you'd like to pretend it's all fun and games, this ISN'T a game. Those were real feds searching my office.

<Kell>Wellll now . . . if you look at it from the right angle, EVERYTHING is a game. I mean, LIFE's a game. Only trouble is, we don't get to know what the solution is until we cross the finish line, and by then it's too late. <;->>

<Dani>I've got to admit, it's got possibilities. But one problem is that a big chunk of the scenario is missing. Larry, since this is now private to just a few members of the list, can you send us the archives?

<Seth>That's a good idea. At least it would help us clarify the back story.

<Larry>Let me think about that. I have to tell you, I'm not crazy about the idea. I don't know if I'm comfortable giving out the archive for something like this. I'm not sure it's fair to the people who aren't part of this private list.

"Oh, come off it, Larry." Anneke leaned back in her chair. "Now he's just being anal," she said to Karl. "Like, they're mine and you can't have them. Should I send them the archive I have?"

"Yes." Karl nodded. "And why don't you post the material I pulled out of it, too."

"Are you sure?" She looked at him dubiously. "Some of the implications are pretty nasty, you know."

"I know. But the implications are there in the archives. One of them would work it out on their own eventually anyway, and I'd just as soon speed up the process. Remember," he grinned at her, "we're leaving for our honeymoon in three days."

"Okay." She created a .zip file of the two documents and sent it out. It would take them a while to digest it all, but when they did she was pretty sure they'd go ballistic.

<Anneke>Sorry, Larry, but this time I think you're wrong. We're the ones at risk here, so everyone has a right to all the information we've got. I have a copy of the archive, so here it is, folks. The file also includes some breakouts from the archive that might be instructive.

<Dani>About clues--in a detective rpg, wouldn't the player go from room to room questioning each suspect? Why can't we set it up the same way?

<Elliott>Sure, it could be like a classic adventure game.

<Kell>Thanks, Anneke. She's right, Larry--you can't work through a game properly if the gamemaster keeps information from you.

<Seth>We'd have to go at it kind of sideways, though. I mean, there's no point in asking about alibis or stuff like that. And we can't investigate things like where someone could have bought explosives. The basic problem is that you've got a limited number of characters you can interact with--you can't go outside the scenario to question ancillary characters like friends or postal work-

ers. It would be tricky to program the right questions so that the player would actually come up with useful information.

    <Kell>How about this.--Each of us writes one question for each of the other suspects. That'll give us five different approaches, and we'll see what we come up with. Maybe the fact that we can't investigate the nuts and bolts will jar something else loose.

"Way to go, Kell!" Anneke cheered.

    <Seth>Sounds like a plan. Let's put it together and see what we've got.

    <Kell>Tell you what.--Why don't you send all your questions to me directly, and I'll put them together so we can take it suspect by suspect, okay? Get them to me by tonight, and I'll get it online by tomorrow morning.

    <Dani>Sounds good. That'll give us time to scan the archives, too.

    <Seth>Okay with me.

    <Larry>All right, I suppose so. But I don't think we should get our hopes up.

    <Jesse>Count me in, gang.

    <Kell>Jesse! You're out! Wecome back!!!!

    <Seth>Hey, man, good to hear from you.

    <Larry>Welcome back, Jesse. Are you a free man?

    <Jesse>Define freedom--are any of us really free? :-) Anyway, I'm back home, and thanks for the support, gang. I really appreciate it.

    <Kell>Okay, now we've got some real incentive. Let's get at those questions, people.

"I assume you'll work out the questions for me to send?" Anneke asked.

"Right." Karl stood and stretched. "Let me go through those pullouts first. And in the meantime, will you do some research on the Bank of Los Angeles, on Gallery3, and on Texonomy Systems? And the people behind Texonomy, if you know who they are."

"In fact, I think Dani named names once or twice." She clicked to open Alta Vista. "I'll see what I can find out."

Goblins live exclusively on human flesh, and you can't spare any of your own to placate them. On the other hand, I suspect that they're going to eat you pretty soon whether you like it or not—you'd better find some way of killing them or driving them away!

—ADVENTURE: THE COLOSSAL CAVE

Karl left then, taking Emma's duffel bag with him, and Anneke opened her planner and examined her wedding file. Only a few entries remained unchecked, thank God and Michael, and most of them had to do with keeping the business running while she was gone. They needed to file a progress report on the inventory program for Ashby Industries; Marcia could be assigned to help Max with the Wave-Assets database; maybe Calvin should shelve "Whitehart" and finish up the Lion Queen Web site first. She'd hoped to finish that one herself before the wedding, but . . . Well, it wasn't her fault if murder had smashed her carefully organized schedule. With a sigh, she annotated the project file she shared with Ken and went through to the outer office.

"I just got control of the infirmary!" Zoe swiveled from the screen, her face flushed with pleasure. Calvin was shaking his head gloomily.

"I think we made it too easy, boss-lady."

"Yeah, yeah," Zoe crowed. "Tell it to the seabots."

Ken was perched on a corner of a nearby desk. "Looks like you're about ready to go to beta," he said to Anneke.

"Just about." She looked at the screen, where a panel blinked blue and amber lights against stark white walls. "Are you sure that doesn't look too much like sick bay on the *Enterprise*?"

"It looks great," Ken assured her.

"I don't know," Anneke worried. "Maybe it's too derivative?"

"Hey, don't go getting cold feet on me now, boss-lady." Calvin reached for the mouse and clicked to bring up the "Whitehart Station" splash screen. "It's cool."

"Maybe. Anyway, we'd better put it aside for the moment. We've got other projects that take priority." She turned to Ken. "How are we coming with the Ashby project? Remember, we promised it by Thanksgiving. Maybe Marcia could work with Max on that database, except she's up to her eyeballs in that online survey, isn't she? And Ken, I'm running late on the Lion Queen site—I thought maybe we should have Calvin do that? Damn. I wish—" She realized suddenly that she'd used the word *maybe* three times. A bubble of panic rose in her throat.

"Anneke, relax." Ken smiled at her. "We really can get along without you for a single week."

"I know that, really. It's just . . ."

"Well, I'll be damned." Zoe's coppery eyes widened and a grin split her face. "I do believe the lady's finally succumbed to pre-wedding jitters."

"Anneke? Nah." Calvin shook his head, looking at her sideways. "Never happen."

"Of course not." Ken shook his head solemnly. "That only happens to people who aren't *organized*."

"And that couldn't be you, could it, boss-lady?"

"All right, all right." Anneke forced herself to laugh. Pre-wedding jitters? That was silly. After all, she and Karl had been living together for more than a year. It wasn't as if the act of marriage was going to change her life. "And *stop* calling me boss-lady." She picked up a foam rubber hammer from Marcia's deskful of toys and tossed it at Calvin, who ducked easily. The hammer continued its trajectory toward the office door. The door opened.

"Oof." Emma took the foam rubber hammer full in the face. She blinked, bent down and picked it up, and turned it over in her hands.

"Oh, Emma, I'm sorry." Anneke hurried forward to retrieve the hammer, trying not to giggle. "Are you all right?"

"Sure." Emma handed back the hammer and looked around the office. "Are you Zoe?"

"Right. And you're Emma. Glad you're here." Anneke could hear the subtext—not "glad to meet you," but, "glad you came to your mother's wedding."

"You're wearing the ring," Emma said.

"I wear it all the time." Zoe held up her right hand, where a heavy band of sculptured silver encircled her fourth finger. The ring had been a gift from Emma, arriving in the same package as a pair of matched wedding rings. "It's maybe the best thing I've ever owned." Zoe's matter-of-fact tone made the statement more convincing than any amount of praise would have done.

Emma broke into the first smile Anneke had seen. "Thanks. I kind of liked it, too. I won't make another one just like it, but I've been working in that style for the last few months and it's going pretty well. I just got an order for two dozen pieces from the Gallery Royale."

188

"The shop on Liberty? Emma, that's terrific." As soon as the words were out of her mouth, Anneke wished she could recall them. She sounded at once too effusive and too condescending, like a mother patting her child on the head for winning a spelling bee. Dammit, why couldn't she be as natural with Emma as she was with Zoe?

Because Zoe wasn't her daughter. Because she didn't worry about Zoe. Because she knew Zoe better than she knew Emma.

The realization was like a bucket of ice water in the face. How could that be? How could she have let that happen?

Well, for one thing, she saw Zoe far more often, spent more time with her. For another, she had more interests in common with Zoe. The admission caused her a pang of regret, but she couldn't deny its truth. And why should she? Motherhood, after all, was about letting your children find their own paths, and in that at least she seemed to have done an adequate job, even if her relationship with them was more superficial than she'd have liked.

She examined the word *superficial* and changed it to *partial*. Or maybe *segmented*. Where their lives intersected, at the level marked "Family," her relationship with her daughters was both strong and deep, and that was all she had a reasonable right to expect. What was it Kell had said? Something like: "Everyone has a different persona that they use with different people." Lives can only intersect on so many points of an arc, after all, even between mother and daughter.

"I'm thinking seriously about opening my own shop," Emma was saying to Zoe. Anneke opened her mouth to speak, then shut it again.

"Really?" Zoe shook her head dubiously. "Won't it take up a lot of time you could use for actually creating?"

"Maybe, but half of what I do now is selling anyway—going to art shows, getting store owners to carry my pieces, trolling for customers. And at least I'd be my own boss." She turned to Anneke. "Mom, how did you decide when you were ready to start your own business?"

"When I realized how much the idea scared me," Anneke replied at once. She laughed. "I figured out that I wouldn't be that afraid if my subconscious didn't know it was time."

"I never thought of it that way," Emma said, thoughtfully. "I'm not scared, though, just undecided."

"There's no reason for you to be scared, at your age," Anneke pointed out. "You've got time to make mistakes. I didn't."

"Mmm. So if I do it, and it doesn't work out, I can always back off, as long as I don't get in too deep." She paused. "Did you do a business plan?"

"I must have done six of them," Anneke confessed. "If you want to see the final one, I have it in a file somewhere."

"Maybe so." She nodded before turning to Zoe. "How about the Cottage Inn at six?"

"Right." Zoe stood and picked up her bookbag. "I'll walk out with you. I've got to get over to the *Daily*. See you later, Anneke."

"See you, Mom." She didn't say when she'd be home—all right, when she'd be at the house.

"See you later," Anneke said, feeling more cheerful. She'd dig out that old business plan, as well as the new one she and Ken had worked up last year. Here at least was something new they'd have in common, another point on the arc.

Yetch—what a mess!

—ADVENTURE: THE COLOSSAL CAVE

"That squirrel can't get into the house, can he?" Rachel's brow furrowed as she regarded the small animal sitting upright on the windowsill.

"Quirrl," Samantha piped, patting a chubby hand against the glass. "Want the quirrl, Mommy."

"No, dear." Rachel hovered over the child. "Squirrels live outside, and we don't touch them, remember?"

"He doesn't come inside," Anneke reassured her daughter.

"Good." Rachel transferred her gaze to the pile of luggage in the hallway. "Marshall, did I remember to bring Samantha's drinking cup?"

"Yep. Also her stuffed kangaroo, the special toothpaste, and the hypoallergenic pillow." Marshall Lang grinned at his wife. He was short and chubby and cheerful; he was also a brilliant attorney who loved his wife to distraction. Anneke was sometimes amazed that Rachel had had the wit to choose so well.

"Want the quirrl," Samantha repeated fretfully. She trotted over to the dining area, grasped one of the heavy Queen

Anne chairs by its leg, and began dragging it toward the window, presumably to climb on. Anneke started toward her, but Marshall got there first.

"How about some juice instead?" he offered.

"She's overstimulated from the plane flight," Rachel explained. "And I'm sure her electrolytes are low."

"There's juice in the refrigerator," Anneke said, "and some cookies in the cupboard. Let me—"

"Cookies! No." Rachel reacted as though Anneke had offered to mix the child a martini.

"I'll see what we can find." Marshall grinned at Anneke and took Samantha's hand. "Come on, sprat, let's get you some juice."

"Make sure if it's apple that it's pasteurized," Rachel called after them. She walked over to the pile of luggage in the front hall and picked up a large carryall. "I'd better get us unpacked." But instead of starting upstairs Rachel dropped the carryall and returned to the living room, where she sank down onto the sofa. "You look frazzled, Mom. Are you sure you're getting enough iron?"

"I have no idea," Anneke confessed. She carefully didn't point out that Rachel was the one who looked frazzled. She was too thin; her heart-shaped face, devoid of makeup, seemed pale and drawn; her blond hair was brushed back from her face and pinned carelessly behind her ears, and her expression seemed tense and anxious. She reminded Anneke of a rabbit foraging just outside its hole, every nerve alert for signs of danger.

"Leave her alone, Sis." Emma swooped into the room and threw herself down on the other end of the sofa. "She looks healthy enough to me." She made a face in the direction of the pile of luggage. "Jeez, is there anything left in Colorado, or did you bring the whole state with you?"

"Some of us have responsibilities," Rachel retorted. "You can't just throw a child in a duffel bag, thank you. And I hope you have something with you besides blue jeans to wear to the wedding."

"I'll find something." Emma leaned back and propped her feet on the glass top of the coffee table, crossing one sneaker-shod foot over the other. "I didn't expect the house to be this big," she said to Anneke. "What do you want with all this space?"

"It's a beautiful house." Rachel answered before Anneke could, sounding defensive.

"Sure it is." Emma shrugged. "It just seems like it'd be an awful lot of work. This is bigger than the house we grew up in. Why should she want the bother, at this stage of life?"

"It's also a lot nicer. And she has a maid, after all," Rachel replied. "And please don't go into that 'no one should have servants' routine. Why shouldn't Mom have household help at her age? She's earned it."

"Are you two quite finished discussing my declining years as though I weren't here?" Anneke asked sweetly. Emma looked at her and grinned; Rachel didn't.

"Yes, but you do need to take care of yourself," she insisted. "You're not a kid anymore, you know."

"Believe it or not, I do know. It's one of the things I'm passionately grateful for. And as for looking frazzled, I think perhaps that can be accounted for by the twin tasks of planning a wedding and trying to solve a murder." Anneke made the statement deliberately, watching their reaction. She'd have to tell them sooner or later, and this seemed as good a time as any.

"Murder? What murder?" Rachel's eyes widened. "Emma, did you know anything about a murder?"

193

"Nope." Emma turned to face her mother. "Has he gotten you involved in one of his cases?" she asked accusingly.

"As a matter of fact, rather the reverse." Anneke spoke more sharply than she'd intended. "At the moment, I'm a suspect in a letter bomb murder."

"A what? In a *what*?" Rachel asked in disbelief.

"You mean that hacker who was arrested?" Emma said.

"He wasn't arrested, and he's not a hacker—at least, not what you mean by hacker," Anneke said. "But yes, that's the murder in question." Briefly, she sketched out the situation, being as matter-of-fact as possible. "I doubt that anyone really thinks I did it," she said at last, "but it would be nice to have it cleared up before the wedding."

"They let Jesse Franklin go." Marshall spoke from the doorway. Samantha, as though sensing something ominous going on, clung to his leg with one hand, holding tightly to a child's drinking cup with the other. "Heard it on the radio in the cab from the airport."

"I know. Thank goodness."

"But that means they'll still suspect *you*," Rachel wailed.

"Jesus Christ. *Cops*." Emma infused the word with utter loathing.

"Mom, have you got a good lawyer? Marshall, don't you know a good lawyer here in Michigan?"

"Why the hell can't *he* get them off your back?" Emma demanded. "As long as we have to have a cop in the family, can't he make himself useful?"

"That's not fair," Rachel said. "He must be doing everything he can. Isn't he, Mom? Just because you hate cops, Emma, you won't even give him a chance, and you've never even met him."

"Yes I did. Met him this afternoon. Big enough to be

about a cop and a half, and he still can't keep our mother out of trouble."

"That's enough." Anneke didn't raise her voice, but both of her daughters stopped dead. My God, I can still do the Mother Voice, she thought, laughing to herself. I guess you never lose it. Aloud, she said: "Karl is on . . . let's say, enforced vacation. That's not a defense of him," she said to Emma, "merely an explanation. And yes, oddly enough, I do have an attorney," she told Rachel, letting a bit of sarcasm show. "I brought this up simply to give you the information, not to ask for your help *or* your opinions. So now that you know about it, let's move on." Rachel opened her mouth to speak, but Anneke plowed over her. "Is dinner at seven o'clock all right?"

"I'm meeting Zoe and some other people at the Cottage Inn," Emma reminded her. "I just came by to shower and change."

"Of course we'll be here." Rachel flashed a look at her sister. "Samantha should be fed and asleep by seven, so that sounds about right."

"Fine." Anneke smiled at them, a Mother Smile. "Michael Rappoport is coming by around nine to go over the wedding procedures, since we're not having a rehearsal. Can you be back by then, Emma?"

"Yeah, I guess." She sounded suspicious but not absolutely hostile, which Anneke figured was as much as she could hope for.

"Good. Then we'll see you later. Rachel, how about my taking Samantha out for a walk now, while you and Marshall unpack and get settled? Come on, Sammy." She held out a hand to the child, and felt foolishly gratified when Samantha let go of Marshall's leg and transferred her sticky clasp to Anneke's own hand.

She hadn't known how dinner arrangements would work out, so she'd kept it simple—salad, beef bourguignonne, and French bread. But Rachel wanted margarine instead of butter, which they didn't have; Marshall wasn't supposed to eat onions; they "didn't ordinarily eat red meat, but since you went to so much trouble . . ."; and they passed on the water because it came from the tap rather than a French mountain spring. Rachel was quite pleasant about it all, but quite firm. "It's different for you," she said obscurely, and Anneke realized that what she meant was: "You're so old it doesn't matter anyway." Only the covert smile on Karl's face kept her from blowing up at her impossible daughter.

"Shall we have coffee in the living room?" Karl suggested finally. "And would anyone like brandy?"

"Yes, please." Anneke said the words so fervently that Rachel looked at her sharply. Oh, shit, now she'll be convinced I'm an alcoholic, Anneke thought, giggling to herself.

"Sounds good," Marshall said. "How about you, hon?" he asked Rachel.

"We already had wine with dinner," she reminded him.

"Take that as a yes," Marshall said to Karl, winking.

"This really is a nice house." Rachel sank into the sofa and accepted the brandy snifter from Karl's hand. "You did have it checked for asbestos before you bought it, didn't you?"

"That was part of the building inspection, yes." Anneke felt a sudden wave of sympathy for her daughter, so buffeted by fearmongers that she could hardly draw a peaceful breath. "Are you still planning to go back to school when Samantha starts preschool?" she asked, changing the subject.

"Yes. I've been looking into a new teacher training program at the University of Colorado."

"Good for you, Sis." Emma made another abrupt appearance in the doorway. "I'd hate to see you turn into one of those soccer moms. You're too bright for that." She remained in the doorway for a moment before stepping into the living room.

"Would you like a brandy?" Karl stood up as she entered.

"Brandy?" Emma wrinkled her nose. "Sure, why not?" She remained standing as he poured from the crystal decanter and handed her the glass. "Thank you." She took a sip. "This is good stuff." The words sounded more like an accusation than a compliment.

"I'm glad you like it." Karl accepted the words at face value. He waited for a moment, but when Emma remained standing he returned to his chair and sat down.

"I never figured you for the brandy type," Rachel said.

"More the beer-and-a-joint type, you mean?" Emma grinned and sat down finally next to her sister. "Hell, I'm always glad to drink overpriced brandy if anyone's dumb enough to pay for it."

"Emma!" Rachel's voice was shocked. Emma's face reddened. Clearly the insult had been thoughtlessness rather than intent, but having said what she meant, Emma would never apologize. Instead, she tightened her jaw and looked away.

Karl threw back his head and laughed aloud.

"You may have a point at that," he said finally. "Why don't we file the question under 'arguments to have later.' We could title it 'The Psychology of Luxury.' "

Emma looked directly at him for the first time. "All right." Anneke thought there was almost a smile on her face. "But let's title it 'Priorities in the Modern World,' okay?"

"Absolutely. But in the meantime . . ."

"Right." Emma's voice was grudging but no longer combative. "Where's the brat?" she asked Rachel.

"Upstairs asleep. You can see her tomorrow," Rachel replied. Anneke could feel some of the tension leaking away. Maybe this won't be so bad, she was reassuring herself, when the doorbell rang.

The troll deftly catches the sword, examines it carefully, and tosses it back, declaring, "Good workmanship, but it's not valuable enough."

—ADVENTURE: THE COLOSSAL CAVE

"That'll be Michael," she said, trepidation returning as she went to answer the door.

He entered in a swirl of drama, a vision in dark blue rayon pants, forest green silk shirt, and dark blue silk bomber jacket decorated with a large gold leaf pin at the neck. Rachel's eyes widened; Emma's narrowed; Marshall looked dubious. Anneke sighed as she made introductions and offered him brandy.

"Yes, thanks." Michael examined the two girls openly. "You're both lucky—you have your mother's bone structure." He sat down in the dark orange chair Karl had vacated and set the brandy snifter on the coffee table. "Now then," he said sharply, calling them to attention. "As I'm sure your mother has explained to you, there will be no walking down the aisle, and no bridesmaids in the formal sense."

"I should hope not," Emma muttered. Michael threw her a sharp glance before continuing.

"There will, however, be an extremely formal ceremony

in front of nearly a hundred people. As you're Anneke's daughters, I'm sure I needn't say more. Now," he went ahead without waiting for a reply, "the groom and his best man will enter from the left. The bride and her attendants will enter from the right. You will proceed to front and center, where you will stand in a flowered alcove. Once the bride is in place, you will take two steps to the side and stand facing forward." He picked up his glass and took another sip of brandy before leaning back with a satisfied expression. "Any questions?"

Emma opened her mouth and then closed it. Rachel shook her head mutely. Anneke grinned.

"Good," Michael said. "Let me remind you of something. During the ceremony, when you will be the center of everyone's gaze, it will be your *backs* that people will be looking at. You might take that into account when you dress and style your hair." Emma opened her mouth again. "The green stripe in your hair is quite perfect," Michael said to her. "It's a beautiful counterpoint to the dark blond, and just visible from the back. Very striking." Emma glared at him.

"Is there anything you want me to do?" Marshall asked. "Will there be ushers?"

"No, because the seating will be in groups rather than in rows. An arrangement of my own devising," Michael said proudly. "Very avant-garde, I promise you." He looked so smugly satisfied that Anneke broke out laughing; he grinned back at her with an air of self-mockery. "You're absolutely *sure* about the doves?"

"Yes, Michael, absolutely. Anything over a dozen would be hopelessly vulgar. And please be sure they're all *perfectly* white."

"My dear, how can you even suggest I'd do anything else?" Michael looked wounded. Rachel looked stunned.

"Doves?" she said faintly.

"Rachel, you always were *so* gullible." Emma giggled suddenly, a sound Anneke had almost forgotten.

"I was not," Rachel denied.

"Oh, right. Remember when I hid Scruffy and told you that Mom had buried him in the backyard, and you spent half the day digging holes looking for him?"

"Emma, I was six years old."

"Is *that* what that was about?" Anneke asked, diverted. Scruffy had been a stuffed rabbit. Anneke remembered the holes in the backyard lawn, and Tim's rage over the desecration, but she'd never known why Rachel had been digging.

" 'Fraid so." Emma grinned at her mother. "Anyway," she said to Rachel, "I don't think we have to worry about being pelted with birdshit at the wedding, do we?" The question was really directed to Michael, who smiled airily.

"There will be . . . surprises," he intoned. He set down his brandy snifter and stood. "I must be off. A maid of honor's work is never done." He winked at Karl, who laughed. So did Anneke.

So, surprisingly, did Emma. When Michael had left, Emma said: "Gee, Mom, I never figured you for a fag hag."

Anneke looked over at Karl before replying. He was grinning openly. "Nor am I," she said evenly. "I promise you—no, I *guarantee* you—that Michael is absolutely straight."

"Oh, puh-leeze," Emma said scornfully.

"Emma, for someone who claims to care so much about inner truths, you're awfully quick to make snap judgments about people based on externals such as how they look, or what they do for a living." She let the last words resonate for a minute before continuing. "I repeat—Michael happens not to be gay."

"How do you know?" Rachel asked.

"I believe," Anneke replied consideringly, "that that's none of your business."

"Do you think they actually believe I slept with Michael?" She was still giggling an hour later, blessedly alone with Karl in her office, the door firmly closed. Rachel and Marshall had gone to bed finally, pleading jet lag; Emma had gone out again almost as soon as Michael left.

"Considering your performance, they could hardly believe anything else."

"Oh, shit. It's just that they made such easy targets I couldn't resist. And they were acting like such . . . like I had one foot in a nursing home."

"Which you definitely do not." He slid his hand across her shoulder and down the back of her arm. "And just in case you have any doubts . . ."

"With my children in the house?" She pantomimed extravagant horror. "If they hear us they really will believe I slept with Michael."

"I take it, then, that you never did?" Karl asked casually.

"You— What?" She turned to face him. "Are you joking? You mean you actually thought . . ."

"Well, let's say the thought did just cross my mind. You and he were friends for a long time before we met, after all."

"Yes, but— Oh, shit."

"Anneke, it's not a problem, you know. We both had lives, and lovers, before we met."

"Yes, but none of yours are planning to show up in our wedding party." She shook her head. "And I promise you, neither are any of mine. Not only have I never slept with Michael, I've never even been tempted." She laughed. "I guess he's not my type."

"Oh, I believe you." He grinned at her. "But don't expect

anyone else to. Especially your daughters. Now," he said briskly, "let's see how our little band of suspects is reacting to the material we sent them."

<Dani>Are you kidding? If that's supposed to be a blackmail threat it sure went right over my head. What's he supposed to be accusing me of, anyway? Sleeping around? Even if it were true, which it isn't, so what?

<Seth>Jesus, that little shit. No wonder they're talking about a full audit.

<Elliott>Im sposed to have done what? Changed my grades? As if. Besids, what culd he blackmail me for, anyway? My Nikes?

"You know, that's a point," Anneke observed. "What *could* anyone blackmail a fifteen-year-old kid for?"

"You'd be surprised," Karl replied. "If it were a serious enough issue, like a prison offense, Elliott's parents might have been induced to pay. Or Elliott might have created a program Vince wanted, or accessed a computer system Vince wanted to break into. There are a lot of things besides money that people can extort from each other." He paused. "Besides, that wasn't even necessarily the point. Blackmail is often as much about power as it is about gain."

"Probably even more so in this case. Vince was definitely on a power trip." She returned to the postings.

<Larry>I take it he's accusing me of some sort of stock manipulation, or insider trading, something like that anyway. The FBI asked me about that, in fact, but luckily it's easy enough to disprove. I actually don't have any Gallery3 stock except what I've acquired through converting stock options, and the rest of my portfolio is almost entirely in mutual funds. Sorry, Vince, but you weren't just crooked, you were also stupid.

<Kell>As far as I'm concerned, he might as well have been writing in Sanskrit--it makes about as much sense. I don't have a clue what he's accusing me of, but it sure doesn't sound like much fun. :-)

<Dani>Shit, I'm in the same position Elliott is--and isn't that a great thing for a 26-year-old woman to admit :-(. I just don't have anything worth blackmailing me for. I guess freedom really IS another word for nothing left to lose.

<Jesse>Poor Vince. What a writhing horror his mind must have been. And we never really got it, did we? When you look at these postings all put together like this, it seems so obvious, but as they came through we all missed it. It doesn't say much for our powers of observation, does it?

<Seth>You know, when you think about it, as far as Vince was concerned we were all characters in a game he was playing, and we never even knew it.

<Kell>Gee, maybe we're all really holodeck creations who've developed self-awareness. Computer, freeze program. :-)

<Elliot>Hahahahahaha!!! <insert evil laugh> Didnt work. Im still here, Captain.

<Dani>Beam me up, Scotty, I don't think I want to play this game anymore.

<Seth>No no, you're mixing generations. This is a Cardassian plot to make us question our reality.

<Jesse>But isn't reality only an agreed-upon construct of the ruling elite?

<Anneke>Computer, freeze reality.

"And we're off again." Anneke's laughter turned to an embarrassed grin when she saw the expression on Karl's face. "Well, what can I tell you? They're gamers."

"Having given up my search for reality, I'm now in the

market for a good fantasy." He quoted the old bumper sticker with an answering smile.

"Okay. Reality." She reached into her briefcase and handed him several sheets of paper. "I did some surfing for the information you asked for, but I don't think I really found anything useful." He took the papers and scanned them rapidly. "There are rumors of a buyout of Gallery Three, but then there are always rumors of buyouts in the high-tech world. And there's another rumor of a merger between the Bank of Los Angeles and BankOne, but the same thing applies." She made a face. "I figure in another ten years there'll only be two banks left in the whole world. I didn't find anything about either company that looked unusual. Both of them reported better-than-expected profits in the last quarter, if that means anything."

"It means that neither company is in a state of panic, at least. Didn't Vince say something about Gallery Three having a red-ink quarter?"

"That was last year. They'd just acquired a small company that had developed a new graphics engine, and they hadn't gone to production with it yet. This year it's supposed to be selling fairly well. Is any of this worth anything?"

"I suppose it clears away some of the underbrush, but not much else." He looked down at the papers and pursed his lips. "I see Dani's former bosses landed on their feet."

"Don't they always?" Anneke felt bitterness for Dani's sake. "One of them is vice president and CFO of Home-Web, and the other two have formed a new software company to develop an Internet shopping service." She glared at the paper in Karl's hand. "Whatever you do, don't invest in either of them."

"I have no plans to, believe me. As far as I'm concerned,

the high-tech stock market is strictly a spectator sport." He put down the papers and stood up.

"Karl, are we getting *anywhere*?"

"Possibly." He sighed, and she felt a twitch of panic.

"This isn't going to be solved before the wedding, is it?"

"I don't know." He shook his head, then grinned suddenly. "Isn't there a rule that the great detective and the gorgeous suspect have at least one steamy encounter in each book?"

"Right," she said drily. "Just before he traps her into confessing and turns her in."

"Well, if that's what it takes . . ."

The sword halts in mid-air, twirls like a dervish, and chants several bars of "Dies Ire" in a rough tenor voice. It then begins to spin like a rip-saw blade and flies directly at the ogre, who attempts to catch it without success; it strikes him full on the chest. There is a brilliant flash of light, a deafening roar and a cloud of oily grey smoke; when the smoke clears (and your eyes begin working properly again) you see that the ogre has vanished.

—ADVENTURE: THE COLOSSAL CAVE

She was late coming down for breakfast Friday morning, after putting on and taking off three different outfits. She decided finally on dark green gabardine pants with an off-white silk blouse and navy blue blazer. She added one of Emma's large, sculptured silver pins to the lapel, and Mexican silver-and-lapis earrings to her ears, looking at herself in the mirror and wondering why she felt the need to impress her daughters.

"Hi, Mom." Rachel was at the dining table, with Samantha on one side of her and Marshall on the other. Karl, sitting in the fourth chair, looked at Anneke and winked. "Here, Marshall's done, aren't you?" Rachel said to her husband. "You can sit here, Mom."

"That's all right." Anneke walked past the table toward

the kitchen, ruffling Samantha's hair as she passed. "I just want coffee anyway."

"Don't be silly," Rachel said sharply. "You have to have a decent breakfast."

Anneke smiled at her daughter without comment and continued to the kitchen, where Helen was refilling the coffeepot. They shared an eye-rolling grin; Anneke filled her cup and carried it and the new pot to the living room. She put the pot on the table and carried her coffee to the sofa, where she set about dosing herself with caffeine. Karl picked up his own cup and joined her.

"Shouldn't you be drinking decaf?" Rachel asked.

"For pete's sake, Sis, leave her alone." Emma strode into the room and plopped herself down in Karl's vacated chair. "Oh good, Zingerman's cheese Danish. Mom, you're not going to need me today, are you?"

"No." Anneke shook her head. "I don't expect to get home from the office until mid-afternoon at the earliest. I would like all of us to have dinner together tonight, though."

"Sure," Emma said around a mouthful of Danish.

"You're going to work today?" Rachel sounded appalled. "It's the day before your wedding!"

"Everything's done." Anneke smiled, trying to ignore the flutter in her stomach that Rachel's words produced. *Was* there anything else she needed to do? Well, only catch a murderer. She saw Karl grinning slightly, and forced herself to ease up.

"But don't you want to spend the day relaxing, getting ready? You'll wear yourself out, and then you'll feel exhausted by the time the wedding starts."

"I'll be fine." In fact, she thought, the only place I *will* be able to relax today is at my office. "Does anyone mind if I turn on the television?" she asked, reaching for the remote without waiting for a reply. "ESPN is doing a preview of Saturday's games, and since we won't be able to go . . ." She flicked on the remote, keeping the sound low and ignoring Rachel's compressed lips. Rachel's lips always seemed to be compressed.

"Isn't there a local morning news program?" Emma asked.

"Depends on what you call news," Anneke replied. "If you want Detroit traffic reports, yes. If you want medical scare stories, celebrity gossip, assorted miseries, and cooking tips, sure. News? Not in this part of the world. At least ESPN tells you what you want to know about sports."

"Why would you want to know *anything* about sports?" Emma demanded. "How can you justify wasting your time watching overpaid postadolescents kicking a ball around? Let alone actually doing it yourself?" The question, Anneke realized, was directed not at her but at Karl.

He looked at Emma and spread his hands. "Justify? Why should I have to?"

"Oh, you don't *have* to," Emma said scornfully. "I just hate to see people wasting their lives."

"Emma!" Rachel spoke loudly and anxiously. "You swore you'd behave." Samantha, energized by the noise, banged her spoon on the side of her bowl.

"Tell me something." Karl spoke to Emma, ignoring Rachel's interruption. "Why do you design jewelry?"

"Oh, here we go." Emma twisted around and threw one arm over the back of her chair. "I've been challenged on that before, believe me. Look, jewelry isn't only personal decoration—it's a form of art, a way of creating beauty while simultaneously making a statement at the deepest levels. It isn't any different from sculpture—in fact, it is a form of sculpture. The difference is, jewelry is more accessible to more people. You don't have to go to a museum to appreciate my art. You can live with it, use it, participate in it."

"You missed my point," Karl said. "I didn't ask you to justify jewelry. I asked you why, specifically, *you* create jewelry."

"You mean, instead of painting, or something like that?" Emma shrugged. "Because it's what I'm good at, I guess. And it's what I love to do."

"Exactly." Karl spread his hands.

"Uh-uh, sorry." Emma saw where he was going and shook her head. "You can't justify every kind of activity simply because you enjoy doing it. There are rapists and serial killers who enjoy what they do, too. And some of them are damn good at it. Does that mean they're in the right line of work?"

"Emma, that's enough." This time Rachel stood up and glared at her sister. "You're being insufferable."

"No, she isn't." Karl not only wasn't offended, he was laughing. In fact, Emma herself was grinning widely.

"Rachel, why don't you take Samantha upstairs and get her cleaned up?" Anneke suggested. Samantha responded to her name with another cheerful anvil chorus of spoon-and-bowl.

"But—"

"I don't think they're going to come to blows," Anneke said.

"Well, not this morning," Emma agreed. "I have two more galleries to visit, and bloodstains aren't exactly a fashion statement."

"In fact, blood is used for self-decoration in a number of primitive cultures," Karl observed.

"Of course it is," Emma pounced. "That's my point— bodily decoration has been a function of human life since the Cro-Magnon days."

"So has game-playing," Karl said. "And competing in games, and watching others compete in games."

"Yes, but . . ."

Laughing to herself, Anneke stood up and quietly carried her coffee cup to the kitchen, leaving them to enjoy their argument.

"Honestly, I love them dearly, but if I had to live with them full-time you'd have to fit me up with a rubber room." She grinned at Karl, sitting next to her desk in the blessed privacy of her office. "I can just about stand living with one person let alone three other adults and a three-year-old."

"A rubber room." He cocked his head. "You know, that might have possibilities."

"Now, now. Let's keep our minds on our work, Lieutenant." She clicked to open her e-mail reader.

<Kell> Okay, I got all the questions. Here's what I did with them. Instead of just listing them here, I've set up a secure Web site where we can all interact. The url is <www.murdermansion.net/foyer>. You should each use your customary handle. The password is: mur33der. Why don't we meet there at noon EDT, which is nine o'clock California time.

"Oh, hell." Anneke checked her watch. "That's two hours away. I wanted to get right on it."

"That's all right. I have a couple of last-minute errands anyway."

"Are you going to talk to Wes?"

"Nope. This is about the honeymoon, not the murder."

"Karl, are you sure we're going to be able to go?"

"Unless they've told you directly to stay in town, yes. In fact, one of my errands is to give Stanley a complete itinerary. If they want you again, they can reach you through your attorney."

"Oh, great." She made a face at him. "So everyone knows where I'll be except me."

"That's why they call it a surprise." He stood up. "I'll be back well before noon."

"There it is." The murder mansion foyer was exactly that—a graphic of a small entry hall, complete with dark green rug, brass chandelier, and coatrack festooned with coats. Seven doors lined the wall, and on each of them was a plaque bearing the name of one of the list members. Across the bottom of the Netscape browser window was a blank text bar and a button marked Send.

Standing in the center of the green rug was a small female figure, with long, curly blond hair, wearing a short red dress. As they watched, the figure twirled around and the skirt of the red dress spun out.

"My God." Anneke stared at the screen wide-eyed. "I don't believe this."

A cartoon balloon appeared suddenly over the head of the dancing figure. "Welcome to Murder Mansion," it read. "Glad you could all make it."

"Incredible. How could she?" Anneke muttered.

"How could she what?" Karl asked.

"How could she put something like this together so fast?" Anneke glared at the screen.

"Is it that difficult?" Karl leaned forward to examine the scene in the monitor. "Couldn't you do it?"

"Yes, I could do it," Anneke agreed, "but not in a few hours. Even if she cannibalized most of the graphics and Java scripts from other places, it's an incredible job. And where the hell would she get all the pieces in the first place?

212

I mean, who has this kind of stuff just lying around on their hard drive?"

"In other words," Karl said, "we're back to our original question—just exactly who *is* Kell?"

The vial strikes the ground and explodes with a violent >foom<, neatly severing your foot. You bleed to death quickly and messily.

—ADVENTURE: THE COLOSSAL CAVE

"We'll go to each room in turn," the balloon over the dancing figure said, "and ask all our questions." The text erased itself and began again. "When it's your room, type your answers in the form at the bottom of the screen." Again the balloon blanked. "Please, no one else enter comments until we're done."

"Incredible," Anneke repeated.

"Since it's my game, I'll volunteer to be the first victim . . . er, subject :-)" the figure said, spinning. "Please click on the door marked 'Kell.' "

Anneke did as she was told, and found herself in a nightclub. On the left side of the screen were three white-covered tables and some simple chairs; on the right, angling across the upper corner, was a stage with stool and microphone. The dancing figure was on the stage; below, clustered around the tables, were six other figures.

"Sorry I couldn't give you a choice of avatars," the Kell-figure said, "but maybe later. Meanwhile, it's showtime."

The Kell-balloon blanked, and a new balloon popped open. Its tail pointed to one of the clustered figures, a football player in a black-and-red uniform. "That must be Seth," Anneke said.

"Have you ever applied for a job with a computer company and been turned down?" the balloon read.

"Nope," the Kell-balloon replied. "I'd rather be a free spirit than a salary drone. I'd make a really lousy Dilbert, wouldn't I?"

The Seth-balloon disappeared and another took its place, hovering over a tall, thin simulacrum with a scraggly beard. The figure was carrying a spear and wearing an odd, pointed metal helmet. ("Don Quixote!" Anneke said, clapping her hands with delight. "That's Jesse.")

"Do you have any roommates, and if so who are they?" Don Quixote's balloon asked.

"Not unless you count two cats," Kell replied, "which you certainly would if they had anything to say about it. My last roommate split with a pretty good stereo system along with a few other things I kind of liked, so now I'm a little more careful. Are you volunteering? That New Mexico spread looked pretty good. ;->"

A new balloon appeared, above a female figure decked out in full wedding-dress regalia. ("I'll kill her," Anneke said, grinning.)

"Are you currently employed, and if so, with whom?" the bride's balloon asked.

" 'Employed' is such a dreary word. :-)" Kell said. "I do some part-time work with a computer company in Chicago, but only stuff I feel like doing."

The next balloon popped open over a small pirate figure,

complete with peg leg, eye patch, and parrot perched on its shoulder—Elliott, Anneke realized after a moment. "Are you a student at Wisconsin, and what are you studying?" it asked.

"Not at the moment," Kell answered, "although I was, and I'm thinking about registering for classes next year. There are a couple of courses in Artificial Intelligence that look fascinating."

The balloon closed and reopened over a figure in military fatigues, standing with legs slightly apart. It had long black hair and Asian features, and it carried an assault rifle held low in its hands.

"Why does that figure look familiar?" Anneke wondered aloud.

"Tania," Karl said at once.

"Tania?"

"Patty Hearst. That's a takeoff of the famous picture of Patty Hearst as Tania, remember?"

"My God, you're right. Talk about a blast from the past."

"What do you dislike most about your life?" the Dani avatar asked.

"Ouch. What a question." The Kell avatar danced and twirled. "I suppose not having enough time to do everything I want to do with my life."

The final avatar was, in its own way, the funniest—a perfectly square figure in a navy blue business suit and gray fedora. He carried a briefcase in one hand and a newspaper in the other. It looked like a concrete block masquerading as a stockbroker. Larry couldn't be too pleased, Anneke thought, laughing to herself.

"What do your parents do for a living?" his balloon read.

"Sorry, but both my parents are dead. My father was a pharmacist, and my mother was a very happy housewife."

The balloon over the Kell avatar disappeared, and nothing happened for a minute. Then the balloon reappeared. "Okay, folks, let's move on to the next room. Jesse, how about you?"

"Sure," Don Quixote replied. "BTW, this is great work, Kell."

"Thanks, Jesse. I figured if we were going to play a Murder Game, we ought to do it up right," Kell said. "Okay, everybody. Back up your browsers to the foyer and let's all click on Jesse's room."

Jesse's "room" was a desert scene, with sand underfoot, two or three large, stylized cacti, and a glowing sunset in the background. The Don Quixote figure stood next to a boulder, while the other avatars clustered on the side of the screen.

"Okay, shoot," Don Quixote said via balloon.

The military figure with the assault rifle spoke first. "Have you made any political or quasi-political contributions in the last year?" Dani asked.

"Yes, of course," Jesse said. "I'm a member of ACLU, I contribute to the Internet Freedom Foundation, and I gave money to the Right to Privacy campaign. (If you answer no to that question, you probably don't deserve to live here, folks.)"

"How much income did you report on your tax return last year?" That was from the football player.

"$45,613." The reply came so quickly, Anneke wondered why Jesse would carry the exact figure around in his head.

"Did you write any more games after Mordona? If not, why did you stop?" the pirate asked.

She was getting used to the process, Anneke realized. The avatars weren't particularly realistic, of course; except for Kell's dancing girl, they didn't move, and they seemed more pasted on than fitted into each scene. But as the questioning went on, she tended to filter the individual avatars and mentally accept the experience as perfectly ordinary interaction.

"Good question," Jesse responded to Elliott. "No, I didn't. As near as I can remember, I just sort of moved on to other things. And I wasn't too thrilled with the direction computer games were taking. Even back then, they were beginning to pander to the worst part of human nature."

"What was your biggest (most lucrative) consulting contract this year?" Larry's square little man asked.

"I'm afraid you won't believe me when I tell you, but it was a government contract—and not only government, but the local prosecutor's office. And now, having shocked you all sufficiently, I'll explain that it was to help them set up a data retrieval system to catch men who were defaulting on child support payments." The avatar, of course, didn't change expression, but Anneke felt she could almost see it smile.

"Has anyone lived in your house with you, even temporarily, in the last two years?" An odd question, coming from Kell's dancing girl.

"Oh yes, often. People come through here every now and then needing a place to stay, and since I've got the space, why not share it temporarily?"

"Do you use any other UIDs online, and if so, what are they?" The bride spoke, looking ridiculous against the desert landscape.

"Yes, I do. I imagine we all do, don't we? But if I told you what they are, I'd hunt you down and kill you :-)

"Well, I figured as much." Anneke shrugged. "Worth a try, I guess."

"All right," Kell's balloon spelled out. "Anneke, why don't you go next."

"Okay," the bride said. Anneke clicked back to the foyer and clicked again, laughing aloud when she saw the background Kell had given her.

The screen showed the outline of a house, silhouetted against the night sky. A ladder leaned against the wall, and the bride stood on its top rung in classic elopement mode. The other figures clustered at the base of the ladder, and Larry's suit-clad avatar spoke first.

"What was the last contract you bid on and lost, and why did you lose it?"

That was straightforward enough. Anneke typed rapidly in the form box at the bottom of the screen. "We bid on an RFP to set up an Internet communications system to monitor shipping in the Great Lakes. We lost it because the agency felt we were too small to handle it—and on reflection, I think they were right. The only reason we bid was because it sounded fascinating, which I guess is the wrong way to make business decisions. :-)"

"Did your fiancé ever serve in the military?" Dani asked.

"Sorry, no," Anneke typed, grinning. A clever question. "He was 4-F because of a bad shoulder he got playing football."

Seth's question was neither simple nor benign. "Why did you get divorced from your first husband, and what is your current relationship with him?" the football player asked.

"This is a little like an advanced game of Truth or Dare, isn't it?" Anneke typed, temporizing. "The fact is, my ex-husband left me for his 23-year-old graduate assistant. The last I knew of him, he was at Arizona State, but I haven't had any communication with him for about 10 years." She was conscious of Karl's presence; nothing he didn't know, of course, but . . .

"What political activities did you participate in during the '60s?" Kell asked.

"It embarrasses me to admit it, but in fact the answer is None. I was busy being a student, and then I was busy being a wife and mother, and except for listening to Dylan and the Rolling Stones I more or less ignored the political scene entirely. God, that sounds self-involved, doesn't it?" She typed the last sentence, then deleted it before hitting the Send button.

"How many employees has your own company had in the last two years, were they all students, and what was their status?" A precise and probing question from Jesse that surprised her somehow. As if he were taking Vince's accusation seriously.

"IIRC, we've had approximately 12 different programmers working for us at one point or another in the last two years, and yes, all of them were students. Of that dozen or so, I think five of them were interns and the rest were contract hires."

And finally, from Elliott: "Where did you learn computer programing?"

"I started out by myself, when I got my first Apple][," she wrote. "Eventually I went through the computer science program here at Michigan." It sounds so simple, she thought, as the words appeared in the balloon over the bride's head. She doubted that any of them would even understand if she tried to describe what it was like—to be the only woman in most of her classes, and a middle-aged woman at that. Well, why should they? Ancient history, thank God.

"Larry, how about you next?" the dancing girl asked.

"All right." Even inside the balloon, the words seemed unenthusiastic.

Anneke clicked mouse buttons, and found herself looking down at a racetrack. She burst into laughter when she saw the creatures lined up at the starting gate—a clutch of rats, waiting to start the rat race. Larry's square little avatar was inside one of the gates; the others were lined along the edge of the track.

The football player went first. "How much did you pay for your house, and how big is the mortgage?" Seth asked.

"$850,000; 80% over 30 years." Larry's reply was terse.

"Why did you leave TerraNova?" the bride asked.

"Because Gallery3 offered me more money and more authority." There was a pause, as though Kell was waiting for Larry to add something, but nothing more was forthcoming, and in a few moments the next balloon appeared over the pirate's head.

"Did you ever write a game all by yourself?" Elliott asked.

"Not since high school. I wrote a board game that I thought was really hot stuff, but when I gave it to my friends to beta-test, it kept crashing their video cards." Talking about games, Larry was more expansive. "I was part of the team at TerraNova that wrote 'The Third Victim,' too."

"Why don't you have any children?" The question was a kind of challenge, appropriate somehow from Dani's military-clad figure. Too much of a challenge, apparently.

"Isn't that a little personal?" Larry said.

221

"Sure it is." The words appeared over Kell's avatar. "But it isn't any more personal than asking Anneke about her divorce. That's the whole point of this. We can ask things the feds won't even think of. You can refuse to answer, of course, but then you're out of the game. If you're going to play, you have to accept the rules."

"All right, all right." Larry gave in. "It's not that we 'don't have children,' it's more that we don't have children YET. My wife is still establishing her career and we both feel we're too busy to do the job right. Children are too much responsibility to just have them and figure you'll work them into your life somehow." There was a pause in the text flow. "Are you happy now?"

"Oh, I'm always happy {:->" the dancing girl replied. "Next question: Is your 1934 Mercedes still for sale?"

"Yes. If you know anyone who's interested, feel free to give them my e-mail address."

The balloon appeared above Don Quixote. "What exactly is your position within the Gallery3 hierarchy? How many people are above you in the organizational chart?"

"Officially, I'm vice president for software development," the suit-clad avatar replied. "There are three other vice presidents, a COO, a CFO, and a chairman of the board. So I suppose there are three others above me."

"Has he ever suggested that he might want to be COO?" Karl asked.

"Not that I recall." Anneke thought about it. "I wouldn't think he'd be a candidate for it, actually. Larry's focused on product, not management."

"Elliott, you're up next," the dancing girl said.

You have jumped into a bottomless pit. You continue to fall for a very long time. First, your lamp runs out of power and goes dead. Later, you die of hunger and thirst.

ADVENTURE: THE COLOSSAL CAVE

Elliot's door opened onto the deck of a ship. Overhead, the Jolly Roger flew; but where the wheel should have been, there was a computer keyboard. The scene beyond, consisting of water and a small, sandy island with a single palm tree, was enclosed in the outlines of a monitor screen.

"Way cool," Elliott's pirate said. "I'm goin to download it for wallpaper."

"Glad you like it," the dancing girl said. "Here come the questions."

"What was your grade-point average last year?" Larry's avatar asked.

"2.3 and who gives a flying fuck? Im pulling As in math and computer science, and thats wat matters. I figure as long as I can make C++ stand up and roll over, nobody's goin to care if I kno the capitol of fucking bolivia, right?"

"What was the last system you hacked into, and what did you do there?" Seth asked.

"Hey, I didn't DO anything, what do you think I am?"

(Even via text in a balloon, Anneke could sense Elliott's real resentment.) "A REAL hacker doesn't mess up systems he visits, he just goes in and looks around. Once I know I CAN do something, why bother to do it?" Elliott didn't answer the question, Anneke noticed, but the others let it go.

Dani's figure spoke next. "What kind of game are you writing and how far along are you?"

"You mean am I relly writing one?" (Now why did Elliott seem so prickly? Anneke wondered.) "Im acually working on two or three different games one is a real-time military sim kind of like Insurrection where you're freedom fighters in Montana, and theres another Im thinking of writing with a friend that would be an adventure/arcade game."

"Who is your best friend?" Jesse's Don Quixote asked.

"What's that got to do with anything? Anyway I guess my best friend is called Wild Willie and he lives in i think Kansas city or st. Louis. Hes the one I said we're talking about riting a game together sort of like Virtua Fighter only set in ancient Rome and with authentic weapons."

"What are your parents' occupations?" the bride asked.

"My father's a stockbroker and my mothers a psychologist."

"Where do you get your spending money?" the dancing girl asked. "Do you get an allowance? Do you have a part-time job?"

"I get an allowance but its just for like books and cloths and stuff. But I do some computer work for a local ISP working on their software front end and some tech support. And some database work for a bookstor here but thats megaboring, you know?"

"Thanks, Elliott." The words appeared in the dancing girl's balloon. "Let's move to Seth next."

A no-brainer, of course—Seth's football-player avatar stood under an old-fashioned H-shaped goalpost. Behind him a grandstand fanned out, and in each seat was a cartoon computer, smiling faces displayed on their monitors. A few of them waved tiny pennants, including a Michigan Block M confronting a red Wisconsin W.

"Why and how did you break up with your last girlfriend?" the dancing girl asked.

"Shit, that's easy. Because she thought Sammy Sosa was the name of the Taco Bell chihuahua and that 'Tomb Raider' was a Harrison Ford movie. And I won't even tell you what she thought a joystick was. Besides, her idea of a good time was to go walking on a beach and have long, long talks about feelings. Did you ever notice that the chicks who talk the most about feelings are the ones who never actually HAVE them?"

The bride's question came next. "How many résumés have you sent out in the last six months?"

"Thirteen, and it'll be a lot more in the next six months, which is why I'm really sweating this murder business." Seth seemed nothing if not frank. "Look, I know I'm no Larry Ellison, but I can do better than stand around pushing buttons for a roomful of suits who don't know a data pod from a doorknob. If I didn't have student loans to pay off I'd walk tomorrow."

"Who did you bet on in last year's Super Bowl, how much, and with whom?" Dani asked.

"Atlanta, two large, and you don't want to know. But

don't worry, it's all paid off. I mean, I may not be the brightest bulb in the chandelier, but I'm not THAT stupid. Look, sure I gamble on sports—it's a way to kind of be part of the action, you know? Just like playing a good computer game. If you've got money riding on a game there's a real buzz that you don't get if you're just a blob on a bar stool. But I never bet more than I can afford to lose." (Easy to say, Anneke thought. Like "I can quit any time I want." But was it true?)

"Do you run a lot of football pools?" the pirate asked.

"Just one, and that's only because I'm using it to model a sports gambling game I'm working on." Again Seth seemed perfectly straightforward. "Running a pool isn't where the fun is, and besides, it's a little risky. Nobody's going to bust a guy who buys a couple of squares in a pool, but they can come down hard on the guy who's handling the action."

"Do you own stock in any bank(s)?" That was Larry.

"Are you kidding? I don't even get my own parking spot in this crummy job, let alone stock options. And even if I did, why would I want stock when I'm planning to grab the next train out of here?"

Jesse's question caused Seth to pause. "What would you like to be doing ten years from now?"

The balloon over the football player's head remained blank for several seconds. "I haven't got a clue," it said finally. "I guess the only thing I'm sure of is what I DON'T want to be doing, and right now I'm doing it."

You could almost hear the plaintive tone before Kell moved them briskly ahead through Dani's door and onto . . .

The bridge of the *Enterprise*? Anneke blinked. It was the

original *Enterprise*, not the later one, but only Uhura sat at her console. In the command chairs, where Kirk and Chekov would have been, were small piles of ash. Dani's fatigue-clad figure stood in the open door of the elevator, assault rifle at the ready, and Anneke could have sworn there was a smile on the tiny avatar's face that hadn't been there before.

The pirate began the questioning. "What sort of revenge did you take on the guys who screwed you over at Texonomy?"

"None." The word sat there inside the balloon for several seconds before the next line of text appeared. "See, what happened is, I was still buying into the good-little-girl rip-off—you know: Work with the system, Dani; don't get a reputation as a troublemaker, Dani; don't always believe the worst about people, Dani. So that's what I did, and by the time I figured out that the only thing I'd bought into was a stack of unpaid bills, it was too late. They were in Chapter 11 and I was out in the cold. Now if you want to know about my revenge FANTASIES, that's another story. My only remaining problem is where to get the polar bear and the handcuffs."

Seth's question was so odd Anneke couldn't imagine what he had in mind. "What's your favorite night spot in Austin?"

Dani seemed to understand his point. "Shit, Seth, you could at least have had the guts to ask the question directly. For the record, my favorite spot is a woman-run café called Janey's; also for the record, Janey's is a gay hangout. And finally, to tell you what you're really fishing for—no, I'm not gay, I just wish I were. Okay?"

"Did you send out résumés after Texonomy folded,"

Larry got back to basics, "and if so, why weren't you hired?"

"Yeah, I sent out a few, but it was a pretty raggedy-ass job search," Dani replied, apparently without rancor. "Look, I kind of went to pieces when Texonomy went under. I did some drinking, and some coke, and some other things I'm not too proud of. I don't blame anyone for not hiring me back then—I was a real mess. It wasn't until I got back to concentrating on art that I started to pull myself together, and by then I didn't really want a job-job, you know? I'm happier making less money and taking less shit." Well, so am I, Anneke thought; so why is a statement like that always so hard to believe?

"Have you ever sold a painting or other artwork?" Kell asked.

"Hell, yes." For the first time, Dani seemed affronted. "And there's a gallery here in Austin that carries some of my multimedia work. AND I've done custom artwork for half a dozen high-end Web sites. What did you think I was, some kid playing with a box of Crayolas? [Although in fact you can do some great stuff with Crayolas.]"

Another off-the-wall question, this time from Jesse. "What's your favorite movie of all time?"

"Female Trouble (or anything else from John Waters); Invasion of the Body Snatchers (the original, please); Dr. Strangelove."

And finally, Anneke's question. "Exactly what kind of work did you do for Texonomy? Not your title or job description, but what you actually did."

"Shitwork." The answer came quickly. "I was supposed to do graphics design and programming—or at least that's what they said when they hired me. But there was always something else that had to be done first, some piece of boring shit that had to be coded, and it was always good old

228

Dani who got stuck with it. They called it 'being a team player,' you know?" Her bitterness poured through the screen.

Just when Anneke thought she was done, a few more lines appeared in Dani's balloon. "DOES anyone know where I can get a polar bear and a pair of handcuffs? ;-}"

The ogre contemptuously catches the sword in mid-swing, rips it out of your hands, and uses it to chop off your head.

—ADVENTURE: THE COLOSSAL CAVE

"I think we're adjourned for the moment," Kell wrote. "Why don't we take some time to process what we've heard for a while." The balloon blanked and new words scrolled into it. "Comments to the murdergame list later."

The balloon disappeared; so did the avatars. Anneke leaned back and regarded the empty bridge of the *Enterprise*.

"Well, I don't know how useful that was," she said finally, "but at least we know a lot more about them than we did before."

"Yes and no." Karl closed his notebook. "We still know hardly anything about Kell."

"Kell. Yes." Anneke shook her head in irritation. "For heaven's sake, it can't be all *that* mysterious. Whatever her secret is, certainly the feds know it. After all, they interrogated her, too." She turned back to her computer. "Look, do you have any objection to just asking her? I can open an IRQ channel and e-mail her to log on to it.

Assuming she's still online, we can talk to her real-time that way."

"It's worth a try. Go ahead."

<Kell>Hi, Anneke. You rang?

<Anneke>Hi, Kell. That was one amazing piece of work you just pulled out of a hat.

<Kell>Thanks. I was kind of pleased with it myself. :-) I did want to have the avatars standing on the ground more firmly than they did, but I guess you can't have everything.

<Anneke>Did you really do that whole thing overnight, or did you have chunks of code you could reuse?

<Kell>Some of both.

<Anneke>Oh, hell. Look, the easiest thing is just to say it. Kell, who the hell ARE you?

<Kell>LOL. That's right to the point, anyway. Okay, I guess I knew it would happen eventually. But would you please not broadcast this unless you absolutely have to?

<Anneke>Promise. Unless you're about to confess to being an ax murderer, I won't tell a soul. [Although if you tell me you're Amelia Earhart it'll be a struggle.]

<Kell>It's almost that bad. <sigh> My name is actually Albert Kelleher.

<Anneke>What!? Are you kidding me?

<Kell>Sometimes I wish I were. :-)

<Anneke>What on earth are you doing on a random mailing list? And why the secrecy? Are you really moving into games programming? And why as a girl? Does Larry know who you are? My God, I'm babbling, aren't I? Anyway, I'm very pleased to meet you, Mr.Kelleher. :-)

<Kell>Because it's fun. Because if people knew who I was, it wouldn't be fun. Yes--because it's fun. Because . . . well, that's a

little more complicated to explain. No. Yes, you are, a little. :-}
Likewise.

    <Anneke>But why--no, sorry. I have no right to pry.

    <Kell>Put it this way. Have you ever heard the phrase: "It's never too late to have a happy childhood"?

    <Anneke>Yes. I guess I see what you mean, Mr. Kelleher.

    <Kell>Please call me Kell, will you? That was my nickname as a child, BTW. Now you know why I want to keep it a secret. So far, the only people who know that Kell Albright is Albert Kelleher are the FBI. They tracked me through Kell's Internet account. And they probably won't leak it unless they see some advantage in it. :-/

    <Anneke>Well, I certainly won't tell anyone, I promise. On one condition.

    <Kell>Which is?

    <Anneke>That I get the first beta copy of your wedding game. :)

"Albert Kelleher?" Karl asked when she had disconnected. "As in Kelleher Enterprises?"

"Albert Kelleher." She was still staring at the screen in astonishment. "Albert Kelleher is . . . well, think of him as the Bill Gates of banking software. Back in the early eighties, Kelleher developed a whole series of packages that pretty much revolutionized computerized banking. Then he went on to revolutionize international trading. And I think he did the same thing for the oil industry. Basically, Kelleher was to industry what Microsoft was to home computing. Oh, shit." Anneke sputtered with laughter. "Kell *said* she 'did a little work for a company in Chicago.' "

She swiveled her chair to face Karl and was surprised to see him looking grimly serious.

"What's the matter?" she asked.

"You realize that what we've come up with," he said, "is probably the best blackmail target out of the whole group,"

"But—" Dammit, he was right. If Albert Kelleher was wandering around cyberspace pretending to be a young woman, that would be News, capital N, in the computer world. "Except there's no evidence to suggest that Vince knew who Kell was. In fact," she realized suddenly, "there's internal evidence to suggest just the opposite. Vince thought Kell lived in Madison, because of the 'uwisc' e-mail account. But in fact, Albert Kelleher lives in Chicago."

"That's true." Karl nodded. "But we don't know if Vince did any more investigating. From what I've heard, it isn't hard to hack into a university computer to get information about an account."

"I suppose." Anneke didn't want it to be Kell; dammit, she *liked* Kell. But then, who did she want it to be? These were her friends. She turned back to the monitor screen, and saw that the clock in the taskbar tray read 2:17 P.M. "No wonder I'm hungry," she said aloud. "Could we get some lunch, please?"

She drove home after lunch along streets brilliant with fall color that she didn't even notice. They'd been fools to believe they'd be able to solve Vince's murder before the wedding, she thought gloomily. She wondered what the feds were doing, and why they hadn't been back to interrogate her again. Or worse, to interrogate Karl. They were probably showing her picture, and his, to clerks in garden supply stores all over the state. We'll never be able to buy mulch in this town again, she thought, trying to laugh.

When she got home, she found Zoe on the floor of the living room, playing blocks with Samantha. "Bigger!" Samantha demanded, pointing at the stack of interlocking plastic squares that already stood as high as her head.

"Why don't we start a second one, and then we can make a bridge between them," Zoe suggested. She handed

Samantha two of the large blocks and scrambled to her feet. "Anneke, can I talk to you?"

"Sure." She dropped her briefcase and sat down at the dining table behind the day's stack of wedding presents. "Where's Rachel?"

"Making baby food." Zoe sat down across from her and made a face. From behind the kitchen door, Anneke could hear the muted whir of the food processor. She only hoped her daughter wasn't driving Helen crazy. "I wanted to ask you . . . Look," she started again, "did you talk to Calvin yet?"

"Not since I saw you last. And Zoe, I wouldn't have the right to tell you anything even if I knew it."

"Oh, I know that. It's just—" Her voice died away, and Anneke felt a pang of guilt. She should have followed up on Calvin, made sure he wasn't in real trouble, found out if he needed help. There just hadn't been time. Besides, anything she did might make things worse; it was a problem that required delicacy. When she got back from her honeymoon . . .

"Oh, shit," she said.

"Oh, sit," said Samantha happily.

"Oh, hell," Anneke said, looking over her shoulder to make sure Rachel was still occupied. Zoe laughed, and after a minute Anneke laughed with her. "I think," she said finally, "that it's probably nothing horribly serious."

"That's what I thought." Zoe sounded relieved. "I mean, you checked him out when you hired him, so it's not like he was an ax murderer, right?"

"Well, I hired him through the University, so I knew he was a student in good standing. I didn't do a background check on him, you know." What *did* she know about Calvin? she wondered. If Kell Albright could be Albert Kelleher,

Calvin could be Saddam Hussein, for all she knew. "I wouldn't worry too much," she repeated, as much to reassure herself as Zoe. "And I made sure he knows there are people who'll help him if he needs it."

"My mom knows some people, too." Zoe's face brightened. "Should I talk to her, do you think?"

"That's a good idea." Knowing Zoe's mother, Anneke felt sure she could deal with anything up to and including a tornado.

"What's this one?" Zoe held up a small parcel, a cube about four inches across, wrapped in elegant gold-and-maroon-striped paper. Anneke took it from her and examined it carefully, as she now did with every package that came through the mail.

"Oh, it's from Jay," she said, reading the return address on the label. It was from the Sheraton Hotel in Seattle. "Karl's old Steelers roommate. He was supposed to be the best man, but he was sent out of town at the last minute."

"It says OPEN AT ONCE." Zoe pointed to the block letters, written in thick felt-tip pen across the front of the package.

"God, I wonder what it is." Anneke looked at the package with foreboding. She peeled off the wrapping paper, opened the white box inside, and withdrew a heavy glass jar filled with cherries packed in a dark amber liquid. "Well, it's not another naked picture, anyway."

"Huh?"

"Never mind." Anneke laughed and looked in the box for a card. "Here. It says, 'Everyone should have a last romantic dinner the night before the wedding. This will help kick off the romance. Jay.' "

"Cherry," Samantha said. She'd abandoned her blocks and now stood peering over the edge of the table. "Want cherry."

"I don't think so." Anneke read the label. "Bourbon-soaked cherries aren't exactly a pre-dinner snack for a three-year-old."

"Want *cherry*," Samantha repeated.

"Oh, Lord, I'd better put these away." Anneke stood and picked up the heavy jar.

"Samantha, are you thirsty?" Rachel emerged from the kitchen holding the child's cup. "I made you some vegetable juice."

"Want *cherry*."

"Where?" Rachel took the jar from Anneke's hand and examined it suspiciously. "These have alcohol in them!" she said. "Mom, what were you thinking?"

"Oh, a few won't hurt her," Anneke said sweetly. "It might even help her sleep."

"Mother! Samantha, *no*! Bad cherries—nasty."

"Rachel, get a grip," Anneke said in exasperation. Zoe was doubled over laughing. "Of course I wouldn't give bourbon to a three-year-old."

"Bourbon?" Emma zoomed into the room and dropped her backpack on the floor with a thud. "Isn't that a little strong for before dinner? And when is dinner, anyway? I'm starved."

"Dinner is at seven." Anneke took the jar of cherries from Rachel's hand and looked at Zoe. "A nice, romantic, pre-wedding dinner." Zoe started laughing again, and Anneke this time joined her.

KILL DRAGON
With your bare hands??
YES
Congratulations! You have just vanquished a dragon with your bare hands!
(Unbelievable, isn't it?)

— ADVENTURE: THE COLOSSAL CAVE

It wasn't exactly romantic, but dinner was more or less cheerful. Karl and Emma continued their argument good-naturedly; Rachel approved of Helen's poached salmon with pasta salad; Emma the vegetarian ate pasta salad and French bread without making a political statement; she and Marshall had a long discussion of the latest assault on Internet freedom. No one talked about the murder, or worried about the wedding.

After dinner Anneke checked the murdergame e-mail, but there was practically none; everyone, apparently, was still getting over the afternoon's question-and-answer session. For once, Anneke was relieved to be able to focus on family.

"They're pretty good kids at that, aren't they?" she said, when she and Karl were alone in their bedroom.

"As a matter of fact, they're terrific." He smiled at her. "You did a hell of a good job."

"I did, didn't I?" She accepted the compliment with real pleasure, not just for herself but for what it implied about Karl's relationship to her family—to *their* family, now. She smoothed the last bit of night-time moisturizer on her face and dropped the small bottle into her travel case. This time tomorrow night she'd be on a plane to—"Karl, should I bring sunscreen?"

He thought for a moment. "No, don't bother," he said. "You can always buy it there." She opened her mouth to ask another question, but he held up his hand. "If you bring everything you might need, you'll miss all the fun of shopping."

"Dammit, I hate not knowing."

"That's the control freak talking, not the blushing bride," he said, grinning. "You need to appreciate the romantic elements of life more."

"Oh! Speaking of romantic . . ." She had put Jay's gift on a shelf in the closet, along with two small dishes and a pair of silver spoons. Now she set them out on the tiny table under the window. "These are from Jay." She handed him the card.

"Amazing. Jay's going mushy in his old age." He put down the card and picked up the jar.

His face went suddenly rigid.

"Karl? What's wrong?"

"Where did this come from?" he asked.

"It came in the mail today. Why? What's wrong?"

"Did you save the packaging?"

"No." Her throat closed in fear. "I—wait, I tossed it in the recycling box. It's still in the basement."

"I'll be right back." He slid his bare feet into bedroom

slippers and disappeared; Anneke sat on the edge of the bed and stared at the jar of cherries as if waiting for a snake to strike. By the time Karl returned she felt almost mesmerized.

He set two transparent plastic bags on the table and pointed to the one holding striped wrapping paper. "Was this the wrapping?"

"Yes." She pointed to the other bag. "And that's the box it was in."

He took another plastic bag out of his bathrobe pocket and slipped it over the jar of cherries. He put the white typewritten card in yet another. Then he sat down and examined the wrapping paper through its plastic casing. "The postmark is smeared," he muttered almost to himself, "but they may be able to get something with infrared."

"Karl, for God's sake, will you please tell me what's going on?"

"Sorry." He shook his head as though coming up for air, and his expression was as grim as Anneke had ever seen. "That jar never came from Jay Banning."

"I gathered as much," she said a little shakily. "How did you know?"

"Have you ever seen me drink bourbon?"

"Well, no, but . . . I mean, I don't drink it either."

"No, I know. I imagine that's why the subject's never come up. But when I was playing football, bourbon was the drink of choice for a lot of guys. I happen to hate the stuff, so when they drank bourbon, I'd drink scotch or beer. For some reason it became a kind of joke—once they even spiked my beer with bourbon to see if I'd notice."

She didn't bother to ask if he had. "Could this be the same kind of thing? I mean, Jay's idea of a joke?"

"No." He shook his head. "While I was downstairs I called the Sheraton in Seattle to ask him."

"And he said no."

"Worse than that. Or better, depending on how you look at it. There's no Jay Banning registered at the Sheraton."

"So it's—what? It's not a bomb. It can't be—I already opened the package. Poisoned? I almost . . ." She discovered she was shaking; she gripped the arms of the chair to stop the tremors.

"It's all right." She was standing up, and Karl was holding her. "Anneke, it's all right."

"I'll kill the bastard." She went from terror to rage in an instant. "I'm going to find out who did this, and I swear to God I'm going to kill him."

"Good." Karl let go of her. "What's more, it's very possible that this is the break we've been waiting for."

"What do you mean?"

"Well, ask yourself this—why you?"

"But—oh. Yes, of course." She shook her head irritably. "I'm not thinking, am I?"

"Someone in that group has a secret worth killing for. And for some reason, he—or she—now believes you know it, too."

"But why would anyone think that?" She still felt muzzy, illogical.

"That is the question, isn't it?" In the soft light of the bedside lamps, Karl's eyes glittered. "Somewhere in your postings since Vince's murder, you must have written something that pushed someone's panic button. Now all we have to do is figure out what."

As a logical deduction it made perfect sense, except that she couldn't even begin to imagine what the trigger could have been. She stared at the jar of cherries in its plastic bag. "Karl, are you *sure* about that jar? Shouldn't it be analyzed?"

"Absolutely." His mouth was a grim line. "I'm going to

take this in to the department right now. And then we're going to wake up the head of the police lab. And *then*, if we feel like it, we're going to notify the FBI." He picked up the collection of plastic bags. "Don't wait up for me."

"No, I won't." She was already well-conditioned to being a cop's wife, she realized. "So much for our fine, romantic pre-wedding night."

"Oh, we'll make up for it tomorrow night." He grinned and kissed her, long and hard. She felt her body respond; she slid her hands inside his bathrobe, and for a moment just gave herself over to feelings. Except . . .

"What about the others?" she blurted.

"So much for my romantic charms." He stepped away from her, grinning. "You mean the others on the list?"

"Yes." She laughed for a second before going on. "Are they in danger, too, do you think? Should we warn them?"

"Let's wait until we have the lab report." He dropped a light kiss on her mouth and then grinned down at her. "Get some sleep. Tomorrow night you won't have time to worry about game-playing."

You attack the ogre—a brave but foolish action. He quickly grabs you and with a heave of his mighty arms rips your body limb from limb.

—ADVENTURE: THE COLOSSAL CAVE

She awoke alone in bed on her wedding day, and the immediacy of it hit her so hard she felt all but immobilized. It was an effort to drag herself out of bed; an effort to force herself into the shower; and getting dressed was an effort utterly beyond her abilities. She slipped into a bathrobe, noting the tangle of blankets on Karl's side of the bed; so he'd gotten some sleep, at least. The simple deduction exhausted her. She tightened the belt of her bathrobe and headed downstairs, drawn by the hypnotic smell of coffee.

The marble art deco clock on the mantle read 7:30. Ten and a half hours until the wedding.

"Gamma!" Samantha waved a chubby hand from her perch on Karl's lap.

"Hi, sprat." She tried to put enthusiasm into her voice, but the only thing she truly wanted was coffee. Black coffee. Very black coffee. Karl, God bless him, was already holding out a cup to her as she reached the table.

"Hi, Mom." Rachel was also in a bathrobe, her hair piled

damply on top of her head. She jumped up from the table at Anneke's approach. "There's oatmeal on the stove. I'll get you some."

"God, no." Anneke's stomach roiled at the very thought. "I just want coffee, thanks."

"But you've got to eat breakfast," Rachel protested. "Especially today of all days."

"Rachel—" Anneke heard the sharpness in her voice and caught herself up. "Rachel, I'll eat something later. Right now I'll just have coffee." She sank into the empty chair between Karl and Marshall, who flashed her a covert smile. Cheered somewhat, she drank coffee in deep gulps, watching Samantha examine Karl's hand with the concentration of an art appraiser confronted by a dubious Picasso.

"Where's Emma?" she asked, when she felt slightly more conscious.

"Still sleeping." Rachel sounded either resentful or envious, Anneke wasn't sure which.

"Boken," Samantha said solemnly, pointing to Karl's middle finger, the one whose tip was out of alignment.

"Courtesy of a man named Fred Biletnikoff," Karl said with equal solemnity.

"Bad man," Samantha announced. "Boke Gampa Karl."

Anneke sputtered into her coffee.

"It wasn't my idea," Karl protested, laughing. "She came up with it herself." His expression was bland, but Anneke could feel the pleasure radiating from him as he looked down at the child.

"Oh, I think it's wonderful," Anneke said. "If I have to be a grandma, you'd damn well better get used to being a grandpa." Out of the corner of her eye, she noted the satisfied smile on Marshall's face, and felt tears prickle at the back of her eyelids. She buried her face in her coffee cup, wondering how to thank him for the finest wedding present anyone could ever have given her.

She looked up at last to meet Karl's eyes, and there was a moment of shared understanding between them so profound it was almost telepathic, an intimacy so deep she felt her face redden. She expected him to smile, but instead he regarded her gravely for what seemed like forever before finally looking away and setting Samantha down on the floor.

"If you're sufficiently caffeinated," he said, "why don't we go into your office so I can fill you in on last night." She nodded, afraid Rachel would ask for an explanation, but her daughter had other things on her mind.

"Mom, what do you want me to do to help?" she asked.

"For the wedding, you mean?" Anneke temporized, searching her mind for something her daughter could do. In truth, everything was done. Michael had the wedding itself under control; she was packed and ready to leave on her honeymoon; her wedding outfit was complete and hanging in her closet. "You might check with Helen about closing up the house," she said. "She'll come in tomorrow, but I was hoping you could make one last check before you leave." Poor Helen; she'd deserve combat pay when this was over.

"Of course." Rachel, looking pleased, stood up immediately and headed for the kitchen. Karl stood also, and Anneke followed him. Marshall, taking his small daughter onto his lap, winked at her as she left.

She closed the heavy oak door. "Was it . . ."

"Yes." He set his coffee cup on the edge of her desk and sat down in the chair next to it. "Preliminarily, as the lab kept insisting, but pretty surely poisoned. A form of cyanide."

She sank into her desk chair and booted up her computer out of habit. "Did you talk to the FBI?"

"Eventually. Unfortunately, all that happened is that I spent about an hour being interrogated." He smiled slightly, tight-lipped. "The chief is about as pissed off as I've ever seen him. He even asked me if I'd postpone my vacation and come back to work."

"Does that mean I'm no longer a suspect? No, of course not." She answered her own question. "Either of us could have sent that package to ourselves, couldn't we?" She looked at him. "Karl, if you do want to postpone the trip, it's all right with me."

For the first time, he hesitated about the honeymoon. "No," he said finally. "Going back to work would just be a gesture—thumbing our noses at the feds. There really isn't anything I can do here. The investigation is entirely in the hands of the FBI."

"Well, not entirely." She turned to the computer. "You said last night that I must have posted something that set the murderer off, right?"

"Right." Anneke dumped the archives of *murdergame* into WinWord, and copied it onto her laptop for Karl. "Do you want a printout?"

"No." He turned the laptop toward him and reached for the pointer. "I'd rather be able to move things around, see how they fit together."

"I'll get us some more coffee," she said.

The clock in her taskbar tray read 8:42 A.M. Nine hours and eighteen minutes until the wedding.

"Anything?" She slid her chair back from the computer finally and stretched cramped muscles. She'd read through the file half a dozen times, concentrating on her own postings and the responses to them. She could probably recite most of them by heart. And if she had written anything threatening to anyone, she sure didn't see it.

"Not exactly." He scribbled something on a pad and set the pen down.

"I'll settle for something inexact." She felt a glimmer of hope at his words, but he only shook his head.

"Why don't we see what's come in since last night," he said.

<Seth>It's too much like Clue, isn't it?

<Dani>Not necessarily. Clue isn't multi-player, for one thing. It's more like one of those murder parties, where one of the guests is the Designated Murderer, and everyone gets to play a different part.

<Larry>You'd have to design a coherent scenario, though, and assign related avatars. It wouldn't make sense to have a pirate and a football player and who knows what else all in the same story.

<Kell>Oh, I don't know. Think of it as Sherlock Holmes Meets the Village People. :-)

<Dani>I think it would work best as an online game, where people could select their own avatars.

<Elliott>It looks good but it doesn't hav enough action. Its too much like one of those old text games, Zork or that stuff.

<Kell>Hey, watch what you say about Zork, or I'll get the Wizard of Frobozz after you. I spent some of the best times of my life in the Great Underground Empire.

<Jesse>Anyone remember an Apple][game called "Hacker"? Maybe the most maddening game I ever saw.

"They've gone off on a tangent again." Anneke sighed and shut down her mail reader.

"What does that mean?" Karl pointed to the][in Jesse's post. "I've seen it a couple of times."

"That's the 'two' in 'Apple Two.'" Anneke laughed. "Typing it that way used to be the sign that you were a real programmer."

"Why was that?"

"Because the Apple Two keyboard didn't have brackets—or a delete key, for that matter. You had to know the escape sequences in order to get the brackets to display, so of course it became a symbol of knowledge. If you typed in the numeral two everyone knew you were a hopeless newbie." She stood up. "I'm going to throw on some clothes. Maybe my brain will function better when I'm dressed."

"I want to go to the department and see if the final toxicology report is in. Maybe talk to some people." He scribbled a final note to himself. "I don't know if I'll be back for lunch."

"That's all right. I don't know if I'll want to eat anyway."

The clock in the taskbar tray read 11:13 A.M. Six hours and forty-seven minutes until the wedding.

She put on jeans and a Steelers sweatshirt and came back downstairs, where Rachel was showing Samantha how to sort plastic shapes into the correct groups, and Emma was sprawled on the sofa reading the newspaper.

"Mom, did you dig out that business plan?" Emma asked.

"No, I'm sorry." Anneke felt a pang of guilt. "Look, let me get something to eat, and I'll run by my office and get it."

"Don't be silly, Mom," Rachel said sharply. "You have to get ready for the wedding."

"I have plenty of time."

"No, she's right." Emma unexpectedly agreed with her

sister. "I'm not in a hurry for it. Why don't you mail it to me when you get back from your honeymoon."

"I'll do better than that. I'll send you the plan *and* the software I used to design it." Relieved, she went to the kitchen and ran an English muffin through the toaster, slathering it with butter and jam and eating it at the counter. Helen, busy making a tuna-and-egg salad for lunch, smiled sympathetically at her but otherwise left her to her own thoughts.

Which, as usual, eventually led her back to her computer, where she read through the murdergame archives yet again, sorting and re-sorting her postings, replies to her postings, and other people's postings. Twice she downloaded mail from the list, but the others were still talking about antique computer games. They seemed to have forgotten about the murder entirely. Well, they didn't know about the poisoned cherries—at least, all but one of them didn't.

"Any flashes of deduction?" Karl arrived while she was comparing Seth's opinion about Vince to Dani's.

"Not even a twenty-watt glimmer." She turned away from the computer. "Any news from your end?"

"Not really." He came around the desk and put a hand on her shoulder. "The feds will try to trace the poison, of course, but it's too commonly available for that to do much good. The one bright spot is that they don't want to make this latest attack public, which at least means we won't become media targets."

"God, I never thought of that." She shivered at the thought. "This wedding is going to be circus enough as it is." She sighed, clicked to shut down her computer, and stood up. "We're not going to pull it off, are we?"

"No." He shook his head.

"Well, if you don't mind marrying a murder suspect, I

guess I don't either." She grinned up at him, determined to be cheerful, and discovered to her surprise that she actually was. "Let's go get married, Lieutenant."

The hands on her wristwatch read 3:52 P.M. Two hours and eight minutes until the wedding.

You fool, dwarves eat only coal! Now you've made him *really* mad!!

—ADVENTURE: THE COLOSSAL CAVE

Calvin looked hot enough to melt concrete. Zoe stood on the bottom step of the East Quad staircase and looked at her handiwork, and found it good. The Sally Army had really come through.

He wore a pair of tuxedo pants, complete with satin stripe down the sides. The jacket was a quasi-military design, from God knew where, with wide lapels and gold braid and a nipped waist that worked perfectly on his tall, thin frame. But the real find was the black silk turtleneck; Zoe was pretty sure it had begun life as an expensive undershirt for skiers, but she hadn't told Calvin that.

If you couldn't afford elegant, go for grunge chic, she'd told him, and that's exactly what they'd done. The total package had cost twenty dollars.

He shifted from one foot to the other, uncomfortable under her gaze. "Do I look all right?"

"All you need is a pair of silver shades, and you'd have people chasing you for autographs."

"Yeah, well . . ." He looked down at his feet, shod in black Adidas. "Wish I had better shoes."

"Not a problem. Nobody looks at shoes as long as they're black." Her own shoes were dark blue platform pumps that added a couple of inches to her height and went with her floaty blue chiffon dress. She thought she looked pretty good herself, but so far Calvin hadn't seemed to notice.

"We better go," he said. "Don't want to be late."

"Okay." She sighed and wrapped her hand-woven stole around her shoulders. Maybe this hadn't been such a hot idea after all.

That had been the deal—she'd help Calvin get the clothes he needed, and he'd "escort" her to the wedding. "I know the art museum's only a block from East Quad," she'd said, "but I don't feel like trudging across campus by myself all dressed up. It'd feel weird, you know?" She'd carefully refrained from calling it a date, and now she was pretty sure Calvin didn't see it as one. Well, maybe he was uncomfortable about going to a formal event. Or maybe he was still worried about the feds.

"Y'know, I really wasn't sure she was going to go through with it," Zoe said, making conversation as they left the dorm.

"Yeah, I guess."

"I wonder where they're going on their honeymoon. The lieutenant wouldn't tell me."

"Dunno." Calvin remained monosyllabic. His long legs ate up sidewalk, and Zoe wobbled on her platform shoes, struggling to keep up.

"Hey." She stopped in her tracks. Calvin, already half a dozen paces beyond, stopped and turned toward her.

"Something wrong?"

"Yeah, something's wrong. In fact, a few things are wrong." They were in front of the Clements Library; she turned into its walkway and sat down with a thump on a concrete bench. "Calvin, sit."

"What's up? We're gonna be late." He followed her to the bench but remained standing.

"Calvin, sit down," she repeated. When he finally did so, glowering, she turned to face him. "Now, give."

"Give what? What are you talking about?"

"You know damn well what I'm talking about. Why did you disappear the minute someone mentioned the cops? What's going on?" When he didn't answer, she said less sharply: "Look, my dad's a criminal lawyer, and a good one. And my mom's—"

Well, what? When asked, Berniece Kaplan called herself an "activist mom," a woman who had a network of political contacts throughout Michigan without ever having held office, or wanted to. Bernie Kaplan, her daughter was sure, could handle anything.

Except, when she'd called her mother about Calvin, Bernie hadn't said what she wanted to hear. "Zoe, there's an old lawyer's adage," she'd said. " 'Never ask a question unless you already know what the answer will be.' " Accustomed as she was to her mother's elliptical advice, Zoe got the message—butt out.

"But Mom, if you and Dad could help him . . ." she'd argued.

"Zoe, people have the right not to be helped." And that was Bernie's last word on the subject.

She's wrong, though, Zoe insisted to herself. Calvin's afraid of something, and that's going to poison his life unless someone helps him. Aloud, she said: "Well, let's just say my mom knows how to get things straightened out." When he didn't reply, she probed, "Why didn't you want the cops to know about Calvin Streeter?"

"Because Calvin Streeter's dead," he blurted out at last. "You satisfied?"

"Dead? What are you talking about?"

"What I said. Calvin Streeter was killed in a drive-by three years ago. He'd already been accepted to Michigan, so I figured, why waste it?" His face remained impassive, but his voice was angry and bitter.

"But . . ." She stopped, so many questions whirling through her mind that they tripped over each other. At least, she thought with enormous relief, he wasn't wanted for some crime, and then realized: How do I know? She looked at him, suddenly aware that she had no idea who he was, and aware also that he knew exactly what she was thinking. She stood up, feeling awkward.

"Let's go to the wedding," she said.

"Wow. Oh, wow." Zoe stopped dead inside the doorway to the museum rotunda, so entranced by the sight that Calvin's problems receded into the background of her mind. Everywhere, silvery light gleamed.

Instead of rows of chairs, there was an informal semicircle of small round tables, each of them covered in silver tablecloths. Above centerpieces of silver baskets filled with white chrysanthemums were glittering strings of tiny fairy lights, and more white chrysanthemums, in huge silver vases, stood on darker, matte-finish silvered pedestals along the walls. At the far end of the room, pairs of chrysanthemum-topped pedestals created an alcove for the ceremony.

It should have been overpowering, Zoe thought, but it wasn't. Michael had sprinkled his silver with a restrained hand, letting the green leaves of the chrysanthemums and the matte pedestals serve as darker accents. And the guests in their bright clothes were themselves accents. She stared and stared, trying to analyze the effect and how he'd pulled it off without going over the top.

"Over there." They were the first words Calvin had spoken since his revelation. He pointed to one side of the room, where Marcia Rosenthal waved at them. Calvin plowed forward, and Zoe hesitated for a moment. He might rather she sat somewhere else; but then again, if she didn't stay with him, would he think she was avoiding him? Sighing with frustration, she followed him toward Marcia's table.

"Isn't this absolutely awesome?" Marcia, in a red silk dress, waved the glass of champagne in her hand, and droplets skittered onto the tablecloth. Across the table, a middle-aged couple were deep in conversation. Zoe and Calvin dropped into empty chairs as Marcia waved once more, this time to a man in a short white waiter's jacket. Shortly, Zoe and Calvin too had flutes of champagne, along with tiny plates of even tinier hors d'oeuvres. "Mmm." Marcia put a puff of pastry into her mouth and chewed rapturously. Zoe bit into a round of toast topped with shrimp and some unidentified spread; it was delicious.

"What's for dinner, do you know?" she asked Marcia.

"No, but if it's anything like these hors d'oeuvres, I can't wait. Calvin, try that one." She pointed to a yellow-and-black mound on a square of cracker. "It's egg and caviar—unbelievable."

"Not hungry." Calvin was looking around gloomily.

"If you don't want it, can I have it?" Marcia nabbed it off his plate before he had a chance to reply. "God, I'm really being a pig, aren't I?" She laughed at herself. "I guess two years of dorm food'll do that to you." Zoe, who'd eaten all the tiny morsels on her plate and was looking around for more, laughed with her. Calvin picked up an hors d'oeuvre at random and put it in his mouth. "Isn't it heavenly?" Marcia asked him.

"It's good, yeah." It seemed to Zoe that Calvin had relaxed fractionally, or maybe it was wishful thinking. Before she could pursue the thought the fairy lights over the tables began to dim, and the music—too tinkly for her taste—rose in volume. The hum of conversation died away. Zoe swiveled toward the flowered alcove just as the wedding party appeared.

"Wow," Zoe said once more under her breath, her eyes fixed on Anneke. Next to her, she heard Marcia breathe, "Oh awesome."

Anneke wore silver. It seemed to float around her, layer upon shimmering layer, drifting and gleaming in the light. Her short brown-and-gray hair was adorned with a delicate ornament of silver filigree, and when she lifted her arm, the flowing sleeve shifted to reveal a bracelet of the same filigree. On her face was the most brilliant smile Zoe had ever seen.

It took her a minute even to notice the others in the wedding party. Emma wore dark green velvet, her sister pale blue silk. Michael Rappoport, just behind them, was gorgeous in a velvet-lapeled tuxedo. Next to Genesko was a cop she'd met last summer—Wes Kramer, that was it—in full Marine dress blues.

Genesko . . . Zoe blinked. She'd never thought of him as handsome, not like Michael Rappoport, anyway. How could she have missed it? Well, she'd never seen him in a tuxedo, looking absolutely scrumptiously perfect. And she'd never seen him with that look on his face. She'd expected them both to look solemn, somehow; instead, they both wore wide, joyous smiles. She blinked again and grinned inwardly. If she weren't careful, she could develop a major crush on a friend's husband.

She was so busy looking at them that she missed the beginning of the ceremony. Judge Esther Grant, in a black suit that looked almost like her courtroom robe, was speaking about commitment.

". . . customary to say a few words about trust, and commitment, and in general, the source of a happy marriage. But I don't think I have to do that here tonight." The judge smiled. "I've heard all the clichés about what makes a perfect couple, and I've never believed any of them. Like a lot of things, I can't define it, but I know it when I see it." She looked down at the book in her hand, and then looked at Genesko.

"Do you, Karl Genesko, take—"

"That's it!" Anneke blurted. "*That's* why he thought I knew."

There is a distant, sourceless screech of incredible anguish! With a sharp >poof< and a small puff of orange smoke, a bent and bearded elf appears. He is dressed in working clothes, and has a name-tag marked "Ralph" on his shirt. "You blithering idiot!" he storms. "You were warned quite clearly not to use that word near water!! I hadn't gotten all of the bugs out of it yet, and now your incredible incompetence has totally destroyed Colossal Cave!! Do you have the faintest scintilla of an iota of an understanding of how much work I'm going to have to do to get the cave rebuilt?!? I'll have to go all the way to Peking for another dragon, and I'll have to convince the Goblin's Union to send me another team of gooseberry goblins; I'll have to sub-contract the building of the volcano out to the local totrugs, and worst of all I'll have to go through eight months of paperwork and red tape!! All because you couldn't follow directions, you purblind and meatbrained moron! I'm rescinding all of your game points and throwing you out! Out! OUT! GET OUT!!$!%#&'@%!!%%!"

—ADVENTURE: THE COLOSSAL CAVE

Not until Karl threw back his head and laughed aloud did Anneke realize what she'd done. And then, to her own surprise, she laughed with him.

"Are you sure?" he asked finally.

"Yes. Probably. I think so." She shook her head in confusion, ignoring the quizzical look on Judge Grant's face and Michael's eye-rolling histrionics. Thank God, she had her back to her daughters. The thought of Rachel's probable expression brought on an attack of the giggles.

"Do you want to proceed?" the judge asked finally.

"Yes." She and Karl answered together, which brought on more giggles. "Oh, by all means," she said. Karl winked at her, and she laughed and said, "Stop that."

"All right." The judge looked dubious, but began again. "Do you, Karl Genesko, take Anneke Haagen . . ."

"I do," he said. And "I do," she said, and instead of the expected lump in her throat there was pure laughter.

"I think you'll do," Esther Grant said, grinning at them.

"Yes. I believe you're right," Karl said.

After which, they posed for photographs, and ate dinner, and accepted toasts, and chatted with family and friends, and said nothing more about Anneke's brainstorm. Not until the celebration began to wind down, and only a handful of people remained in the rotunda, did Zoe sidle up to them, with Calvin in tow.

"Was that blurt what I think it was?" she asked.

"I'm afraid so." Anneke laughed again at the memory.

"Oh, well." Michael appeared at her side, his face flushed with triumph. "Think of it as a small birthmark on an otherwise perfect face. It provides character, a defining point, so to speak. Since every other element of the wedding was pure perfection, your, er, blurt may therefore be considered charming."

"Why, thank you for your forbearance, Michael." She stood on tiptoe and kissed him on the cheek. "I do mean that, you know. Thank you."

"Is there going to be a break in the case?" Zoe kept her focus on the main issue.

"I don't know." She looked at Karl and sighed. "It's reality time, isn't it?"

He touched the silver filigree in her hair. "Oh, this is real, I promise you. But I suppose we need to deal with alternate realities, for a little while."

"In that case," Zoe said, "Calvin has something to tell you."

"That's the way we're going to play it, Mr. Winstead. The suspects will be told that you're online, but you will not participate until we're done." Karl listened to the voice on the other end of the phone, shaking his head. "Sergeant Kramer of the Ann Arbor Police Department will also be reading along, as will a reporter for the *Michigan Daily*." He listened again, longer this time. "She will not print anything without my permission." Another pause. "I'm afraid you'll have to take my word for that."

The conversation had been going on for a while. FBI agent Hal Winstead was livid. As near as Anneke could tell, he wanted both to control the interrogation *and* keep his presence secret; she didn't know how he thought he could do both, but it didn't matter anyway because he wasn't going to get to do either. Only when Karl had an ironclad guarantee, with Zoe on the extension as a witness, did he give Winstead the password to Kell's murder mansion.

He hung up at last and asked: "Is everyone ready?"

"Yes." She turned to the computer and typed in the password. "Damn," she said, as her sleeve caught on the edge of the desk, the fine layers of silver tissue wrapping themselves around a drawer handle. "I should have changed first."

The limousine waiting on State Street had taken them back home instead of to the airport, with Zoe along at Karl's request. Ignoring Rachel's expressions of dismay, they had gone directly to Anneke's office, where Karl had called the Ann Arbor police chief, and the FBI, in that order. Anneke, meanwhile, had e-mailed the circle of suspects and arranged a meeting in Kell's mansion.

"So that's why you wanted me along," Zoe said, grinning. "To make sure the feds don't take credit for solving it."

"Not exactly." Karl shook his head, and then smiled slightly. "Well, not entirely, anyway."

"Here we are." Anneke pointed to the monitor, where the scene was once again the furnished foyer. There was a new door this time, ornately carved and with a large brass plaque that read PARLOR. "I guess it's showtime." She stood up and moved away, silver fabric floating around her. Karl slid into her chair, picked up the mouse, and clicked on the parlor door.

Anneke, looking over his shoulder, laughed. The centerpiece of Kell's parlor was a huge desk. Next to it was a red leather chair; other chairs were drawn into a semicircle in front of it. On one side of the desk was a tray containing two bottles of beer and a pair of stemmed pilsner glasses; on the other side, a vase of orchids. The avatar behind the desk was a huge man in a dark blue suit and yellow shirt.

"At least now I know how Kell can be this good," she said.

Three other avatars were already in place. Seth's football player, Dani's military girl, and Elliott's pirate hovered slightly above chairs in front of the desk. As she watched, Kell's dancing girl, Larry's square man, and Jesse's Don Quixote flicked into view, and words appeared in the balloon over the dancing girl's head.

<Kell>Glad you could all make it. Tonight we get to play out one of those classic mystery scenes--the one where the Great Detective gathers all the suspects together and reveals the killer. And of course, there's always a cop lurking in the background, so consider yourselves warned.

For the first time, Anneke noticed a shadowy figure in the background, not an avatar but drawn into the scene. The balloon over Kell's head blanked, and new lines of text appeared.

<Kell>Fortunately, we have our own Great Detective, in the person of Lieutenant Karl Genesko of the Ann Arbor Police Department. He'll be starring in the scene using Anneke's account. All right, Lieutenant, let the games begin. :-)

Karl had already begun typing a string of words into the form at the bottom of the screen. Anneke leaned forward tensely as he clicked the Send button and then continued to type.

<Anneke>[Lt. Genesko]Thank you all for coming. I'm sure you're as anxious to end this as we are. First, I'd like to fill you in on an event that hasn't yet been made public. Yesterday, Anneke received a box in the mail purporting to be a wedding present from a friend of mine, Jay Banning. Inside the box was a jar of preserved cherries that contained a lethal dose of cyanide.

Karl hit Send again and then paused. "Let's give them a chance to jump in," he said.

<Kell>Yow. Since you and Anneke are both here, I'm assuming you didn't eat any of them. How'd you figure out they were poisoned?

261

<Elliott>Hey, dosn't that let us out? How wold we know anything about a friend of yours?

<Anneke>[Lt. Genesko]Luckily, they were something I knew Jay would never send me--details aren't important. And unfortunately, Jay's name came up when Kell was asking Anneke about our wedding. All of you were told that he had to cancel because he was being sent to Seattle.

<Larry>Are you sure the two incidents are related? I mean, except for being sent through the mails, the two things are awfully different. And you are a policeman, Lieutenant. You'd have to have a fair number of enemies.

<Dani>You've got a point, Larry. How about it, Nero? Why couldn't the poisoned cherries have come from some gang you busted up?

<Seth>Or maybe the enraged wife of a crook you sent away.

<Kell>Or a master criminal who can't proceed with his nefarious scheme until he's gotten rid of the one man clever enough to stop him. ;->

<Anneke>[Lt. Genesko]Enticing as they are, I'm afraid none of those scenarios will work, for one simple reason--the package wasn't addressed to me, it was addressed to Anneke. I'm afraid the poison was sent by the same person who sent the mail bomb to Vince Mattus--and for the same reason.

<Jesse>So we're back to the blackmail game.

<Dani>I'm still not convinced about that, Sherlock. I mean, we may not be a group of happy little Mother Teresas here, but we're pretty ordinary people, barring a sick sense of humor. I'm having trouble believing any of us have anything in our backgrounds worth blackmailing over.

<Jesse>I'm having the same problem. Not only serious enough to blackmail over, but serious enough to kill over? It just doesn't track.

<Anneke>[Lt. Genesko]The thing to note about blackmail is

this: Even if the actual secret isn't all that serious, the EFFECT OF DISCLOSURE may be. Let me recap, and I think you'll see what I mean. (Please note--at the moment, let's put aside the issue of whether any of these accusations is in fact true.)

Now, three of Vince's targets were accused of real crimes. First, Jesse. The technical term for what Vince accused him of is industrial espionage, and it's no joke. If Vince had evidence, Jesse could find himself facing a long jail term.

The same thing is true of Larry. If Vince could prove he was involved in insider trading, he'd not only be out of a job, he'd very likely wind up in jail.

And if Anneke really did falsify government tax forms, she'd be looking at the loss of her business at least, and also possibly prison.

Now, let's move on to accusations that didn't involve actual crimes, starting with Seth. Suppose we accept his statement that he never bets more than he could afford to lose, and moreover, that he doesn't associate with a criminal gambling element. Even if all that is true, what would be the result if his superiors at the bank became aware of his gambling? Well, they might decide that he was simply too high-risk to have around. Even in the absence of any actual wrongdoing, Seth could well find himself out of a job--and with unpleasant whispers going around about him.

Dani is an artist, which I admit isn't an easy profession to blackmail. But what happens if it's revealed that she tried to sleep her way to the top AND FAILED? Well, for one thing, she suddenly isn't such a sympathetic figure anymore. In fact, she becomes a figure of pure ridicule.

And finally, Elliott. Now even if Vince had proof that Elliott changed some grades, so what? He won't be arrested, and I don't think Elliott cares about grades, or school reprimands, or anything else the official world could do to him. But there is something he cares about, something he might very well lose if he were exposed--his computer. The likelihood that his parents would confiscate his computer system might be the worst thing Elliott could imagine. That's what I mean by "effect of disclosure."

<Elliott>That's stupid. I could always get a hold of a computer somewhere. Besides, my dad would never do that. I do computer work for him howd he get it don without me?

<Seth>Your problem is that at this point I really don't give a rat's ass whether they fire me or not. Not only wouldn't I kill to keep this job, I might kill to get out of it.

<Jesse>It's an interesting way to look at it, Lieutenant. The trouble is, your motives fall apart in the face of innocence. Since I never DID steal data, there's no way Vince could have "proof" that I did. That's ultimately why the feds had to let me go-- because if Vince got it wrong, there's no motive to kill him.

<Anneke>[Lt. Genesko]Not necessarily, Mr. Franklin.

<Dani>What's that supposed to mean, Hercule?

<Anneke>[Lt. Genesko]Remember this--Vince really DIDN'T know any secrets about any of you. He was, as we stated, playing a new version of "I know what you did." In addition, he had to be careful to phrase his accusations in such a way that the victims would understand them, but nobody else would. The result was that his posted accusations were so obscure it was impossible to be sure exactly what he was accusing anyone of.

<Jesse>In other words, I might be innocent of data theft, but guilty of something else that Vince seemed to be implying. Possible, Lieutenant, definitely possible.

<Anneke>[Lt. Genesko]Looked at in that way, it was an almost impossible puzzle. The trigger could have been anything-- a phrase, a reference, a joke. It could even have been a single word. We might never have solved it if the murderer hadn't sent those poisoned cherries.

<Dani>Okay, I'll play straight man. And why was that, Ellery?

<Anneke>[Lt. Genesko]Because it meant that the murderer

believed Anneke knew the secret. And since she DIDN'T know the secret, she had to have written something in one of her postings that replicated the trigger phrase. What's more, it had to have been something she posted since Vince's murder; otherwise she'd have been targeted at the same time he was.

<Elliott>Okay, okay. How long are you gonna drag this out? What is this freaking trigger word?

<Anneke>[Lt. Genesko]SOURCE.

<Kell>You mean source as in source code?

<Anneke>[Lt. Genesko]Exactly. Source code--one of the most valuable properties in the computer world. The word SOURCE--capitalized--shows up in only one of Vince's postings--to Larry. And Anneke used the word only once, also in capitals, and also in a posting directed to Larry.

Everyone got hold of the wrong end of the stick, didn't they, Larry? They were so focused on your activities since you've been with Gallery3, that they didn't bother to investigate your activities BEFORE you signed on with them. Specifically, nobody bothered to ask what you brought to the table when the money men put together the company. You didn't have their kind of capital to contribute, and you're a good programmer but not that good. Your contribution was the source code for a high-end graphics library, wasn't it? The graphics library that a whole team of programmers had developed at TerraNova, just before it went under. Since you headed the team, it would have been easy for you to tell them the program wasn't going to make it, and then simply walk off with the pieces of code each of the other team members had developed.

<Kell>Larry, is any of this true?

<Seth>But how did Anneke find out about it?

<Anneke>[Lt. Genesko]She didn't--that's why it took that poisoned jar for it to fall together. When she used the word SOURCE, it was an absolute coincidence. Unfortunately--or fortunately, as it turned out--Larry thought she'd figured out Vince's threat.

Once we realized someone thought Anneke knew the truth, we went back and examined all her postings since the murder, and compared them to Vince's. And there it was.

<Jesse>Larry, if you've got anything to say, now's the time.

<Dani>Come on, Larry. Say something.

<Agent Winstead>I can now inform you all that Larry Markowitz has been arrested for the murder of Matthius Vincent. He was apprehended while trying to flee his home in Sunnyvale, California, and a collection of disks in his possession has been confiscated.

<Kell>I'll be damned. He thought he was so smart, and he turned out to be Yet Another idiot suffering from Clue Deficit Disorder.

<Seth>Definitely an RS232C brain with a DIN connector.

<Elliott>Yeah, he keeps Sending back packets, but the check-sums are wrong.

<Dani>His brain really is in need of a ROM upgrade, isn't it?

<Jesse>Afraid so. The wheel's spinning but the hamster's dead.

Anneke leaned across Karl, laughing, and reached for the keyboard.

<Anneke>I guess we're all agreed that Larry is definitely a case of cranio-rectal inversion. I think we're adjourned, gang.

A sepulchral voice reverberating through the cave, says, "Cave clos-
ing soon. All adventurers please report to the treasure room via the
alternate entrance to claim your treasure."

—ADVENTURE: THE COLOSSAL CAVE

"If he hadn't tried to run, would they have been able to
make a case?" They were airborne at last, a day late but
heading west on a flight to San Francisco. Anneke was
delighted with the destination, but Karl still hadn't told her
any details.

"I doubt it." Karl shook his head, took a sip of champagne, and made a face. Airline champagne, even first-class
airline champagne, was a lot like carbonated vinegar. "It's
lucky that he was stupid enough to have the original Terra-
Nova disks when they grabbed him."

"He had some luck, too. Like the smudged postmark on
that jar of cherries."

"Oh, that wasn't luck. First, he took it to a post office in a
place called San Carlos. It's in the general area of Sunnyvale, but enough off the beaten track that he figured the feds
would never get around to questioning the postal workers
there. He handed them the box, they postmarked it, and
then he asked for it back so he could write 'Open at Once'

on it. While he was writing, he licked his thumb and smudged the postmark with it."

"Clever. I guess. And quick—he must have sent it almost the same day I posted that message with the word *source* in it." She turned slightly to look at him. "Did he really decide to kill Vince that quickly, too? Just because of a single scattershot posting?"

"Oh, no. He e-mailed Vince, and they went back and forth for a while. Apparently, when Vince discovered he'd hit a nerve, he decided to play it out. He didn't ask Larry for money; instead, he threatened to tell the original programmers that Larry had stolen their work."

"Did he." Anneke felt truly sad for Vince for the first time. "So he wasn't really a blackmailer. What he was, was a hacker." It was the highest compliment she could pay him. "I'm glad we caught the bastard."

"Yes. If you hadn't hit on the word *source*, I'm not sure we ever would have."

"If Esther hadn't used the word in the wedding ceremony, I probably wouldn't have." She shook her head. "Even so, it was awfully tenuous. If Larry had just sat tight, instead of trying to dispose of those disks, he'd probably have walked."

"I think it never occurred to him that the FBI would be staked out right outside his house. As far as he was concerned, he was all alone, talking to people who were thousands of miles away."

"No, I suppose not." She looked out the window at the jagged landscape of the Sierras 30,000 feet below. It had the insubstantial quality that great distance always lends; Kell's virtual parlor had felt more real than those distant peaks. "Larry never quite thought of us as real," she said aloud.

"No. Cops see that too often—the ones who think of

other people as nothing but props in their own personal dramas."

"As though everyone else was just an avatar." She nibbled on a cashew and pondered the notion of reality. "I'm glad you didn't have to destroy Kell," she said.

"Destroy?"

"Well, it would have, wouldn't it? If her—his—real identity came out, Kell Albright would no longer exist. I'm glad to have met Albert Kelleher, but I'd miss Kell if she vaporized." She sighed. "Reality isn't as simple as it sounds, is it? Not even when it's standing in front of you."

"Calvin, you mean."

"What's going to happen to him?"

"I don't know. Zoe's going to have him talk to her father. Assuming he isn't in trouble otherwise, they should be able to get it sorted out."

"As soon as we get back, I'll call Zoe's father and see what I can do for him."

"Not very flattering, you know." He grinned at her. "Brides aren't supposed to be so anxious to get their honeymoon over with."

"Hush." She saw the stewardess coming toward them. "If you dare let anyone know this is a honeymoon, you'd better be prepared for separate hotel rooms." She handed the stewardess her nearly full champagne glass, asked for a Diet Coke, and looked out the window again. "Oh, look." She pointed. "Is that Lake Tahoe?"

"Yes. San Francisco should come into view in about twenty minutes."

"I can't wait." She stretched her legs out in front of her. "Do you have anything specific planned?"

"I wondered when you were going to ask." He reached into the briefcase at his feet and pulled out an envelope.

"We'll spend the first three nights at the Ritz-Carlton, in the city. From there . . . here." He handed her the envelope.

She opened it and withdrew two shiny multicolored pieces of pasteboard; tickets, to . . .

"GameDev? Are you serious?"

"You did want to go, I believe?"

"Yes, but . . ." She stared at him. "What about you? You can't want to spend two days examining video cards and attending programming seminars."

"Oh, I'll keep busy." He pulled another envelope out of his jacket pocket and handed it to her. This one also contained two pieces of shiny pasteboard, each bearing the word "Guest" and a scrawled signature. At the top was the helmet logo of the San Francisco 49ers. "The Forty-niners' practice facility is only about a mile from your convention center," he said. "Their linebacker coach is an old friend of mine."

"But . . ." She looked at the football passes with longing. "Damn. How fast can I get myself cloned?"

"I don't think I can handle two of you." He laughed. "But there's no reason you can't do some of both. And your convention ends Saturday." He withdrew two more pieces of pasteboard from the envelope. "Sideline tickets for Sunday's game at Candlestick."

She sighed with pure happiness, and then giggled. "A honeymoon at a computer convention and a football game—for God's sake, don't tell Rachel. But you really do know how to put on a honeymoon, Lieutenant."

"Oh, you haven't seen anything yet," he said.

"Is it going to be all right?" Zoe asked. "Dad's going to fix it, isn't he?"

"I think so." Bernie Kaplan's voice on the phone was matter-of-fact, the way she approached any problem.

"He isn't . . ." Zoe hesitated. "I mean, he's not wanted or anything, is he?"

"No. It's just a matter of working things out with the University."

"That shouldn't be all that hard, should it? I mean, he's already a junior, and he's got something like a three-five GPA."

"Well, it may be a little more complicated than that," Bernie said. "For one thing, he never graduated from high school. And then, there's the fact that what he did really does constitute fraud."

"But . . ."

"Don't worry, dear. Your father will take care of it. If necessary, Calvin's story could be turned into a national tearjerker. Not that Calvin wants that, but neither would the U—especially if they wound up cast as the villains."

Not bad, Zoe thought. "So it'll be all right, then." She sighed, part relief, part something more. "I haven't had a chance to talk to him much in the last couple of days," she said casually.

"No. I know." There was a moment of silence from Bernie's end of the line. "I'd give it some time. Right now, I'm afraid, you're a reminder of the mess he's in. He feels embarrassed and awkward, and that makes him uncomfortable, and *that* makes him angry."

"But that's silly," Zoe protested.

"No, just human." This time it was Bernie's turn to sigh. "That's why they say no good deed goes unpunished."

Author's Note

In case you hadn't noticed, this is a mystery in which neither the reader nor the detective actually "meets" any of the suspects face to face—f2f, as they say online. Now, this is the sort of thing that's fraught with danger for an author. If it works, it's called a tour de force; if it flops, it's called a disaster. (If it just sort of lies there, of course, it isn't called anything because nobody bothers. :-)

One of my favorite people in the world is a woman who lives in New York, three thousand miles from me. We chat nearly every day; we swap books, and videotapes, and restaurant experiences; we talk about our work, and our hobbies, and our families. We have never met f2f. Is she a friend? By any definition I can imagine, she is.

It's true that, if she were sick, I couldn't rush over to her apartment with a container of homemade chicken soup (although as anyone who knows me can tell you, I'd be a lot more likely to pick up a container at Zabar's anyway). But virtual hugs are still hugs, and after a particularly painful 49ers loss, we did indeed share a consoling box of virtual chocolates, just as heartwarming and a lot less fattening than the "real" kind. (No, I'm not making this up—check out *www.virtualchocolate.com*.)

Now it's perfectly possible that she is, in fact, not the person I believe her to be. For all I know, she's actually a Seattle bus driver, or a British soccer thug, or a Russian cosmonaut. It's all part of the risk, and the reward, of this astounding global village we find ourselves in.

Besides, f2f encounters are no guarantee of anything. I have a good friend here in the Bay Area. I know she's a woman of about my own age, because I've seen her. I know what she does for a living, because I've seen her do it. But everything else I "know" about her is simply what she's told me. For all I know, she's actually a '60s radical living underground, or a mob wife hiding from her husband, or a CIA agent with a license to kill.

The point is, we "know" a lot less—and a lot more—about people than we think we do, whether we've met them in cyberspace or live space. We know kindness when we see it; we know hostility when we see it; we know decency, and bigotry, and cheerfulness, and all the other qualities by which we decide who our friends are.

Of course, it takes a while for these qualities to manifest themselves, and only an idiot would jump into a relationship—whether f2f or virtual—without caution. So obviously you don't wander into a strange chat room and give people your home address, any more than you'd wander into a strange bar and do the same. Common sense is common sense, and too often uncommon, no matter what the milieu.

But in the end, there's something liberating about meeting people online. All the physical cues—the ones most responsible for prejudice and other knee-jerk reactions—are missing. Instead, we can focus on intrinsic qualities of character, and intelligence, and humor, and all those things that really matter.

I've been online since 1981, and I'll admit that, like Anneke, I suffer from a certain nostalgia for the Good Old Days, when Usenet was a community instead of a marketing opportunity. But I also have to admit that it was a very narrow community, composed almost exclusively of hackers (the good kind) and computer gurus. My friend in New York—and a lot of other friends I've made online lately—would never have logged on to that kind of Internet. So I guess, in that great British phrase, what you lose on the swings you make up on the roundabout. And I wouldn't trade my current network of friends for anything—not even freedom from scumbag spammers.

NOTE: I have taken a few, but only a very few, liberties with online communication in this book. For one thing, I've eliminated the convention of copying a piece of the preceding message into a post. And for another, I've organized the postings in a more absolutely sequential manner than they might normally arrive in one's incoming mailbox. But it's not unusual, when a major event occurs, for list members to remain online for hours at a time, reading and replying in almost real-time.

Also, some but not all of the newsgroups and websites referred to in the book are actual newsgroups; occasionally it was necessary to invent a particular newsgroup to suit a character. If you're interested in finding a newsgroup about a particular topic, check out *www.deja.com/*, where you can browse newsgroups by categories, search for postings about a given subject, and even post replies of your own.

And if you're interested in finding an online mailing list that deals with a particular topic, there's a huge database of them at *www.liszt.com/*.

A final note about the chapter headings: These are taken

from the wonderful, seminal grandfather of all computer games. If you want to know more, there's a playable version online at *http://www.stanford.edu/adventure/*.

The history of "Adventure: The Colossal Cave" is murky, because it was developed, expanded, and ported to a dozen different systems in a dozen different computer languages over the years. But the most accurate history I've been able to find attributes it first to Willie Crowther at the Xerox Palo Alto Research Center, Don Woods of Stanford University–Artificial Intelligence, and Gary Palter of Massachusetts Institute of Technology. Gentlemen, we thank you.

—Susan Holtzer